New York Times bestseller Jill Shalvis is the award-winning author of over four dozen romance novels, including her sexy, heart-warming contemporary 'Animal Magnetism' and 'Lucky Harbor' series. She won a RITA for *Simply Irresistible* and is a three-time National Readers Choice winner as well. Connect with Jill on her website www.jillshalvis.com for a complete book list and to read her daily blog, where she recounts her Misplaced City Girl adventures, or visit her at www.facebook.com/jillshalvis or @JillShalvis for other news.

Praise for Jill Shalvis:

'Packed with the trademark Shalvis humor and intense intimacy, it is definitely a must-read . . . If love, laughter and passion are the keys to any great romance, then this novel hits every note' *Romantic Times*

'Heartwarming and sexy . . . an abundance of chemistry, smoldering romance, and hilarious antics' *Publishers Weekly*

'[Shalvis] has quickly become one of my go-to authors of contemporary romance. Her writing is smart, fun, and sexy, and her books never fail to leave a smile on my face long after I've closed the last page . . . Jill Shalvis is an author not to be missed!' *The Romance Dish*

'Jill Shalvis is such a talented author that she brings to life characters who make you laugh, cry, and are a joy to read' *Romance Reviews Today*

'What I love about Jill Shalvis's books is that she writes sexy, adorable heroes . . . the sexual tension is out of this world. And of course, in true Shalvis fashion she expertly mixes in humor that has you laughing out loud' *Heroes and Heartbreakers*

'I always enjoy reading a Jill Shalvis book. She's a consistently elegant, bold, clever writer . . . Very witty – I laughed out loud countless times and these scenes are sizzling' *All About Romance*

'If you have not read a Jill Shalvis novel yet, then you really have not read a real romance yet either!' *Book Cove Reviews*

'Engaging writing, characters that walk straight into your heart, touching, hilarious' *Library Journal*

'Witty, fun, and sexy – the perfect romance!' Lori Foster, *New York Times* bestselling author

'Riveting suspense laced with humor and heart is her hallmark, and Jill Shalvis always delivers' Donna Kauffman, *USA Today* bestselling author

'Humor, intrigue, and scintillating sex. Jill Shalvis is ... original' Suzanne Forster, *New York* ...

'Fast-paced and ... Cherry Adair, *New York* ...

By Jill Shalvis

Animal Magnetism Series
Animal Magnetism
Animal Attraction
Rescue My Heart
Rumour Has It
Then Came You
Still The One

Lucky Harbor Series
Simply Irresistible
The Sweetest Thing
Head Over Heels
Lucky In Love
At Last
Forever And A Day
It Had To Be You
Always On My Mind
Once In A Lifetime
It's In His Kiss

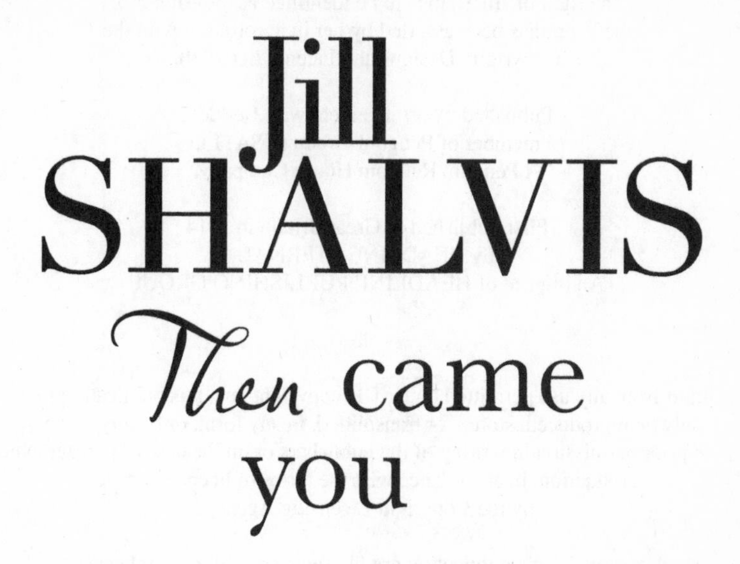

headline
ETERNAL

Published by arrangement with Berkley,
a member of Penguin Group (USA) LLC.
A Penguin Random House Company.

First published in Great Britain in 2014
by HEADLINE ETERNAL
An imprint of HEADLINE PUBLISHING GROUP

1

Cataloguing in Publication Data is available from the British Library

ISBN 978 1 4722 1728 8

Offset in Times by Avon DataSet Ltd, Bidford-on-Avon, Warwickshire

Printed and bound by CPI Group (UK) Ltd, Croydon, CR0 4YY

HEADLINE PUBLISHING GROUP
An Hachette UK Company
338 Euston Road
London NW1 3BH

www.headlineeternal.com
www.headline.co.uk
www.hachette.co.uk

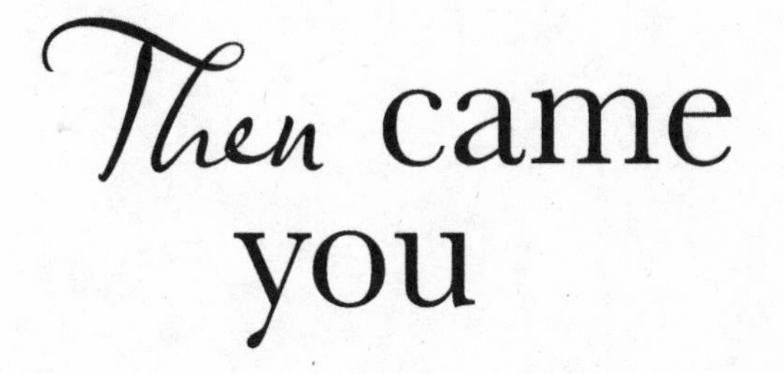
Then came you

One

"I wanted to thank you for having me, Dr. Connelly—" Emily Stevens broke off and shook her head. Not quite right. She tightened her grip on the steering wheel in the parking lot of her new job. "I really hope to make a positive impact—" Nope, even worse. No one liked a brown-noser. She cleared her throat, looked into her rearview mirror and forced a smile. "I'm thrilled to be stuck in West Nowhere, USA."

Your own fault.

She drew in a deep breath, applied lip gloss—because everyone knew *that* was the same thing as courage—and got out of the car. It was early autumn, and the chill in the early morning air only served to remind her just how far from Los Angeles she really was. She looked around, taking in the towering, intimidating Bitterroot mountain range, backdropping what could only be described as a vast, wide open valley of the most pristine, remote land of meandering rivers and lakes she'd ever seen. Emily figured it was filled with bears and wild mountain lions, and probably Bigfoot for all she knew.

Having come from the land of freeway overpasses and interchanges, the wildest animals she'd ever seen were of the two-legged variety.

In front of her was Belle Haven, a wood and glass building housing an animal center run by Dr. Dell Connelly and his two brothers, Brady and Adam.

If only Belle Haven had been her number one choice on her list of dream jobs.

Or even last.

But it hadn't been on her list at all.

She sucked in a breath. She could do this. She *had* to do this. In her first year of vet school, she'd accepted one of only two available grants. The repayment was a year of internship at either of the two animal centers who'd donated the money, and she always paid her debts.

She'd hoped for L.A., not Sunshine, Idaho, but that's what happened when your mom's multiple sclerosis flared up right before you left for college and you ended up doing school half-assed while trying to keep the rest of your life together—the other scholarship recipient got their first choice.

Shit happened, and Emily knew that better than most. Shit happened, people got sick and died, you picked yourself up and kept going.

What was one year anyway? And besides, by tonight it would only be three hundred and sixty four days left . . .

Pulling out her phone, she accessed her calendar, the one she'd labeled *The Plan*. It kept her sane, listing everything that had to be done, including her goals. More recently she'd added a list of the pros and cons of Idaho, though so far only the con column had anything in it.

Under today's goal she'd typed: *make a good impression*.

Huh. Not nearly as helpful as she'd hoped. Next time

she'd have to be more specific. She slipped the phone back into her pocket and kept moving.

The property was immense. Besides the big, main building, there was a barn, and pens off to the side. There were three guys in the first pen, two of them working a few horses, one leaning against the fence taking notes. All looking like they'd walked off a Marlboro Man photo shoot.

Not something she saw in L.A. every day . . . She pulled back out her phone and added her first check to the pro column—*hot guys*. She was still smiling when she entered the front doors to a large waiting room area.

Sprawled out in various positions on the floor were a golden retriever, a collie mix, two pissed off cats in carriers, and . . . a Shetland pony.

The pony stood next to a chair, calm as you please, while the woman holding his reins sat flipping through the latest *Women's Journal*.

Not something you saw every day . . .

The front counter was a wide half circle, behind which was a woman working two computers and her phone at the same time. She was a strawberry blonde, beautiful, cool as a cucumber as she ran her world. A parrot was perched on her printer and a cat dozed in her lap.

This tugged another smile out of Emily. Animals owned her heart, always had. Hot guys and animals . . . a damn fine combination. Feeling better, and far more confident, she moved toward the counter.

The biggest St. Bernard she'd ever seen came around from behind it and gave her a friendly "wuff."

Emily patted it on the head, and the St. Bernard "wuffed" again.

"Gertie wants you to pay the toll," the receptionist said, nodding to the jar of doggie treats on the counter.

Emily gamefully pulled one from the jar and offered it to Gertie. The dog took it, slobbered her thanks, and lumbered back around the counter, where she thudded to the floor, making the ground shake.

"Graceful Gertie," the receptionist said with a laugh.

"Wuff," said Gertie.

"*Wuff!*" said the parrot in a perfect imitation of the dog.

The receptionist smiled. "No cookies for you, Peanut."

"Boner," Peanut said.

The woman slid the parrot a long look. "We've discussed your language."

Peanut gave a startlingly human sounding sigh and fell silent.

The receptionist turned back to Emily with a smile. "How can I help you?"

"I'm Emily Stevens, the new intern."

"Oh good." She looked vastly relieved. "Dell's been asking every five seconds if you're here yet. It's been chaotic since Olivia left to have her baby last month—"

A man stuck his head in from a hallway off to the left. Emily recognized him as one of the guys from out front, the one who'd been taking notes.

"She here yet?" he asked.

"As a matter of fact," the receptionist said, and pointed to Emily. "Emily, meet Dr. Dell Connelly," she said.

"Great to have you," he said. He had the coloring of a Native American, with dark eyes that cut straight to hers. "Sorry ahead of time, but we're jumping right into the fire this morning."

This only made her feel even more comfortable. "I live in the fire," she said.

"Perfect. We need two extra hands in delivery. I'll catch up with you later on everything else." He gestured for her to go down the hall.

So down the hall she went. She passed a few exam rooms, an x-ray room, what looked like a staff room, and then a surgical room.

The back door was opened, flapping in the wind.

"He's in the last pen," someone in scrubs said, pointing outside.

Feeling a little bit like Alice in Wonderland must have after she'd fallen down the rabbit hole, Emily headed out the back door and to the last pen.

A man was there, on his knees, at the back end of a sheep. He wore cargo pants and a doctor's coat over broad shoulders, his wavy sun-kissed brown hair a few weeks past needing a cut. There was something oddly familiar about it, something familiar about *him*.

The sheep's head was down, her belly was clearly swollen with pregnancy, her sides heaving.

"You're doing great, Lulu," he murmured, stroking her sides. "Such a good, sweet girl."

Lulu bleated weakly.

"I know, baby," the man said. "Almost there, promise." His tone changed then, still low, but now he was talking to Emily. "Welcome, New Girl. Can you come closer, or are you going to help by osmosis?"

At the sound of his voice, Emily felt the shock of familiarity reverberate through her as she moved into the pen.

"Glove up," he said, still not taking his eyes off his patient. "Back pocket." Keeping his hands on the sheep, he elbowed his jacket off one hip.

Emily stared at his butt, now revealed. It was a great butt, as far as they went. Really great. "Um—"

"We doing this today?" he asked.

Biting her lower lip, she reached out and snagged the gloves from the back pocket of his cargoes, doing her best not to cop an accidental feel while she was at it.

"Good," he said. "Now get ready to help catch."

She pulled on the birthing gloves as the sheep emitted another bleat, this one sounding so pain filled that she winced in commiseration with mama sheep.

"Hurry up, New Girl," the guy said. "Find your sea legs. Poor Lulu here isn't going to wait for you."

Emily eyed the muck in the pen, and then her new pants suit, which had been bought with the Beverly Hills clinic in mind, where she'd envisioned herself treating the pets to the stars and looking glam while doing it.

Shit happened.

He moved over to make room for her and she kneeled at his side in time to literally catch the baby sheep and lower it to the ground.

The next half hour was a bit of a blur. The second lamb arrived in the wrong position, so she found herself up to her elbow in sheep. Literally.

"Close your eyes," her mentor instructed.

She did, and he was right. It was much easier to "see" with her hands when her eyes were closed. The uterus tamped down hard on her arm, hard enough to bruise for certain, but she managed to guide the baby out. She stared down at the wiggly mass of goop and felt her heart stutter with the miracle of birth.

They helped Mama get her babies cleaned up, helped the babies get on all four wobbly, stick-thin legs, watching as they took their first sips from Mama. Covered in hay and muck, and sweating like crazy, Emily's eyes misted with the beauty of it all.

Then she became aware that the man next to her had gone still. She felt the weight of his gaze. Yeah. At some point in the past half hour he'd figured it out, too.

Taking a deep breath, she looked up and met his familiar whiskey-colored eyes, which were narrowed at her in a squint. He was as filthy as she, but somehow he still looked hot as hell.

He opened his mouth to say something just as someone joined them. Dr. Connelly crouched low at her other side, grinning at the sheep. "Nicely done, Lulu."

No longer in pain, Lulu bleated happily at the praise.

He turned to Emily next. "Sorry we didn't get acquainted before we threw you to the wolves. I'm Dell Connelly."

Extremely aware of the man still on his knees next to her, staring openly at her now, Emily started to thrust out her very messy, still-gloved hand to Dell. "Oops— Sorry."

Dell smiled. "No worries."

"I wanted to thank you for having me here, Dr. Connelly," she said, struggling to remove the gloves. She was about as graceful as Gertie.

"*Dell,*" he corrected, and eyed her new and now filthy business suit with a quirk of his lips. "We're pretty casual here. Try jeans tomorrow." He nodded to the man on the other side of her, the one who'd carefully settled the new lambs with their mother. Emily could see his T-shirt beneath the opened doctor coat now, stretched over his broad chest, loose over his abs. The shirt said: *Trust Me, I'm a Vet.*

"So you met Dr. Wyatt Stone," Dell said. "He's going to be your immediate supervisor for the duration of your internship, and you'll be shadowing him. I'd trust him with my life, and certainly to have my back in any situation that arises here, and you can, too."

Oh boy. With no choice but to actually finally face this head-on, she looked Wyatt in the eyes. Oh yeah, it was him. Her one and only one-night stand from her one and only vet conference three months ago in Reno.

Two

Wyatt was exactly as Emily remembered—flat-out, dead sexy.

Dammit.

He was built all big and rugged and tough. Great eyes, great smile, both of which advertised that he was up for anything, especially trouble.

While he squinted those mesmerizing eyes at her, Dell snorted and shook his head. "You lost your glasses *again*? Man, Jade's gonna staple them onto your nose."

"They're in my coat pocket," Wyatt said, his voice sliding with smooth heat over Emily's every single female nerve ending. She hadn't forgotten the gruff huskiness of it in her ear, whispering all sorts of naughty promises of what he planned to do to her next.

And he'd kept every promise.

Every.

Single.

One.

All night long . . . She must have made some sound because both men raised their brows. She bit her lip and shook her head. Nothing. Or at least nothing she wanted to share with the class. Especially since she was remembering how her supervisor felt buried deep inside her body.

Dell reached forward and patted Wyatt's pec, pulling out a pair of glasses, shoving them on for him, adding a face shove while he was at it. It was a guy thing to do and spoke volumes about how well they knew each other.

Wyatt blinked, presumably putting his world into sharp focus. Then he took another long, careful look at Emily and his mouth went grim.

He could join her club. This was the stuff nightmares were made of. Going to school in your Spiderman pj's. Giving a public speech naked.

And discovering you'd accidentally slept with your boss.

She got to her feet and backed up, right into the fence. Yep, graceful to the end, that was her.

Dell rose to his full height. "You okay?"

"Yes, I just have to . . ." She put her hands out, letting the two men—one a little confused, the other completely flummoxed—assume she needed to wash up.

Which she did.

And then she needed a quick escape out of here and a one-way ticket to Timbuktu.

She hustled into the clinic and straight into the first room she came to.

A small bathroom. Perfect. There she scrubbed up, staring at herself in the mirror over the sink. "Good going, Doc. You slept with a perfect stranger for the first time in your entire life and now you have to look at him every day for a year." Not that *that* was going to be a hardship.

She tapped a second round of soap out of the dispenser and scrubbed up some more. It was Reno, Nevada's fault, she decided. It had been her first vet conference, and she'd loved it. She'd just graduated, been high on that and the joy of her future, and for the first time since her mom had died, she'd decided to let her hair down.

And oh boy had she done just that.

She'd had the night of her entire life; hot, torrid, *amazing* sex, but the next morning when she'd left his hotel room and made the walk of shame back to hers, wearing her clothes from the night before, heels in hand, she'd been embarrassed at her lack of control.

She, the woman who had to interview dentists before choosing one, she who couldn't buy a new pair of shoes or an outfit without thinking about it at least overnight, had slept with a perfect stranger. Except now he wasn't going to be a stranger at all.

Karma was such a bitch.

Behind her, the bathroom door opened. With a surprised squeak, she quickly whirled around. "I'm in here—"

"I know," Wyatt said. The room was so small that his body bumped into hers when he closed the door. The last time this had happened, she'd ended up in his bed. Naked.

"Step back," she said in a voice that wasn't nearly strong enough.

He didn't step back. To be fair to him, he couldn't. But he didn't have to get closer—which is exactly what he did. So much closer that she could have taken his pulse. With her mouth.

He was wearing glasses and though she'd never given it an ounce of thought before, a guy in glasses was sexy as hell.

Or maybe it was just *this* guy.

He dropped his birthing gloves in the trash, and then washed and dried his hands, his gaze holding hers prisoner in the mirror the entire time. Then he turned to face her and backed her into the wall. One of his hands settled beside her head, the other by her hip, trapping her in. "It's really you."

She gave him a little push, but did the big lug move? *No.* "I'm using the facilities here, Wyatt."

"Good to know."

"That I'm using the facilities?"

"That you remember my name."

It was just about the only thing she did know about him, and that he'd pointed it out only emphasized how big a mistake she'd made. And if she was regretting it, sleeping with him, how must he feel? She knew why she'd done it, but why had he? What kind of a guy picked up a woman in a hotel bar at a vet conference?

Okay, so just about every guy on the planet would be up for that. But still . . .

She was close enough that when she tilted her head up to stare at him, a strand of her hair stuck to the stubble on his jaw. She stared at it, at the way his mouth quirked slightly, revealing an easy humor.

And she realized maybe she knew a little bit more about him than just his name. Thanks to the past hour, she also knew he was a vet like her, and a really good one at that. He was early thirties-ish, definitely young enough that the faint lines fanning out from his eyes were clearly from the sun and laughter, not age.

This wasn't the problem. The problem was the other stuff she knew about him, things no one should know about people they worked with. Like the fact that he kissed amazingly. And he did . . . other things amazingly too. He liked to talk when he was in bed. Dirty talk that had shockingly turned her on. With nothing more than his voice, he'd been able to coax her into forgetting everything except what he'd been doing to her. And she'd liked what he'd done to her.

A lot.

He'd been an intuitive, giving, demanding, *fantastic* lover, and now she worked for him. Good sweet baby Jesus.

Those whisky eyes on hers, he hit the bathroom lock, the sound of the bolt sliding into place as loud as her accelerated breathing. "Oh, no," she said, shaking her head. "No way." They weren't going to have a second one-night stand no matter how hard her nipples had gone. He'd already wielded his magic over her, with nothing more than that low-pitched voice and sex-on-a-stick smile. They were over and done.

Done. Done. Done. "Absolutely *not* doing it again."

He grinned. "It?"

"You know what I mean." She poked him in the pec, momentarily distracted by how firm it was. "And how is it you work here? Are you stalking me?" She gasped as another thought occurred to her. "Did you guys take me on because of— Oh my God. Is it because I"—she lowered her voice into a horrified whisper—"got *naked* with you on the first date?"

His lips twitched. "Sweetness, that wasn't a date." His voice went a little dry. "But yeah, I found you so irresistible in Reno that I hired a PI, got your last name and where your internship would be, and then applied to the same place to have a job as your supervisor all in order to continue having sex with you."

"Okay," she said slowly, staring up at him. "You're right. I'm being ridiculous." Now that she was thinking again, logic thankfully took over. She'd accepted this internship long before she'd ever gone to Reno. "Sorry about that."

"Yeah, you almost overreacted there for a minute," he said on a smile.

"Ha." But she was overreacting to his smile, holy cow. He hadn't shaved that morning, and she had good reason to know that the stubble on his sexy jaw wasn't too soft or too rough, but juuuust right. She closed her eyes and tried to shake off that memory, but it was far more difficult than she'd have thought possible. "I have a plan," she said. "A life plan. And this isn't on it. *You* aren't on it."

Getting back home to L.A. was on it. Marrying her college study partner John was on it—though probably it would help if she was actually dating him for real instead of their vague promise to "maybe" reconnect in Los Angeles once he'd passed the bar exam. Paying off her college debt and buying her dad a house was also on her plan. As was getting herself a nice, comfortable, stress-free life. The only thing regarding Idaho on the plan was the three-hundred-and-sixty-four-day countdown she had going.

Wyatt had been watching her think too hard and his smile faded at whatever he saw on her face. "Your academics and work ethic earned you this internship, Emily. What happened in Reno—"

"—stays in Reno?" she asked hopefully.

He stared down at her for a long beat, and then nodded slowly. "If that's how you want to play it."

"So . . . it's my call?" she asked, needing the verification.

"Your call."

"Really?"

"I'm a lot of things," he said. "Not all of them good, but if I give my word, then it's gold."

She nodded, and some of her relief must have shown because he cocked his head at her, looking genuinely surprised. "What did you think I was going to do?" he wanted to know. "Take out an ad in the newspaper about our night?"

Oh God. "Sunshine has a newspaper?"

"Well, no," he said. "But there's a bulletin board outside the Stop And Go. Good as gospel."

She dropped her head and laughed a little, and then realized her forehead was on his chest. His *hard* chest. She quickly lifted her face. "I'm sorry. I shouldn't have touched you."

His eyes darkened a little bit, and she knew he was remembering the other things she'd touched that night.

And kissed . . .

Oh this was bad. Very, very bad. "We have to go back to being strangers," she said.

He just stared at her.

"We *are* strangers," she said.

"Yeah. Strangers who know what each other's O-face looks like—"

She covered his mouth but it was too late. And great, now she was sweating again. "We wouldn't know that," she said through her teeth, "except *someone* insisted on keeping the lights on!"

He smiled, wrapped his fingers around her wrist and pulled her hand from his mouth. "I like the visuals."

And there went the bones in her legs. "Okay," she said shakily. "We're going to need rules."

He grinned. "Like?"

"No. No smiling! These aren't fun rules."

"Damn."

She forgot about the no touching, and poked him in the sinewy pec again. Her finger practically bounced back. "One of the rules is that you can't look at me like that," she said. "We aren't going to repeat what happened in Reno."

He laughed softly. "It'd be hard to repeat it since you can't even say what 'it' is."

"I'm serious! I work under you, that's it—" She broke off at his wicked expression and realized that she'd sounded . . . dirty. "You know what I mean!" She said this in no uncertain terms, firmly, and she meant it. Or, more accurately, she *wanted* to mean it. She'd have to work on that. "So you can just keep those sexy looks to yourself."

"Sexy looks?"

Like he didn't know. "Yes!"

"All right," he said in his slow, warm voice. "I'll stop giving you sexy looks. Anything else?"

"We ignore what happened in Reno. It never happened. We stay professional because Belle Haven is my job, my livelihood."

His smile faded. "We're in accord there."

She let out a breath of relief. They could do this. "Okay,

good. I'll go out there first." She started to turn to go around him, but there wasn't room.

"Here," he said, and his hands went to her hips as he turned, too, trying to make space.

Now they were sandwiched up against each other and she sucked in a breath.

"We're going to have to stop meeting like this," he said, good humor in his voice.

"If you weren't so big, it wouldn't be a problem."

He gave another sexy low laugh and she replayed her words, heard the unintentional innuendo, and blushed. Well, hell. He *was* big. *Everywhere.* And in spite of being knees deep in muck not fifteen minutes ago, he smelled good. Really good. Warm and sexy good, which was just damn unfair. "Are you doing this on purpose?" she asked.

He gave her a look of utter innocence. "Doing what?"

"Blocking the door!"

"Why would I do that?" he asked.

She closed her eyes, sucked in a breath, and squeezed past him, brushing her breasts against his chest, her thighs to his, and everything in between—all of which contracted hopefully—as she finally got to the door.

"Emily."

She didn't look back. "I think we've said everything there is to be said, Dr. Stone. I really think it's best if we completely ignore each other for now."

"I get that, but you've got a . . ."

She felt the brush of his fingers at her ass, and she craned her neck and glared at him in disbelief. "Are you serious? We just agreed that this"—she waggled a finger between them—"never happened." God help her but she couldn't do this without his cooperation. "That's the plan. Remember the plan. *Stick* to the plan."

He stared at her for a beat through those sexy glasses, then lifted his hands in surrender.

Turning away, she peeked out the door. Seeing no one, she stealthily slid out and took a deep breath. Shook it off. Just a minor setback on The Plan she told herself. Just a little hiccup, and a huge mark in the con column of Sunshine. About six-feet-two-inches huge.

Trying to be cool, she walked down the hallway, and had just passed the staff room when the woman from the front desk stuck her head out.

"Hey there," she said. "I didn't get to introduce myself before. I'm Jade Connelly."

Emily shook her hand. "Are you related to Dr. Connelly?"

"Married him. Did you know you have a birthing glove stuck to your ass?"

Three

Bemused, feeling a little bit like he'd been hit by a tornado—a cute, feisty, sexy-as-hell tornado named Emily, Wyatt stepped into the hallway. He was just in time to catch sight of Jade pointing out what he'd tried to tell Emily—that she had a birthing glove stuck to her very sweet ass.

Her own hands on that sweet ass, she was twisting around to try to see herself. She went still, and then yanked off the glove. She stared down at it, and then, from the length of the hallway, lifted her head and caught his gaze.

He raised a brow.

She blushed.

Someone should probably point out to her that in order to ignore someone properly, you didn't blush every time you caught sight of that someone. But it wouldn't be him, since they weren't going to talk. Not about their personal lives, and certainly not about that night.

And yet he remembered it, every detail. Sometimes he'd

flash to the feel of her lips on his skin, her breath warm on his neck, her bare legs wrapped low and tight around his back, hardened nipples pressed to his chest as she arched up into him. And the sound of her sweet, needy gasp in his ear on that first thrust . . .

He blew out a breath and shook it off. He knew what she wanted from him, and he agreed. They needed to ignore what'd happened in Reno, for *lots* of reasons, not the least of which was that like her, working at Belle Haven was everything to him. No way in hell would he put it in jeopardy. He knew how to be professional, and for both of their sakes, that's exactly what he'd be.

The center's tech, Mike, came down the hall, his eyes going to Emily. "Pretty," he said to Wyatt.

"A good vet," Wyatt said.

Mike smiled. "Even better." He handed over a file. "Exam room two. First timer. Has a . . . *unique* problem."

Wyatt slid him a look. "Care to share?"

From exam room one came the sounds of a scuffle, and then Dell's voice calling out for Mike.

"Oh shit," Mike said. "Gotta go."

"Hey, what's the unique problem?"

But Mike was gone.

Instead, Emily was moving back toward him. Someone, probably Jade, ruler of their universe here at Belle Haven, had given her a lab coat to put on over her suit. He wasn't sure why she'd been in a suit in the first place when her job was wading knee deep in questionable shit all day, but hell, he had sisters, two of them, both bat-shit crazy, so he knew better than to question a woman's clothing choice.

Besides, she'd looked sexy as hell in her fancy suit, with her pretty blazer offering peek-a-boo hints of some lace thing beneath, as she helped Lulu give birth.

In general, Wyatt didn't have a "type" of woman. For him it was about a certain gleam in her eye, a spark that said she knew life was hard as hell but that it could also be fun as hell, and she could make it work in either scenario.

Right now the look in Emily's eyes was *bring it on*, and damn if he didn't like that, too. He tore his eyes off her and opened the patient file in his hands. He read Mike's prereport and smiled.

"What is it?" she asked as he came to a stop before her.

"Gonna be fun." He handed her the file and walked into the exam room, hearing Emily's sharp intake of air behind him.

She was a fast reader.

Lady was a year-old Tibetan mastiff. She was sitting next to her owner, Sally Feinstein, humping Sally's leg.

Sally was calmly ignoring this behavior, thumbing through Facebook on her phone. At the sight of Wyatt and Emily, Sally put her phone aside and gestured to her hundred-pound dog—who looked twice that at least, thanks to her crazy, thick fur. "I'm on a road trip to my parents' house down south. I've only had Lady about two weeks. They've never met her before, and I can't take her there while she's doing this to . . . everything."

Lady had switched from Sally's leg to the table leg.

Wyatt crouched low and introduced himself to Lady by offering his fist for her to sniff.

Lady took a polite sniff, licked his knuckles, and went back to her humping.

"I try to ignore her," Sally said. "I didn't want to reward this embarrassing behavior by bringing attention to it."

Jade must have briefed Emily on protocol because she pulled a pen from her coat pocket and began to ask Sally the usual questions about their patient. What did Lady eat, had Lady been exhibiting any odd behavior lately, etc.

"I call trying to screw my mailbox odd behavior," Sally said. "You've got to fix this."

Emily made a note.

"She even humped my pastor," Sally said, distressed. "She humped the little old lady who lives next door. She humped my other neighbor's prized gardenias, and her husband nearly shot Lady."

Emily made some more notes.

Wyatt listened to the ongoing conversation with one ear while he sat next to Lady and began to examine her. He found the problem in about ten seconds.

"Could it be some sort of odd vitamin deficiency?" Sally asked hopefully.

"That seems unlikely," Emily said, and put down the file. She crouched at Wyatt's side, meeting his gaze.

He gestured for her to go ahead and make her own assessment. She looked at him for a long beat, and he knew he hadn't completely hidden his good humor from her because her eyes narrowed.

Smart girl.

He waited as she turned her attention to Lady, examining her in the same manner he had—thoroughly. So he saw the exact second she realized what he'd already discovered. Her mouth curved, then her teeth chewed into that bottom lip to try to hold it back, but her hazel eyes were laughing when they met his across the length of Lady's body.

The moment was brief but oddly electrifying, broken when Sally dropped to her knees beside them. "What is it?" she asked, sounding deeply concerned.

"Mrs. Feinstein," Emily said. "You said you adopted Lady two weeks ago?"

"Yes, I've got a friend who's got a cousin whose sister-in-law's brother breeds Tibetan mastiffs. Lady was the last in a long line of winning show dogs. I don't have her paperwork yet. It's been delayed for some reason. It doesn't matter. I'm not going to show her, no matter how expensive she was. I just love the breed because they look like teddy bears. No ugly reproductive parts showing all the time." She shuddered distastefully.

Emily bit her lip harder.

Wyatt rubbed Lady's tummy, and the dog went boneless on its back, spread eagle. Lady *did* indeed resemble a teddy bear. In fact there was so much hair everywhere the dog might have been a stuffed animal from a child's room.

Except for the huge erection between its hind legs, sticking straight up in the air.

Sally stared at it. "What in the Sam Hill is *that*?"

"A penis," Wyatt said.

"I was really hoping you were going to say tumor," Sally said. She paused. "Why does my girl dog have a penis?"

"Lady isn't a female. And there doesn't appear to be a thing wrong with him—other than he hasn't been neutered."

Sally shifted her shocked gaze from dog to vet. "Lady's not a she."

"Not in the slightest."

Tired of being flat on his back, Lady leapt to his feet and panted happily at them. Then he tried to hump Emily.

Wyatt rose, pulled Emily up with him, and then Sally.

Lady wasn't bothered by being disrupted in mid-hump. He went back to dating the chair.

"We could take care of this for you," Wyatt told Sally. "Dr. Connelly is doing the surgeries today, I could check and see if there's an opening for Lady."

"Good gracious," she said faintly, a hand to her heart, still staring down at Lady like she'd just discovered she was the owner of a green-striped pig. "Yes, please. I'd like to get this . . . taken care of."

Wyatt took Emily through two straight hours of patients before giving them a moment to breathe in the staff room, where they inhaled the plate of sandwiches Jade had put out for them. They stood at the counter, and though Wyatt didn't know about Emily, *he* was giving the whole ignoring her thing a good ol' college try.

Mike broke their uneasy silence when he poked his head in and held out their next file. Wyatt gestured for Emily to take it. She reached out for it and a birthing glove fell from beneath her white lab coat.

Mike grinned. "You don't have to hoard those, Doc, we keep 'em in every exam room."

When he was gone, Emily looked at Wyatt. "You could have told me I had another stuck to my butt."

"That would've suggested that I'd looked at your butt."

She pulled off her coat and one last glove fell from her. She made a noise from deep in her throat that suggested she blamed him.

This wasn't a surprise. Something else having sisters had taught him—blame was easily assigned to the nearest male in the room.

They went back to work and saw twenty-seven more patients before the end of the day. He sent an exhausted Emily home with the rest of the support staff, and then went to Dell's office, where Dell and Adam were waiting on him.

Adam was Dell's brother, and while not a vet, he helped run Belle Haven. He was a search and rescue expert, an S&R instructor, and taught all the local dog obedience classes.

"How did the new girl do today?" Dell asked.

"She's smart," Wyatt said.

Dell nodded. "And?"

Sweet. Cute. Hot . . . "Good with people and animals," he added.

Dell smiled. "We already know all that, it's why we took her. Tell me something I *don't* know."

"She's a quick thinker, and knows her stuff when it came to the domestic animals."

Dell nodded.

Adam hadn't moved. He remained sprawled back in his chair, as still as a cat, just as intelligent as his brother. "But?" he said.

"I already know," Dell said. "We all know. She's not used to this kind of work, she's a city vet. She startled when you treated Sergeant and he nearly took off her hand."

Sergeant was a bad-tempered sheep who'd come in today with a stomachache. "Sergeant has nearly taken off all our hands at one point or another," Wyatt said.

"How about Crazy Charlie?" Dell asked. "He throw her off her game?"

Crazy Charlie had come in with his even crazier parrot who tended to shout all sorts of racial obscenities.

Like owner, like parrot.

Turned out, Emily wasn't all that good at corralling her emotions. Annoyance, embarrassment, fear. Wyatt had seen each and every one of them as she felt them. So had everyone else.

She was going to have to do better there. "She's finding her footing," he said.

Adam arched a brow, but didn't say a word.

Dell smiled. "You're defending her."

Wyatt shrugged. "You like her, too, or she wouldn't be here. You already know she was worth it."

Dell nodded. "But it's good to know you feel the same."

"Yeah," Wyatt said. "I feel the same." Aware of Adam's quiet, knowing gaze, he left and went to his office to handle the mountain of paperwork waiting for him.

He was still at work at seven o'clock, stomach growling, hunched over his computer when his cell phone buzzed an incoming text from Zoe, his older sister.

So as it turns out, the gas stove isn't working. No worries, the fire department said all is well now.

Jesus. He grabbed his keys and headed out. Someday in the near future, *home* would be the house he built on the land he'd purchased earlier in the year—ten acres out near the lake on the outskirts of town. For now, home was the place he and his two sisters Darcy and Zoe shared, the house that the three of them had inherited from their grandparents.

And *home* might actually be the wrong word. Money pit. Yeah, *money pit* was definitely right. The huge, rambling old Victorian was falling off its axis, but it was the only home the three of them had ever known. The plan was to fix it up just enough to get out from beneath it. They'd divide the profits, and each would go on their merry way with their lives. But it had been a year and they were still stuck with each other.

Zoe was the oldest at thirty-two. The classic oldest, she was driven, bossy, and a perfectionist. Wyatt, the middle child, was only eleven months behind her, and the baby, Darcy, had just turned twenty-six and . . . well, she was as crazy as they came. Not three-day-emergency-hold crazy so much as . . . uncontrolled, uninhibited, and scary as hell.

The three of them had grown up quickly, and at the mercy of their foreign diplomat parents, whose jobs had taken them all over the world. Liberia for two years. Bolivia for three. Jordan. Hungary. Indonesia . . . It was mostly a blur now, but the lifestyle of being ripped away from everything you knew every few years, or even every few months, had left its toll in varying ways on each of them.

In Wyatt's case, all he'd ever dreamed about was putting down roots and staying somewhere long enough to be on a sports team, and maybe get a pet while he was at it.

The bright side to his early years had been his grandparents. Born and raised in Sunshine, they'd never left. He and his sisters had often been sent here for summers. Though both grandparents were gone now, they'd left their legacy—the deed to the money pit.

The deed was worth squat.

The house was worth squat.

But the memories of the time spent here was deeply rooted, and as the commercial went—priceless. After all the years of forced upheaval, Wyatt was here in Sunshine to stay.

He pulled into the driveway just as the sun was setting

behind the Bitterroot mountains. There was nothing like fall in the mountains. A brilliant cornucopia of colors in every hue flashed beneath the last of the sun's rays. He parked his truck and noted that there were no fire trucks. A bonus—the house was still standing— Well, somewhat. All good signs, he figured.

Zoe opened the door as he hit the top step. "'Bout time," she said.

"Fire?" he asked.

"There was no fire. I just was getting tired of waiting on you."

He glared at her, but she was unaffected. It was hard to intimidate someone who'd seen him wear a Superman cape to bed until he was eight.

"Dammit," she said. "You look exhausted."

"I'm fine." If *fine* was half a minute from falling asleep on his feet.

She narrowed her eyes and studied him, her fingers clutching a pad of paper that he knew held the dreaded "to-do" list.

The list had to be tackled, was being tackled, one item at a time. Nightly. By the person least done in by their life that day. He and Zoe had a little who-was-busier competition going. She was a pilot at the small, local airport, and worked long hours. Wyatt worked long hours. So usually, it was a toss-up.

"How was your day?" she asked casually. Too casually.

But this wasn't his first rodeo. He knew how to stay on the bull. "Delivered two baby sheep, expressed anal glands, cast a leg, cut the nuts off a sheperd," he said. "You?"

"Crop dusted, and dropped the mayor at Yellowstone for an interview."

They stared at each other, waiting to see who would crack first.

"Jesus," came a disgusted voice from the couch. "Whose penis is bigger?"

Zoe hugged the list to her chest. "Mine is."

Wyatt snatched the list from her for pride's sake, for his entire male race.

Darcy, prone on the couch, cackled.

Wyatt pushed his way in and stood in the center of the living room, hands on hips as he studied his baby sister, still recovering from her accident nine months earlier, and the five surgeries she'd required in the time since. "Thought we agreed, you're using your powers for *good* these days," he said.

"But evil is so much more fun."

Four

Emily was hanging upside down from the pull-up bar across the foyer doorjamb when her sister walked in the front door, stifling a little scream.

"Jesus," Sara said, hand to her chest. "You look like a vampire."

"Vampires don't sleep in the open daylight," Emily said. "How do you use this thing every night? I've only managed one stomach crunch."

"That's because your idea of exercise is reading in bed until your arms hurt from holding up your Kindle," Sara said.

Unfortunately true. She righted herself and jumped down. "But I want a stomach as flat as yours."

"Then you need to do more than hang upside down," Sara said. "Burn some calories."

"Calories," Emily said on a sigh. "The evil tiny creatures that live in my closet and sew my clothes a little tighter every night."

Sara laughed and pulled off her sweatshirt, shedding a layer of sawdust as she did.

"Hey," Emily said. "Did you hear anything funny when you drove up?"

"Like the sounds of my sister vampire snacking on the mailman?"

"Ha-ha," Emily said. "No, I mean I keep hearing some odd howling. I don't know if it's a dog or coyotes—"

Sara dropped her sweatshirt to the couch. She wore cargo shorts, heavy-duty work boots, and a men's wife-beater tank that showed off her tats. Her short, spiky hair was still dusted in sawdust—as was most of the rest of her. She'd come to Idaho with Emily as a show of support, the both of them putting on a show of being psyched for the wild, wild west that they'd imagined Idaho to be.

Emily was still missing Los Angeles.

Sara, not so much. She'd recently had her heart run over—and backed up on and run over again. She was open to the idea of staying if it turned out that Sunshine, Idaho had a place for a rock chick, broken-hearted lesbian who'd collected degrees like some women collected shoes and yet chose to be a carpenter instead of using any of those degrees.

Sara kicked off her badass boots and more sawdust flew everywhere, drifting slowly to the floor of their rental house.

"Meow." This came from Q-Tip, the ancient fuzzy gray cat who'd come with the rental. She'd appeared out of the shadows on move-in day, looking deceptively sweet—until she'd bitten both Sara and Emily within the first half hour for having the audacity to try to pet her.

No one wanted to claim the old cat, and the landlord had suggested they take her to the shelter. Sara, who wasn't crazy about cats, and bleeding from the bite, had been on board.

But Emily had looked into Q-Tip's eyes and known the truth. Q-Tip was old, grumpy, and set in her ways. No way was anyone going to adopt her, which left only an incomprehensible future ahead of her.

Emily had refused to do it, and so they now owned a cat. Correction, they were now *owned* by a cat.

Sara, a forgiving soul, reached down now to pet Q-Tip hello. The cat accepted this like it was her due . . . for about three seconds. Then she bit Sara's hand—not too hard, more like a warning—and then, head high, the feline moved a few feet off and began to clean herself.

"Queen to peasant," Sara said, shaking off the bite as she looked at Emily. "We feed her again why?"

"Because when we don't, she yells at us."

"Ah, that's right," Sara said. "So . . . how was your first day on the job?"

"Terrific," Emily said.

"Really?"

"No. Guess who my supervisor is?"

"Uh . . . a werewolf?" Sara asked. "A zombie?"

"Wyatt."

Sara blinked, looking confused. "Who?"

"My one-night stand."

Sara stared at her then thrust both hands high in the air. "Score!" she yelled.

Q-Tip jumped about a foot, glared at Sara, and stalked off down the hall.

"No," Emily said to her sister. "Not score. How'd you like it if your one-night stand was suddenly your supervisor?"

"My supervisor is a six foot three, three hundred and fifty pound, hairy, chunky, twice married, serial hetero male," Sara said.

"You know what I mean."

Sara moved to the kitchen, pulled open the fridge, and stared at the contents.

Q-Tip came running in, belly swinging to and fro. She could hear food coming from five miles away.

"Chicken or spaghetti?" Sara asked Emily. "And what did you do when you saw him?"

"Spaghetti," Emily said. "And I made a fool of myself." She paused and mentally groaned. "I accused him of stalking me."

Sara gave a bark of laughter, grabbed salad makings, set them on the counter, and then went to the sink to wash her hands. She was an amazing cook, which was a good thing because Emily could burn water.

"And how did *he* take this turn of events?" Sara asked.

"He thinks it's funny."

"It is."

"No, it's not." Emily sighed.

"You gonna sleep with him again?"

"No!" Emily said. "And would you focus on the real problem here? I now have to work with someone I got naked with."

"So?"

"So, it's unprofessional!"

Sara out and out laughed at this. "Only if you accuse him of stalking you again."

Emily opened her mouth, but realized Sara was grinning. And it had been a long time since her sister had been happy. Since she'd dumped her model girlfriend Rayna in fact. Six long months. There'd been times Emily had despaired of ever seeing Sara happy again. "Well I guess it's nice to see you smiling, even if it's at my expense."

Sara shrugged. "Like you always say, life sucks and then you move on."

Did she say that? Had she really taught her sister that? "No," she said slowly. "Life doesn't suck."

"Uh-huh," Sara said. "Let me see your calendar."

Emily strode to her purse and pulled out her phone. "Here. Why?"

Sara accessed The Plan.

"Hey," Emily said. "That's just for me—"

"Right here." Sara had gone back to the day Emily had found out where her internship was going to be. All that was typed in the square was "life sucks."

"Okay," Emily said. "But that was a really bad day. Sara, life doesn't suck."

"Then why does today's page say: three hundred sixty-four days left until—"

Emily made a grab for the phone, but Sara was quicker. And taller. Sara held it out of reach. "—until I'm back in L.A.," she continued reading, "at a great job and can reconnect with John." She frowned. "John?"

"John Number *Two*." She didn't talk about John Number One, the cheating, lying, rat-fink bastard. At Sara's blank look, she added, "My college study partner."

"Yeah, but that was for what, two minutes?"

"A whole semester," Emily said defensively. John had taken her out for pizza in exchange for help in their psych class. He'd been handsome and smart, and he'd seemed genuinely interested in her. Plus he'd always paid for her meals, a huge bonus since she'd been on a budget so tight anything other than ramen had been a treat.

After he'd gone to law school and she'd gone to vet school, they'd lost contact. But it could still happen.

Maybe.

Okay it was highly unlikely, even she knew that she used the abstract idea of getting together with John as a way to give herself security, and something to look forward to on her plan.

After a very complicated, not to mention emotionally draining, last few years, she wasn't up for the complication.

In any case, Sara didn't look impressed. "Wasn't he the guy who had his life all compartmentalized out? In a planner?"

"Hey, there's nothing wrong with that."

"Uh-huh," Sara said.

She could do worse. John was driven, smart, kind, and

yeah, he liked a good plan as much as she did. "He's a good guy," she said.

"Does he know that you tell people you're planning on putting a ball and chain on him?"

Emily bit her lip. "I don't tell people that."

Sara rolled her eyes and handed back the phone. "And some say *I'm* the oddball sister."

Whatever. It was a good, solid plan, and that was important to Emily. It gave her security, which she'd lacked for some time now. It gave her a road map to follow, and she wasn't going to take any detours. She'd had enough detours to last a lifetime. The plan was in motion, period. And it did *not* include having a hot affair with a hot vet. She shoved her phone back in her purse. "I don't mock your dreams."

"My dreams are to get laid by the weekend," she said. "What's to mock?" She paused. "Em, maybe you should just keep things simple, you know? Simple works. No expectations, no worries. No plan. Just wing it for a change."

Sara had *always* just "winged it." It was the motto of her entire family, just so accepting of whatever came their way. Emily sighed. "I can't operate like that, I can't be like you and Dad."

"There's nothing wrong with how we operate," Sara said. "And Dad's doing good, Em. He's never going to stop grieving but he knows Mom had the exact life she wanted. She died content."

Emily didn't buy this. Refused to buy this. When their mom had gotten sicker, Sara had been away gathering one of her three degrees. She'd been spared seeing the illness grip their mom. She hadn't had to help her out of bed, get her dressed, fed . . . Emily knew her sister meant well, her heart was in the right place, but like their dad, she had no clue.

None at all.

Five

Wyatt got up before dawn. Normally this wasn't a problem, but he'd stayed up late the night before working on the roof over the back patio, number three on Zoe's to-do list.

Number one was supposed to be the leaky kitchen sink, and number two a misfiring smoke alarm, but the patio roof had been relegated to numero uno when it had collapsed after dinner.

Using a halogen light he'd worked late into the night. He still wasn't finished, but he'd gotten the framing fixed, so at the very least no one was going to die if they walked through the patio. He considered that a success.

Ass dragging even before his day got started, he showered—which involved trying to fit into a bathroom filled with his sisters' lingerie hanging on every surface to dry—dressed, put on coffee for Zoe—a necessity as it turned her from evil witch to somewhat human—started the water for Darcy's oatmeal, and then made his way back down the hallway. He knocked on Zoe's door, shoved it open, and flipped on her light.

"You are such an asshole!" she yelled at him.

Yep. "Coffee's on," he said, ducking out of the way of the pillow she sent sailing in his direction. He moved to the next bedroom. Wash and repeat with the knock, opening the door, and flipping on the light.

But Darcy's bed was empty.

"Shit," he said, knowing this meant that once again, she'd been unable to sleep.

"What?" Zoe called from her bedroom, still sounding morning rough. "What's wrong?"

"Wild Girl's gone," he said. "Again."

Zoe's sigh said it all. She appeared in the hallway in her pj's with crazy bed hair. "It's my turn to track her down," she said. "You get to work."

"Text me when you've got a status," he said, feeling more than a little grim as headed to work. Darcy was a lifelong problem that neither he nor Zoe had yet figured out how to handle. She was smart, and ever since her car accident, lost. So damn lost.

Maybe if either of their parents had given her the time of day instead of being baffled by their own offspring, but they'd been—and still were—too busy saving the world. What he did know was that he and Zoe were all Darcy had, and they were stuck with one another, for better or worse. And hell if Darcy was going to go off the deep end on his watch.

He stopped in town for a donut and coffee, breakfast of champions, and to his utter shock, found Darcy's beat-up Toyota in the lot.

But when he didn't find her in the bakery, he stepped outside again. To the right of the bakery was a preschool. No way in hell was Darcy in there, though at the moment she had the right mental capacity for the age level.

To his left was the old general store. That had been

turned into a bookstore, and then, most recently, a marijuana dispensary. Fuck. He strode inside and there she was at the counter, talking to a guy in a medical lab coat over a Hawaiian print shirt and board shorts slipping off his scrawny ass. His hair was in a do-rag and he wore round, wire-rimmed sunglasses with pale purple lens.

"All you need is a card, man," he was saying to Darcy. "And then I can get you—"

"Oh, *hell* no," Wyatt said.

Darcy turned, eyed her brother, and sighed.

He grabbed her walker in one hand and lifted her in the other, carrying her out of the store.

"Seriously?" she asked when he'd set her down on the sidewalk and shoved her walker at her. She glared up at him, steam coming out of the top of her head.

"Seriously," he said at a much lower decibel than she. "You're on the mend, Zoe. Don't fuck it up now."

She blew out a sigh and stared down the sidewalk. "You're a pain in my ass."

"Ditto, Wild Girl." He paused, softened his voice. "You're getting so much stronger," he said. "You got out of the wheelchair when they said you wouldn't. You're off the pain meds—"

"But I still have pain."

He knew it, he hated it. "Your PT says you're doing better every day."

"My PT's evil."

Her physical therapist happened to be AJ Colten, one of Wyatt's oldest friends. AJ owned and operated Sunshine Wellness Center, both a gym and a physical therapy facility. He was a big bear of a guy who'd been through his own hell, and one of the best men Wyatt knew. "That's bullshit, Darcy. And so's this." He gestured to the dispensary behind them. "I know it sucks, but—"

"Do you?" she challenged. "Do you know what it's like?" She rolled her eyes again and lifted a hand when he would've spoken. "Forget it," she said, and blew out a sigh. "How about donuts? You going to object to donuts for breakfast?"

"No," he said, aware that he'd won the sprint but not the race. "I'll even buy."

Belle Haven was still quiet when Wyatt arrived for work. The sun's sleepy rays were just peeking over the rugged, majestic mountains at the other end of the valley as he strode around the back of the building to the barn.

As a kid, he'd never owned more than could fit into a backpack. He'd been ten the year he'd attempted to stow away a lizard. It had died on a train in Africa, and he'd learned a valuable but painful lesson.

No pets.

He'd spent years aching for that to change, rescuing injured animals, begging to keep them.

It had never happened.

He walked up to the first pen and greeted the horses. Reno and Kiki, who belonged to Adam and Dell. And Blue. *His*. He and Adam had rescued her from a shitty hellhole of a horse ranch about two hundred miles south of here, and after doctoring her up, he'd fallen in love.

Blue nickered at him and pressed against the fence to get closer, blowing in his face, fogging his glasses. Wyatt wasn't sure if the show of affection was because she loved him back, or because he carried treats.

"Miss me?" he asked, stroking her.

She snorted, and he couldn't help but smile. The thrill of owning something that didn't fit into a backpack hadn't faded one little bit. Like the land he'd bought himself, Blue represented another tie to Sunshine. He was growing roots, and he wasn't done.

He saddled up Blue while she frisked him for the treats, prancing in place with anticipation.

She loved to run.

So did he.

They took the hills, and only when they were both satisfied with themselves did Wyatt turn them back to Belle Haven.

By the time he'd cooled her down, put away the riding gear and entered the animal center, it was nearly seven. They didn't open the doors until eight, but the place was showing signs of life. Dell was there, prepping for the morning's surgeries. Mike hadn't arrived yet, but he would soon.

Same with Jade. And, presumably, the new fiercely determined intern that he was going to do his damnedest to ignore, as dictated by the fiercely determined intern herself. It made good sense, for both of them. Problem was, he'd never been all that down with being good.

Emily parked in Belle Haven's lot and gave herself day two's pep talk. "You can do this." Yesterday she'd been thrown off her game by one sexy Dr. Wyatt Stone, but not today. Today she was prepared. No matter how hot he looked with his rumpled hair, glasses, and cargo pants filled with goodies—not all of which were in his pockets—she was sticking to The Plan.

Totally doable. Of course, it would be a heck of a lot easier if she hadn't dreamed about him last night and how he looked *without* the cargoes. Tall. Broad. Built . . .

"Oh boy," she whispered and banged her head on the steering wheel a few times. She lifted her head and stared at herself in the rearview mirror. "You can do this."

Her reflection didn't look as sure as she'd like.

Blowing out a breath, she got out of the car and headed inside. Jade was at the controls, and smiled at her. "I've got coffee on in the staff room," she said. "And your day's schedule in your inbox. We had a surprise patient show up early, so Wyatt's already at it in exam room one. Dell's in surgery, the poor guy had to get up extra early to handle today's insanity."

Emily smiled. "It's nice that you two get to work together."

Jade laughed. "Nicer for me than him."

"Dell doesn't enjoy having you run his world?"

"Well . . .. you'd have to ask him. But maybe don't ask him today." She grinned. "I had to transfer some funds, and let's just say that sometimes I like to get creative with the label I put on the transfers. Today's was 'grocery money for the Guatemalan hookers.'"

Emily burst out laughing. "Because they don't feed themselves?"

"Exactly!" Jade grinned. "You should've heard him when he saw it." She lowered her voice and affected a Dell-like tone. "'You know this appears on our formal bank statements, right? Our accountant sees this, Jade.'"

Emily was still smiling when she entered exam room one, momentarily forgetting her nerves about seeing Wyatt again.

Until her eyes landed on him.

He was sitting on the floor, long legs stretched out in front of him. Between them was an opened crate, and he was sweet-talking a terrified, pissed-off tabby at the back of the crate, who, given her long, howls of protest, absolutely did *not* want to be sweet-talked.

"Where's her owner?" Emily asked.

He pushed up his glasses and glanced up at her. "Missy can't handle this."

"I can see that."

"No, Missy's the owner. Sweetie's the cat." He was wearing another pair of cargo pants, battered steel-toed work boots, at least a size twelve, and today's shirt under his open lab coat read: *Vets Do It With a Lot of Heavy Petting.*

He should've looked ridiculous sitting on the floor, leaning into the crate making kissy-kiss noises at the cat, but he didn't. He looked . . . mouthwatering.

"Hey, sweet thing," he said in a low cajoling voice. "Come on out. I'm gonna love you up, I promise. You know you want some of that."

"Oh, please," Emily said on a laugh to cover up the fact that her bones melted at the sound of him. "That's never going to work—"

But hell if the cat didn't shift ever so slightly closer to Wyatt and sniff at him.

Wyatt flashed both Sweetie and Emily a smile. "Aw, that's it," he crooned to the suspicious, wary cat. "Come on, baby girl, all the way. I'll be good to you, I promise."

Emily laughed again, even as she felt her nipples tighten. She crossed her arms over her chest. "Honestly, Wyatt, no self-respecting female—cat or woman—is going to—"

But Sweetie walked out of the crate and into Wyatt's lap. He cuddled the cat in close and eyed Emily over its head. "*All* females react to that."

"Not all," Emily said. "*I* wouldn't."

He just smiled at her.

"I don't," she repeated. *Liar, liar* . . . "I'm . . . seeing someone." Holy crap. *Where had that come from?*

Wyatt raised a brow at her.

"It's true," she said.

He totally didn't believe her, she could tell. "We met in college. John," she said, clarifying. Good Lord, *stop talking!* But her brain receptors refused to carry the message to her mouth. "He's concentrating on his career right now, but . . . yeah." She bit her tongue, hard, to keep from saying anything else. She'd bite it off if she had to.

Wyatt had gone back to checking out the cat in his lap, feeling her lymph nodes, looking in her ears and eyes. Somehow he got Sweetie to open her mouth for him. Emily would've sworn Sweetie was actually purring.

"So . . ." Wyatt said, continuing the conversation from

hell. "You and your boyfriend are on a break. So he can concentrate on his career."

"Um . . ." Emily wasn't sure how John Number Two had gone from boyfriend fantasy to fake boyfriend but she wanted off this subject. "Yeah." The. End.

"In the meantime, who's concentrating on you?" Wyatt asked.

Not the end. "Me?" she asked, trying to sound bored.

Wyatt looked up from his exam of Sweetie. "Yes. You."

"I . . . don't know what you mean."

"Say you need something," he said. "A spider removal, someone to hold you after a bad dream, help with your car. Or maybe just some company, seeing as you're new to town."

She stared at him. "I handle my own spiders. And I don't have very many bad dreams, but when I do, I turn on all the lights and watch *Say Yes to the Dress* on Netflix. My car's in okay shape but if I need help, I'll call a mechanic. And I don't get lonely."

Again with the liar, liar thing. Because the truth was, sometimes, she *did* get lonely.

But hell if she was going to admit to it.

Wyatt's gaze said he knew she was full of shit, but he didn't call her on it. Instead, he shocked the hell out of her by responding seriously.

"If you were mine," he said. "I'd want to do those things for you. Just for future reference."

"Well . . ." Gulp. "Good to know." Something in the way he'd said *mine* had her taking a second look at him. He had that whole laid-back look going, but he had a good amount of protective alpha in him. "Are you with someone?" Oh, please don't let her have slept with someone else's man.

A small smile twitched at the corners of his mouth as he read her expression through those hot smart-guy glasses. "Worried?" he asked, stroking Sweetie into a puddle of goo in his lap.

"It's a legitimate question," she said.

His smile faded. "I wouldn't sleep around if I was with someone."

She nodded and then squirmed a little at the implication. "Listen, regarding my . . . boyfriend." Oh boy. She squirmed some more. "The truth is, the relationship is sort of . . ." Nonexistent. "Silent."

"Silent."

"Yeah. Like the *K* on knight. Actually, to be honest, it's more of an implied thing."

Wyatt was looking amused again. "As in made-up?"

She sighed.

And he laughed. "You're a nut."

Yes. Yes, she was. A complete nut. "Let's go back to ignoring each other," she said a little desperately. "Can we?"

"Absolutely," he said. "I'm good at ignoring nuts."

She sighed again.

Six

Emily worked hard over the next few days to maintain some sort of professional distance with Wyatt, to varying degrees of success.

Or failure, depending on how she looked at it.

On Monday of week two—three hundred and fifty-eight days left—Emily and Wyatt went over their schedule and got right into it. Their first patient was a female boxer, approximately one-year-old, with a runny nose.

"'Morning, Martha," Wyatt said to the dog's owner. "This is Dr. Stevens, our new intern. What's up with Gracie today?"

"She's sick," Martha said, wringing her hands. "So sick. She whistles when she breathes."

Emily took a look at Gracie, who weighed around fifty pounds. Solid girl. Currently she was rolling in ecstasy in Wyatt's lap, loving up all over him.

And she did indeed whistle when she breathed.

"Gracie's new to Martha's family," Wyatt told Emily.

"Which includes four kids and two other dogs. She's very playful and obsessed with all the toys she can get her mouth around, as we learned last month when she swallowed Martha's son's coin collection," he said, stroking Gracie. "She came from a shelter, so I think she's just trying to make up for lost time, aren't you, girl?"

Gracie licked his jaw, whistling with each inhale.

"Why don't you do the assessment for us, Dr. Stevens," Wyatt said, voice calm. She knew that was to keep both patient and owner calm. He always spoke calmly, even through the tough ones, like Friday's tricky feline birth, or the extremely pissed-off pit bull who hadn't wanted his shots, or extracting a nickel from the back of a yellow Lab's throat.

But Emily knew that his casual 'tude had nothing on his sharp intelligence. No doubt he already knew exactly what was wrong with Gracie. But happy to learn and gain new experiences, she moved closer. Gracie sniffed her hand before turning back to Wyatt.

Wyatt smiled and held Gracie for her, taking on the role that she'd taken for him her first week. First thing she did was look at the dog's extreme runny nose. Interestingly enough, it was only dripping down one side. This was a blatant clue that either something was anatomically incorrect, or there was a physical blockage. She turned to Wyatt and found him watching her.

Yeah. He was way ahead of her.

Her first thought was maybe the dog had broken a tooth, and she looked into Gracie's mouth. Nope, not a broken tooth. But it was something she'd never seen before and again met Wyatt's gaze.

"Yeah," he said. "It's a new one for me, too."

"What? What is it?" Martha asked, crowding in.

"Well," Emily said after Wyatt nodded at her. "It appears Gracie swallowed a Kong toy whole." She turned Gracie's head to face her worried human mama so that she could see down the dog's throat. The length of the Kong lined up along Gracie's throat, the larger end nearest her nose.

"Oh my goodness," Mrs. Coleburn said. "I suppose that's why she whistles."

Emily slid a look at Wyatt.

His eyes were flashing good humor. "Yep, that's why she whistles."

"But why the runny nose?"

"Because she can't swallow," he said.

"Oh my— Is she going to die?"

Had the Kong gone down sideways, Gracie most certainly could have, but Wyatt gently patted Martha's hand. "No, we can get the Kong out. Emily here will take real good care of her, I promise."

"But . . ." Martha glanced at Emily, gave her a nervous smile, then turned back to Wyatt. "She's new," she whispered, like Emily didn't have ears.

"She's also good," Wyatt whispered back, and patted her again.

Martha melted for him the way Gracie had.

Dr. Wyatt Stone, animal whisperer, woman whisperer.

An hour later, Gracie had been sedated and the toy removed from her throat. Emily was washing up when both Dell and Wyatt walked into the staff room.

"Nice job," Wyatt told her. "Really nice job." He turned to Dell. "She's got a good touch."

"Glad to hear it," Dell said.

"Because it means your money was well spent?" Emily asked.

Dell laughed. "Well, that, too. But it's nice to have you on board. I'm hearing great things from the staff."

Emily slid a look at Wyatt, who was watching her with that easy, calm confidence he exuded in spades.

"She handled herself with Blackie earlier," he said. "Without getting nipped."

Dell laughed, and at Emily's confusion, he said, "*Everyone* gets nipped by Blackie the first time."

"And some of us, the second time as well," Wyatt said wryly, rubbing his thigh as if in memory.

Dell just grinned. "Man, that last time she just about ate your pants right off of you."

"Which was the last time I kept a carrot in my front pocket, I can tell you that," Wyatt said. "But Emily had her eating out of the palm of her hand in five seconds."

Emily felt her face heat with embarrassment as she soaked up the praise she hadn't realized she'd been desperate to hear.

Dell reached up into a cabinet and pulled out a box of cookies. Jade walked into the room and without missing a beat, took the cookies from his hand and replaced them with an apple.

"How the hell do you know?" Dell asked, baffled.

Jade smiled, kissed his jaw, and left.

Dell sighed and bit into the apple.

That must be love, Emily thought.

"We need a welcome to Belle Haven dinner," Dell said to Emily. "How about tomorrow after work, Wyatt?"

"No go," Wyatt said. "Adam's running an S&R class, and we're both working with him. You promised."

"Yeah. And then Jade's got me signed up for a couple's cooking class for the next three nights after that." His face was carefully neutral as he said this, and Emily loved that, though he was clearly not thrilled about this, he kept it to himself, not discrediting his wife in any way.

"Friday then," he said.

"Sounds good to me," Wyatt said, and both men looked at Emily.

No socializing, she'd told herself. Just ignoring. Wyatt, his back to Dell, smirked at her clear internal battle. It was the smirk, she decided, that disconnected her mouth from her brain. "Dinner would be great."

Dell left and she stared at Wyatt. "Does he know about us?"

"Know what?"

She felt herself flush again. "You know."

He laughed, low in his throat.

"You think this is funny?" she asked in shock.

"What's funny is that you can't say 'sex' but you could put your mouth on my—"

"We can't have dinner!"

"Hey," he said, lifting his hands. "Not my idea."

"No, but you could've told him you were busy."

"I wasn't."

"And you never lie?" she asked in disbelief.

"Only when it suits me."

She absorbed that for a moment, thought about their night together, specifically their good-bye, and then sucked in a breath. "Did you—"

"Like when I told you as you left my hotel room that it'd been the best night I'd had in a long time?" he asked.

Actually, he'd pressed her against the hotel room door, cupped her face, given her a *wow* good-bye kiss, and then whispered in her ear. *You're going to be hard to get over, sweetness. That was a night I won't forget.* She cleared her throat. "Yeah," she said. "That."

He was still smiling, but there was more to his gaze, a sudden intensity. "No," he said. "That was one hundred percent honesty." He met her gaze. "You're not the only one thrown off their axis here, Emily. We never intended to see each other again. Hell we didn't even know each other's last names. And that worked for me."

She absorbed the unexpected jab, and then shook it off. If she was being honest it worked for her, too. After her internship, she was going to leave Sunshine and go back to her real life. She had a whole lot of plans, none of which included a sexy but laid-back vet who apparently had his own secrets. "Which is why we need to really work at ignoring our sordid past."

His lips quirked. "Especially since you have an almost sort of boyfriend. The . . . silent kind."

She refused to let him bait her. "And how about *your* reason for not wanting to be with someone. Let's hear about that."

He didn't answer. Just flat out said nothing.

If she hadn't been so flipping curious about him in spite of herself, she'd have taken the time to admire his ability to do that so effectively. Only a man, she thought. "I suppose this is your charming way of saying none of my business?"

He shrugged.

"Got to tell you," she finally said. "It's a little annoying, not being able to read you, and you not speaking in full sentences. Or in *any* sentences."

He smiled at that. "When you first started here. I wondered how a cute little thing like yourself had ever been pushy enough to make it through the world of animal medicine, but you've got grit, sweetness. You were born for this job."

"And you should've become a politician for your ability to dodge a question."

He tipped back his head and laughed. It was a good laugh, and did something to her belly. Not good.

"I'm not opposed to being with a woman," he said. "As you very well know." He met her gaze, and she felt yet another blush rise up her cheeks.

"As for settling down with *one* woman," he went on. "I work morning to night, I live the job, and on top of that, I've got two bossy, nosy sisters, and we share a large ancestral home that's falling apart. It all requires a lot of my time and attention. A woman would be crazy to want me right now."

Emily thought maybe that was unfair to the woman who

fell for him—which absolutely would not be her. But surely, whoever *did* could see through his schedule to the man beneath, and just as surely get that he was worth working around his busy life.

"Now you," he said.

"Me what?" she asked warily.

"When I complimented you in front of Dell, you just about fell over in shock and embarrassment. Why?"

"I didn't." But she had, and they both knew it.

Wyatt waited her out with the same calm patience he'd shown every animal they'd seen together.

"I guess I didn't expect you to notice how hard I was working, because you were working just as hard," she finally said.

He looked at her for an eternal beat, during which time it felt like he was seeing all her inner thoughts. And as some of these inner thoughts involved him naked on a platter, this wasn't a comfortable feeling. But she also had a lot of insecurities and self-doubts, and wasn't used to the kudos.

"Why did you become a vet?" he finally asked, voice quiet.

And just like his patients, she fell right into his eyes and tried to please him. "I'm a third generation," she said. "My grandpa was an army sergeant turned vet." She smiled at the memories of him. "There wasn't an ounce of gentleness to him for people, but he had endless vats of it for an injured or sick animal. He inspired me."

Wyatt smiled. "Was it your mom or dad to follow the tradition?"

"My dad. He's not army," she said. "But he's just as pragmatic and stoic as my grandpa was. He's a rescuer, always was. He spent most of his career working for the local shelters, doing whatever needed to be done without much thought or care to anything else." Like his personal life.

Including his family.

"Makes sense," Wyatt said. "He was raised by a military

man." He paused. "It's not easy to make a living working just the shelters."

"No." Though they'd always had the bare necessities, there'd definitely been a lack of comfort. "He doesn't practice much anymore," she said. "Hasn't since my mom died."

Wyatt was quiet a moment, and she was extremely aware of his gaze on her face, and the fact that she'd given him a lot more than he'd given her.

"Broken heart?" he asked.

"More like a lack of interest," she said. "She was his drive. He still rescues animals though."

"I meant what I told Dell, you know," Wyatt said. "You're good. And it's nice that you're following your father's footsteps. Nicer still that you're taking the less obvious route by coming to Idaho instead of the Beverly Hills gig."

She could have just not said anything, but unlike him, she didn't have a tier for acceptable lies. "I wanted the Beverly Hills gig."

Something changed in his eyes, but he didn't say a word about her choices or the reasons for them. He merely gave her another smile. "Maybe things work out for a reason. Maybe you'll like it out here."

"Maybe," she said.

And look at that. Apparently she had a tier for lies, after all.

Seven

One week after Wyatt's and Emily's first real conversation in the staff room, he got up even earlier than usual and ran to the store for everything he needed. Then he dragged Darcy out of bed. Too tired to deal with her walker, he carried her down the hall to the kitchen.

"What the—" she started grumpily, stopping when she saw the balloons, flowers, and blueberry muffins he'd just gotten.

"Oh, good catch," she said yawning. "It's Zoe's birthday."

"Yeah, and you're going to help make a stupid big deal out of it." Wyatt had long ago learned that the way to a woman's heart was through gestures he didn't always understand, so he knew enough not to question the power of celebrating a birthday in a huge way.

This, through some trial and error over the years, had come to mean decorations no matter how "Hallmark," and something delicious that wasn't allowed on a normal day.

Zoe had been claiming to be fighting five pounds all year, and had banned muffins from the house.

But he knew she'd want one today, because according to her, calories didn't exist on birthdays. Just like they didn't exist for any dessert that had fruit in it.

He shoved Darcy's walker at her and gathered up all the decorations. Then he got them both down the hall and to Zoe's room.

There, they flipped on her light and sang "Happy Birthday" to her while she fought her tangled sheets to sit up, swearing at them the whole time.

When that didn't stop them from singing as loudly and off-key as they could—a sibling tradition—she threw her pillows at them.

And then the book on her nightstand.

Wyatt ducked in time, but the book knocked a lamp over. Of course it broke, and then Darcy cut her finger on the glass. They yelled at each other over the lamp, the glass, Darcy's cut finger, and then Wyatt shoved Zoe's present beneath her nose.

A gift certificate to an entire day's pampering at the spa.

She went still, and then, oh Christ, her eyes filled. She chucked her last pillow at him. "How did you know I needed this more than my next breath?" she demanded.

Wyatt smiled and tossed her a box of tissues.

Darcy punched him on the arm. "Don't you dare take credit for knowing," she said, and then turned to Zoe. "He knew because you left us a very specific list, as you damn well know. You e-mailed, texted, and put it on Facebook."

Zoe laughed. "Oh, yeah." She held out her arms.

Wyatt and Darcy both took a mistrustful step back. Well, Wyatt did. Darcy, gripping her walker, ducked reflexively.

"No, I mean it," Zoe said, and waggled her fingers in a "come here" gesture. "I want a damn hug."

"You need a Midol to go with it?" Darcy asked warily.

"No!"

Hoping to avoid yet another physical altercation, losing any more furniture—or his head—Wyatt shoved Darcy ahead of him. Naturally, the "hug" included some noogies and lots of bone crunching, but hey, there was no more bloodshed.

And then he heard the telltale sniff. Grimacing, he pulled back and gave Zoe a pained look. *"Again?"*

She swiped a tear. "Dammit! I didn't expect to get all sappy. I don't know what's wrong with me."

"It's because you're old now," Darcy said.

Wyatt wrapped an arm around her neck, covering her mouth with his hand.

"Mmffl!" Darcy said.

"Zip it, I'm saving your life," he said. He looked at Zoe. "You okay?"

"Yeah." She sent them each a watery smile. "I know this is a birthday, but I gotta say, the crazy makes it feel a lot like how our first Thanksgiving together with just the three of us went, doesn't it?"

They'd never celebrated Thanksgiving growing up. They'd never been in the States in November. But they'd celebrated this year, and not surprisingly, had fought like cats and dogs. Being here together now, fighting like cats and dogs yet again, he agreed that this was exactly what Thanksgiving had been like—crazy as shit. And crazy wonderful.

The next few days at work with one adorably sexy Dr. Emily Stevens flew, and he was getting pretty good with the ignoring thing. Or at least he'd done a good job with the faking of the ignoring thing.

Because she, with her tough, smart ways, was pretty damn difficult to ignore.

Except she wasn't going to stick. She had one foot out the door. He didn't have to work at remembering that—he couldn't forget it. "So," he said conversationally as they scrubbed up for their first patient. "How many days left?"

"Three hundred and forty-seven."

He'd been just teasing her, but her ready answer was a sober reminder. Like his parents, like his ex-fiancée, like at least one of his sisters, she was yet another person in his life with one foot out the door. He needed to remember that.

The day was long and challenging as they saw twenty-two patients. They'd done their best for each of them, and each of them had appreciated it. It had been in every soft, warm lick, every tail wag, and in some cases, a rumbly purr.

It was the people who *owned* his patients who were the pains in his ass.

Mr. Thicket hadn't appreciated being kept waiting and had bellowed at Jade behind the receptionist desk.

Since Dell had flown north to a client's ranch to inoculate horses that morning, Wyatt was in charge. When he heard Mr. Thicket go off, he excused himself from a patient's room and strode out to the front, standing in front of Jade's desk, hands on hips to face Mr. Thicket. "Problem?"

"You have incompetent help." He jabbed a finger at Jade.

Wyatt couldn't see Jade, but he could feel her narrow her eyes. Jade was a lot of things, and maybe impatient was one of them, but incompetent? Hell, no. In fact, she was just about the most competent woman he'd ever met.

"You need to fire her," Mr. Thicket said.

Wyatt had a very long fuse, but that fuse didn't extend to a guy taking his frustration out on a woman, no matter that the woman in question had a baseball bat behind her desk and knew self-defense moves that could take down a man twice her size. "You have two choices," he told Mr. Thicket. "Wait outside while I treat your dog, or go somewhere else to be treated."

Mr. Thicket glared at him, weighing his options. There weren't many. Everyone and their brother knew that there was no comparable animal center to Belle Haven for two hundred miles.

"It's cold out there," Mr. Thicket said. "Effing fall arrived."

"Two choices," Wyatt repeated, unmoved.

In the end, Mr. Thicket huffed and puffed, but went outside, where he proceeded to bitch to every person who walked in or out the front door until Wyatt finished seeing his dog.

The day didn't improve when he was assisting Emily in treating a ferret named Franko and Franko's owner—a teenage girl—grabbed the animal incorrectly. Franko lashed out, going right for Emily's face. Wyatt caught him in mid-air, and got his finger bit nearly to the bone for his efforts.

Emily treated him in the staff room. He could tell she was shaken—not at the blood, she had nerves of steel—but that it was *his* finger and not hers. "You shouldn't have done that for me," she said.

In all truth, it had been instinct. He'd have done it for anyone.

"Does it hurt?" she asked softly when she was done with him.

"If I say yes, you going to kiss it better?"

She rolled her eyes and cleaned up.

Wyatt had no idea why he baited her.

Okay, he knew. After being near her for the past couple of weeks, and then remembering how good their long-ago night had been, seeing that they still had chemistry and knowing it would be that good again now, he wanted her. He wanted her naked beneath him, her tongue in his mouth, her legs wrapped around his back, her hips rocking up to meet his until they both came so hard they saw stars.

And she could take or leave him. The fucking story of his life.

A few hours later, Franko's owner was back. The teenager had bought Wyatt a present—a tie with puppies and kittens on it. Jade made him wear the tie for the rest of the afternoon.

Much later, he stood at the front desk after their last patient, getting his messages from Jade and giving Gertie some love. His day was topped off when Cassandra Hastings came in carrying a casserole dish.

Cassandra was in her forties, unhappily single, and a regular at Belle Haven. She always paid on time and was polite. And warm and friendly.

Very warm and friendly.

"Here she comes," Jade warned him beneath her breath. "The cougar, at six o'clock."

"Cougar!" Peanut the parrot yelled, and ducked dramatically.

Wyatt turned his body away. Cassandra had a problem with roaming hands. And sure enough, she set the casserole dish down on the counter to give him a hug.

He pretended he'd dropped something, and evaded, a maneuver he'd gotten good at.

"Brought you lobster ravioli," she said. "Your sister said it was your favorite."

Wyatt was going to kill Zoe. Or maybe Darcy. Hell, he'd just kill them both and be done with it.

Jade, behind her counter, gave him the laughing eyes. She knew damn well that the last time he hadn't turned away fast enough, Cassandra had copped a feel. Not something he cared to repeat.

Cassandra patted the casserole dish. "I've been told I make the best lobster ravioli this side of the Mississippi. Why don't I come out to your place tonight to gather the dish?"

"Your place," Peanut said.

Wyatt glared at the parrot. Jade was no help, she'd ducked behind her computer screen, shoulders shaking with silent laughter, the ingrate.

Taking his silence as consent, Cassandra shifted closer. "Poor baby, I bet you're exhausted, what with how hard you work and all."

"I'm not tired," he said. He'd passed tired about three hours ago. "But I am busy later."

"No problem." She smiled and winked. "I'll come early."

He heard what he'd have sworn was a gagging noise behind him, and when he craned his head, he met Emily's gaze.

She nudged Wyatt out of the way and offered her hand to Cassandra. "Dr. Emily Stevens," she said. "The new intern. Why don't I go in the back and transfer the dish to another container for you right now so you don't have to bother Dr. Stone tonight?" It was worded as a question but everyone knew she wasn't asking, including Cassandra.

She stared at Emily for a long heartbeat before pulling her hand back. "Not necessary," she finally said. "I'll get the dish back from him another time."

"Boner!" Parrot yelled merrily as Cassandra left.

Jade put out her finger and Peanut high-fived her with one of his parrot feet. Then Jade grinned at Emily. "You're good." She turned away to answer the phone and then said, "Hold on a sec, they're both right here." She hit Speaker. "Go ahead, babe."

Dell's voice filled the room. "I can't get back in time for dinner," he said. "You two go on without me."

Their welcome to Belle Haven dinner for Emily. Wyatt had forgotten that was tonight.

Emily stared at him and gave him a wide-eyed head shake that he got loud and clear. She wanted him to get them out of this. It made perfect sense.

But he said nothing.

Emily narrowed her eyes at him, and he found himself smiling.

"Problem?" Dell asked into the silence.

"No," Emily said. "Of course not."

"Use the company card, Wyatt, this one's on me."

"Got it," Wyatt said, watching Emily bite her lower lip. The same lower lip he'd once sucked on until she'd moaned his name.

"You should come with us," Emily said to Jade when Dell had disconnected.

"Oh, that's sweet, but I can't. It's book club night and it's at our house. You'll have to join us next time, Emily. Sorry, Wyatt, chicks only." She stood up and began her closing up routine. "Shoo," she said to both of them. "Go have dinner. After the day we had, you both deserve it."

Which is how Wyatt ended up in his truck driving Emily to dinner.

"This is silly," she said. "You should've let me take my car. We could've left at the same time, and each gone our own way. No one would've ever known that we didn't do dinner."

"We're doing dinner," he said.

"Why?"

Yeah, genius. Why? "We're going to be working closely together," he said. "Ignoring each other isn't going to work for a whole year."

"Three hundred and forty-seven days."

"Or that," he said. "We might as well settle in and get to know each other."

She slid him a look. "We already know each other. Far more than we should."

He laughed. This was true, to an extent. He did know certain things, such as she had a warm, perfectly curvy bod that fit his perfectly. He knew what she tasted like—heaven. And he knew the soft, erotic little sounds she made when she was desperate to come. And *those* thoughts weren't helping one little bit. He shifted in his seat. Yeah, definitely, he shouldn't be remembering any of those things. "We could get to know each other on a *conversational* level," he said.

Her gaze dropped to his mouth, and he did his damnedest not to do the same. "How is *that* a good idea?" she wanted to know.

"We can learn each other's tics and idiosyncrasies."

She stared at him. "You think that if we get to know each other, we won't like what we learn, and that will put a coolant on our chemistry?"

He laughed a little, unable to help it. But there was a fat chance in hell that they could put a coolant on this thing.

Over there in the passenger's seat, she turned to face him, arms crossed, clearly having taken his amusement in the wrong way.

"Oh my God," she said. "You think you won't like *me*. Why not?"

He was still smiling. "You already know you don't like me all that much, so why the hell do you even care?"

"Humor me," she said, eyes narrowed.

"All right." He shrugged again. "I don't want to fall for a woman who has one foot out the door."

She opened her mouth, and then closed it and turned to the window.

Conversation over. Clearly he was right, which didn't give him any satisfaction. But he was glad they'd gotten that out in the open. His parents had chosen their life's calling over their own kids. His ex's career had meant more than anyone or anything in her life, including him. And here was Emily, giving off that same vibe.

Good thing he learned from his mistakes.

Usually.

"Sounds like you've been hurt," she said softly. "What happened?"

He didn't like that she read him so easily. And as attracted as he was to her, he knew she wasn't going to be his, so he had no intention of sharing his own fucked-up life with her.

She surprised him by suddenly seeming hugely relieved at his lack of response. "This is good," she said, leaning back. "We can't talk to each other. You know what that means? It means we're totally unsuited. So all we have to do is not sleep together again, and it'll be okay." She glanced over at him. "We can do that, right?"

No, he was pretty sure they couldn't. His expression must have answered for him.

"Crap," she said finally. "We're in big trouble, aren't we?"

He was saved from having to answer that when his phone rang. He answered on Bluetooth and was shocked as hell when his mother's voice filled the cab of his truck.

"Wyatt, darling," she said. "So glad I caught you before I head into the Rome embassy."

To hear from her was rare enough that his first question was the obvious. "You okay? Is Dad okay?"

"Of course," she said. "We just wanted to wish you a happy birthday."

He felt Emily look at him in surprise. "Mom," he said, pinching the bridge of his nose. "It's Zoe's birthday, not mine."

There was a long pause. "Are you sure?"

Wyatt choked out a laugh. "Yeah, I'm sure."

"Huh," his mom said. "Okay, well, tell her I said happy birthday."

His eye twitched. "Mom, you should tell her yourself."

"No time now, darling. Call her for me, okay?"

"I don't need to call her, I live with her," he said.

"You're still in Sunshine then, at Nana's?" she asked with a whisper of disbelief.

Wyatt understood her confusion. His parents thrived on

constantly being in motion, moving on to the next great place. They'd given their kids the world, all of it, every single corner, and they couldn't comprehend them not loving that lifestyle.

"In Nana's house," she said. "In that crazy old place. I can't even believe it's still standing. How in the world are you managing? And Darcy, with all those stairs?"

None of these were real questions, they were purely rhetorical. His mom cared about the general well-being of her children, she really did. She just never needed the details. "We're managing fine," he said.

"But you all fought so much as children," she said.

Still did, Wyatt thought, remembering the lamp.

"I just figured you'd sell that monstrosity and move on," she said.

Yeah, definitely, an eye twitch. He put a finger to it. "Mom, I told you and Dad both when I first got here last year, I'm staying in Sunshine."

"In Idaho," she said, adding bafflement to her disbelief. *"Idaho."*

"Idaho's beautiful," he said.

"Yes, but how many people can say they've seen the seven wonders of the world before the age of eighteen? And out of all those places, you end up in Idaho."

"I'm happy here," he said, very aware of Emily's gaze on him. Guess she was going to get to know more about him than he'd counted on. "I'm staying."

"The three of you, together. It's so . . . domesticated," she said, still confused.

The truth was, just about everything Wyatt had ever done had confused her. Trying to collect animals wherever they went, wanting to stay in the same school for more than a month, insisting on attending college and vet school in the States. Vet school! That had *really* baffled her, and now here he was, living in Sunshine, which barely showed up on a map. "I realize your offspring living in nana's house, fixing it up together, boggles your mind, Mom. But Zoe's still flying the friendly skies and seeing the world, and I can assure you, Darcy's as wild and untamable as ever. You did good there, real good."

"I'm sensing sarcasm, Wyatt James Stone," his mom said. "You know I don't like sarcasm."

He bit his tongue, which went against the grain for him. But talking to her never failed to remind him of why he led the life he did. Growing up, he'd had zero choices. But he had choices now, and no one could take them away.

"I've got to run," his mom said.

The story of his life. But at least he no longer had to pack up and run with her.

"Send my wishes to the girls," she said.

"Will do—" But she'd disconnected.

Eight

Emily found herself fascinated by the inadvertent peek into Wyatt's personal life. Fascinated, and full of a surprising empathy. "Your parents live in Rome?" she asked.

Wyatt kept his eyes on the highway as he drove. "This month."

Interesting that while at first glance he appeared to be relaxed and in his driving zone, his mouth was a little grim, his hands tight on the wheel.

He drove to the next town over from Sunshine, where there were more restaurant options. He parked, and they walked the short distance to the heart of downtown.

"Thai, Mexican, Sushi, or American cuisine," he asked, gesturing to her choices.

Thai was good, but it always gave her a stomachache. Mexican was even better, but then she'd have pico de gallo breath. Sushi could go either way.

No, wait. A stomachache or bad breath didn't matter.

Because they weren't going to sleep together again.

Nope, that ship had sailed. Completely. Gone, over the horizon never to be seen again.

Even if for some crazy reason she wanted to hug him—which was a little like wanting to hug a polar bear—cuddly but rather dangerous.

"Emily?"

Her gaze went to his mouth. Did he know he had a great mouth? "American cuisine," she heard herself say.

His lips curved. "Emily."

She lifted her gaze to his and winced at his knowing smirk. Busted. Had she thought he needed a hug?

"Better," he said.

"Hey, maybe you have something on your mouth," she said. "Like a crumb or something."

"Do I?"

She bit her lower lip. Save face and lie? Or come clean and admit she was lusting after him. *Lie*, she decided. "Yes," she said.

"Where?" He swiped his forearm over his mouth. "Better?"

She couldn't explain herself in a million years, but she shook her head and went up on tiptoes, touching his lips with her fingertips. "Here," she whispered, and then, clearly in the throes of a psychotic break, she pressed her mouth to the spot.

Wyatt's hands went to her hips, tightening their grip when she pulled back.

"You get it?" he asked, voice low but tinged with amusement as well as heat.

Not trusting her voice, she nodded, and telling herself that was absolutely the *last* time she touched—or kissed—him, they went inside the restaurant. They ordered bacon blue burgers and seasoned sweet potato fries, and some locally brewed beer.

The food was fantastic.

So was the company.

In Emily's world, there were pretty much three levels of existence; bad, okay, and good. *Bad* was having her mom slowly die over a five year period from complications of MS. *Okay* was attending vet school after earning her undergraduate degree, but nearly killing herself to do it, because she had to keep a job on the side to pay for such luxuries as eating and helping her dad with medical bills. *Good* was pretty much the same, but school was finally over and she was actually working at her dream job—albeit about a thousand miles away from where she'd planned. In one year though, she could have her dream job, in her dream location. Life might achieve great status.

She didn't see room for a distraction named Wyatt. She understood the attraction—she'd have to be dead and buried not to be attracted to him, but he was a damn big deviance from her Plan.

Too big.

One beer loosened her tongue, two beers separated it from her brain. So naturally she had two. "Your mom's interesting."

"She's something," he said.

"What does she do?"

"She and my dad are foreign diplomats."

"Wow. Impressive." From what she'd heard, it sounded like he and his sisters had been on their own for a long time. And on top of that, his mom had seemed downright disinterested in his life.

Her own mom had been the opposite. She'd been snoopy, nosy, bossy, and . . . amazingly wonderful.

It had been several years since her death but Emily still got a lump in her throat just thinking about her. "You must've had a very interesting childhood," she said.

"Sure," he said. "If you call moving twenty something times between the ages of five and seventeen interesting."

"So I guess you're good on a plane," she said.

"Planes. Trains. Mules . . ." He smiled at her laugh. "Ah. You've never been to Morocco."

"No. I'm a shaky traveler," she said. "I can't even sleep through a flight, I have to be awake for the crash."

Now it was his turn to laugh.

He had a great laugh. And did he know that when he laughed, his eyes laughed, too? Or that his hair curled over his ears in a really sexy way? She forced herself to stop noticing and blamed beer number two. She pushed it away from her.

"Travel enough and it gets easier," he said.

"We used to vote on our family vacations. Land or sea." She smiled at the memory. "Land meant driving to the desert and camping out. Sea meant driving twenty minutes to the Los Angeles reservoir. We'd sit on the concrete shore in our drug store beach chairs and pretend we were on a deserted South Pacific island."

"Hey, at least you got a vote," he said.

"You didn't, I take it."

He shook his head. "I'd come home from school and say, 'Hey, Mom, just joined the Bolivia soccer team,' and she'd say, 'Sorry, Son, we're going to be in Greenland by this time next week.'"

She couldn't even imagine. "Did it screw you up?" she asked.

"Nah." He let out a low rueful laugh and scrubbed a hand over his stubbled jaw. "Well, maybe a little."

"Don't worry, you hide it well," she teased, trying very hard not to notice that the sound of his hand on his stubbled jaw made her nipples hard.

This wasn't good. This was the opposite of good. He was open and fun and charming, but he was also being very professional—as she'd requested—and she needed to be, too. Which meant absolutely no more noticing that he smelled good. Or that she wanted to hug him again . . . and climb into his lap. *Dammit.* "We're *all* screwed up by our parents. What are your sisters like? Are they like you?"

"Like me how?"

She bit her lower lip, and he gave her that sexy laugh again. "Oh, don't hold back now," he said. "Here's your chance to tell me what you think of me."

She thought he was sexy as hell, but she wasn't about to share that. The truth was, he was wonderful. He came off as laid-back, deceptively carefree, even playful.

But he was much more. At work, he was intuitive, sharp, and also incredibly demanding, expecting the best for his patients, expecting the best out of the staff.

He'd been all those things in bed, too, and at the memory, her body quivered. If she closed her eyes, she could still remember what his hands had felt like on her, guiding her where he wanted, his mouth at her ear, his words turning her on every bit as much as the rest of him.

"No words?" he asked. "Nothing?"

"Maybe a little annoying," she said primly, and he flashed that knowing smile again.

He knew her way better than was comfortable.

"Your sisters," she said. "You were going to tell me about your sisters."

"They're crazy," he said. But his tone was affectionate, and there was laughter in his voice. "Zoe's only eleven months older than me, but she's been playing mom since she could walk. Darcy's the baby, and managed to party her way across the planet. They're both colossal pains in my ass, but for the most part we make it work."

"You live with them."

"For now. They needed me." He shrugged. "Family."

At the simple statement, and the deep loyalty in it, she nodded. She got that. Learning about his family, how he'd grown up, how he took care of his sisters, it was yet another layer to him that she hadn't expected.

As for their little experiment of getting to know each other in order to derail their attraction . . . if the low-level hum of arousal buzzing through her system accounted for anything, they hadn't derailed a single thing. And now, instead of liking him less, she liked him more.

Epic fail.

"I really wanted you to be a jerk," she admitted softly.

"You wanted to work with a jerk?"

"No, I wanted to not be attracted to you anymore." She reached for her beer, needing the liquid courage. "Is it just me?" she asked softly into his silence, knowing she shouldn't. "I'm the only one struggling here?"

He looked at her for a long moment, but didn't respond to that, either. Instead, he dropped some cash on the table, stood up, and pulled her with him.

Mr. Professional.

She should appreciate the effort. She should replicate his effort. "Where are we going now?"

"Home," he said, taking her back to his truck, opening the passenger's door for her. "To bed."

She went still and assessed her feelings. Her girlie parts were on board. Standing so close to him between the truck and his big, warm, strong body, she gave in. "Okay, good. Maybe just one more time—"

"In our *own* beds," he said.

"Oh." She blew out a breath. Nodded. "I knew that."

Nine

They didn't speak much on the drive back to Belle Haven. The lot was dark and empty when they pulled in. Emily grabbed her purse and slid from the truck almost before Wyatt even stopped, needing to get out of his sexy air space ASAP.

But as chill as he was, the guy could move like lightning when he wanted. And apparently he wanted, because he caught up with her in the blink of an eye.

"You don't have to—"

"Yes," he said firmly, setting a big hand on the small of her back, vigilantly taking in their surroundings as they moved. "I do. There's been some break-ins this year. Not here, but at other animal centers, addicts looking for drugs. I'm not taking chances with you."

"Oh. Well, thanks." At her car door, she hesitated. If this had been a real date, she'd be wondering if there was going to be a good-night kiss. But this wasn't a real date. "And thanks for dinner," she said.

He dipped down a little to see into her eyes. "We good?"

Oh, great, and now he felt sorry for her. "Yep." She added a super enthusiastic nod. "We're good. We're great. We're super-duper." She bit her tongue to shut herself up, but he was already frowning.

"You're toasted," he said.

"What? No, of course not. I only had two beers." Or was it three? "Okay, maybe I'm half toasted. I'll call my sister for a ride."

He wrapped his fingers around her wrist and turned back to his truck.

"Hey. *Hey*," she said, tapping him on the shoulder to slow him down. "What are you doing?"

"I'm driving you home." He hustled her back up into the truck's passenger's seat.

"I can't ask you to—"

"You didn't ask." He shut the door on her next protest and walked around the hood to the driver's side. He slid behind the wheel and turned to her, an arm up along the back of their seats. His other hand came up and he stroked the worry lines between her brows. "Don't worry about the car, Emily. I'll get it to you."

She nodded. She didn't trust her voice. He was sitting there, still wearing his puppy and kitty tie. And those glasses that made her want to steam them up. The combination should've made him look utterly ridiculous, but it didn't. Instead, it gave the big, leanly muscled, sexy-as-hell guy an unexpected softness, and she wanted to kiss him. The kind of kiss where you tasted each other for a good long time, where you tried not to bite but maybe you bit a little anyway.

"You're staring at me," he said.

"Am not."

She could practically hear him smile. Good Lord, she was out of control. He was over there being all Captain Platonic, and she wanted to rip that tie off and use it to bind him to her bed.

It was the beer, she decided. It had awoken her inner slut. He had one hand up on the headrest behind her, the other on the steering wheel, his thumb idly strumming back and forth.

She could remember that thumb doing the same over her nipple. "This is never going to work."

"What?" he asked.

"Nothing." *Get a grip.* The night was dark around them, pitch-black in a way that she never really got to see in Los Angeles with all its city lights.

Here, there were no lights at all, nothing but stars littered like diamonds across a blanket of black velvet. It took her breath away. "It's really beautiful here."

"You sound surprised."

She turned to him and felt herself brush up against the inside of his forearm where it rested behind her. It was shockingly like being in his arms. She felt his fingers brush her bare arm and she shivered. "What are you doing?" she whispered.

"Waiting for you to tell me where you live."

Oh. Right. "I live off Highway 29, between Rancher's Way and Fisher Creek Road."

"I own some land out that way," he said, turning the truck's engine over and pulling out of the lot. "Ten acres."

"You live there?" she asked, wondering if they were neighbors. "With your sisters?"

"No, the land is just mine. I'm going to build a place on it eventually." He glanced at her. "Just out of morbid curiosity, what did you think I was doing back there?"

"Trying to turn me on."

He smiled. "I don't have to try."

Damn, he was right about that. In fact, he was doing it right now. She squirmed a little, and his smile turned to a grin, which made it easier to ignore him for the rest of the drive home.

The house she and Sara rented was on the end of a short

cul-de-sac that backed up to at least thirty acres of wilderness. There were a few other properties scattered throughout the area, but not many. The closest house was fifty yards in one direction, and twice that in the other. She'd not met a single neighbor.

Her house was dark. It was karaoke night at the local bar, and Sara loved karaoke. She wouldn't be home for hours. "You do realize that I totally blame you," she said, breaking the silence.

"For?"

"Sitting there wearing a goofy-ass tie, driving like you do everything else, which is so stupid sexy I can't think."

He swiveled his amused gaze her way. "Anything else?"

She blew out a breath. "Fine. Mock me. Just . . . keep your hands to yourself."

He lifted them in surrender.

"And your mouth."

Said mouth quirked, and he mimed zipping it closed.

God, she was out. Of. Control. She covered her face with her hands and took a deep breath. "I'm going in now."

She didn't go in.

"This is so ridiculous," she finally whispered.

She felt his fingers grip hers. He lowered her hands from her face. "It's fine," he said. "You don't want anything to happen, nothing's going to happen."

She stared at him. "It's not?"

"Well, not unless you want it to, and then instigate things in a big way."

She stared at him, and then dropped her head back to stare at the roof of the truck instead of into his mesmerizing eyes. "Well that's just great."

"You changed your mind. You *want* something to happen," he said, sounding like maybe he was smiling again. "You're the one who made the rules, sweetness."

"I know, but . . ." She sank in her seat a little bit and sighed. "It's just that I've never really mastered being the instigator in the man department when I don't know how that instigation will be received."

There was a horrifyingly long beat of silence, and she sunk in her seat a little lower, wishing she could *poof*, vanish.

"The problem isn't whether I'm attracted to you," he finally said. "But this isn't about attraction."

Her head came up, both startled and relieved to hear him admit the attraction was mutual. "It's not?"

"No," he said. "You have a grand plan. I'm not on it."

"And I'm not on yours," she said, grasping at straws. "Right?"

"Right."

She ignored the little stab of disappointment. "Right." Nodding, she stared at him in the ambient light. So strong, inside and out. He was so much more than she'd known on that long ago night.

"Emily," he said, his tone low. A soft warning.

"I know." She looked at his mouth again. And his Adam's apple. And his throat. And his shoulders, covered by his shirt. Which didn't matter because she knew what he looked like without that shirt. "It's just that I hadn't had an orgasm in forever," she blurted out.

"What?"

"That night. I hadn't had an orgasm in six months." She hesitated. "Or since," she whispered, and then clapped a hand over her mouth. "Oh my God. Shut me up. I'm begging you."

He laughed, that low, sexy sound that never failed to make her nipples hard. He slid his hands to her arms and gently squeezed. "How about we just say good night."

"And pretend this conversation didn't happen?" she asked hopefully.

He gave a slow shake of his head, eyes flashing good humor. "Afraid I can't make that promise. This conversation was good for me."

"Okay, now I'm really going in." She thrust out her hand. "Good night."

Still looking vastly amused, he took her hand. His was warm, callused. Big. She held it for a moment too long, and then, oh God and then there was more eye contact. Nobody did eye contact better than Wyatt Stone.

"I like having you at Belle Haven," he said. "I hope you get a lot out of this year, Emily."

She stared at his square jaw, at his dark, thick eyelashes that were totally not fair and so wasted on a man, and then . . . and then somehow she tugged on his hand a little, to kiss his cheek.

Except she missed his cheek and got his mouth instead, dislodging his glasses, which fell between the car door and the seat.

"Uh-oh," she murmured, but didn't move away.

His hands went to her arms. "Emily."

Maybe it was the way he squinted just a little, maybe it was the gruff warning in his voice, but she quivered again. Big-time. As if he felt it, he tightened his grip on her arms, then his hands glided up into her hair on either side of her head as he roughly whispered her name.

That was when she lost her tenuous hold on her sanity, reaching for him at the same time he tugged. She landed in his lap, straddling him. "Hi," she said against his lips. "I'm instigating.

"Jesus." Wyatt captured her wrists, wrapping his arms—and hers—behind her back. But this only served to press their torsos together, and she moaned helplessly at the contact.

So did he. And then he kissed her hard and long, until they were breathing wildly, breaking off only to stare at her in the ambient light of the dash.

She did her best to look like something he had to have.

"We can't do this," he said firmly, voice raspy like he

wasn't buying his own words. "It's not Reno. Now you work under me. There could be a lawsuit—"

"I doubt Dell's going to sue me for having sex with you."

"Smart-ass." He was still holding her wrists pinned behind her back. She could feel him hard and ready beneath her. Definitely, he wasn't buying what he was saying.

"And I *couldn't* sue," she said. "Because this is consensual."

He blew out a breath.

"Oh my God." She felt herself freeze in horror. "Wyatt, say it's consensual."

"Killing me," he said on a groan, dropping his forehead to hers.

"Say it!"

He huffed out a laugh, which was just about the best aphrodisiac she'd ever heard. "You're crazy," he said.

"Yeah," she said. "But crazy hot, right?"

"Hot as hell." Releasing her wrists, he cupped her face and stared at her for a good long beat. "What are you looking for?" she asked.

"Tell me you're sober," he demanded.

"I'm sober."

"All the way sober?"

"Yes!"

"What about that guy?" he asked. "Is he still the silent boyfriend, like the K in knight? Like the kind that isn't really a boyfriend at all but a guy you use as a shield to hold off the other guys?"

She felt herself flush. He was totally on to her. "Yes," she whispered.

He held her still another moment, then groaned. "Killing me," he said again, but he finally moved, sliding his hands beneath her sweater. "Last chance," he said gruffly, his fingers sliding north. "Last chance to stop me."

She reached down and hit a lever, and his seat flew back.

Flat on his back, Wyatt laughed, and then her shirt was

gone, over her head, *gone* and his hand was on her jaw, turning her where he wanted her, which was close, and finally.

Finally.

They were heading in the right direction. She pulled his shirt from his jeans and shoved it up, revealing the mouth-watering torso she'd been dreaming about. She ran her fingertips over his abs counting ridges of muscles, loving how they quivered beneath her touch. "Six," she whispered, and reached for his belt buckle.

This tore some more colorful swearing from Wyatt, and she bent low, nipping his lower lip. "Are you going to talk all the way through this?" she asked.

He choked out a laugh. "I might."

"Good," she said, trembling as she remembered last time. Not only had he talked, uttering rough, erotic nothings in her ear, he'd made her to do it, too.

And she liked it.

One hand in her hair, he seared his mouth to hers, hard and fast, his tongue demanding entrance. When she parted her lips, a low growl sounded in the back of his throat. Her bra went the same direction as her shirt, and then he filled his hands with her breasts.

Still straddling him, her head fell back and she oscillated her hips. Her butt hit the horn, startling the crap out of her as it went off, loudly.

Wyatt laughed again. Grinning against her, he pulled her down over him, his hands going to her ass. His kiss was heady stuff, all deep and hot and wet as they went at each other. In Reno, they'd been perfect strangers, and that'd been hotter than she could have imagined.

This time, knowing him now, was even better. It was like coming home.

"Kick off your shoes," he said against her mouth.

She rushed to do that while he busied himself peeling her jeans to her thighs. "Lift up, Em."

Bossy as hell, just like last time, and damn. It still turned her on. He lent his hands to the cause, tugging the jeans the rest of the way off, leaving her in just a little itty-bitty neon green bikini panty. "Pretty," he said, hooking his thumbs in the sides. "I'll owe you."

And then he tore them off.

She just about had an orgasm at that.

But now she was completely naked and he was wearing way too many clothes, especially since hers were littered around them. She tugged at his shirt and he pulled away to yank it over his head.

She got less than a second to admire his naked chest before he jackknifed up with a ripple of his gorgeous abs so that his tongue could do things to her nipples that should probably be illegal.

She couldn't stop the helpless moan that escaped her mouth, though the sound seemed to trigger something inside Wyatt because the next thing she knew, he was swearing again, fighting one of the pockets of his cargo pants for his wallet.

When he produced a condom, she nearly sobbed in relief.

Then he was hauling her up his body.

From working with him, she knew something unequivocal. He handled an animal, any animal, with cool, calm, gentle-but-firm care. Always. In fact, she'd discovered she could watch him for hours, and he never failed to awe and amaze her. No matter if an animal was furious in its pain, or simply terrified, Wyatt had an unmistakably authoritative way of holding himself that made every four-legged creature innately trust him.

He had the same talent with two-legged creatures as well, even flat on his back in the pitch dark of his truck.

She hugged her knees to either side of his hips and he groaned in her ear at the contact. The sound of it, rough and ragged, was foreplay in its own right.

Hearing him rip open the condom was more foreplay. The last time she'd slept with him all the little nerve endings in her body had stood up, done the wave, marched around the room, and then sung the "Hallelujah" chorus.

She could feel that starting to happen again.

By the time he gripped her by the waist and drove himself all the way inside her, she was more than halfway gone. And if his ragged breathing was any indication, so was he.

"Oh fuck, Emily," he growled, head back, eyes heavy-lidded, throat exposed, enticing her to lean down and lick him there. "So good." He wrapped one arm low around her back, the other braced on the steering wheel behind her for support as he thrust up hard and deep inside her.

The horn sounded again, tugging a muffled laugh from him. Muffled because his face was buried in her neck now as they moved together in a rhythm that felt all the more intimate for the close proximity, and she supposed, the added danger of possibly getting discovered.

The pleasure built hard and fast, in thick layers. She couldn't stop herself from whispering his name in need, in desire, in hunger.

His throat worked as his eyes slid shut. His lips were parted, his chest rising and falling with each long exhale. She whispered his name again and he opened his eyes, lifting his head to watch her body engulf his.

"God, Wyatt."

"Just Wyatt'll do," he said, and when she let out a breathless laugh, he fisted a hand in her hair, bringing her eyes and mouth to his.

"Good?" he murmured, lips to hers.

"So good," she managed. "More, please."

He thrust into her with just enough force to rock her world. "Ask like that and I'll give you anything you want."

Riding his movements, arching into him, she was peaking when the horn went off again. "Dammit!"

He snorted but patiently worked her up again, nothing

stopping him this time, not the obnoxious blast of the horn, nor the lack of space, nor the fact that she bumped their noses together trying to kiss him.

He was a man on task, and as she already knew, he was good on task. It took only a few more masterful strokes for him to bring her back to the edge of sanity and then beyond, and as she came, clenching tight around him, she took him right over that edge along with her.

Hot and fast and dirty.

And amazing.

And without a doubt, the most erotic experience of her life.

Ten

Wyatt could hear himself still panting for breath when Emily finally lifted her face from where she'd plastered it to his throat.

He tried to see her expression but she was a blur. Reaching down, he searched for and found his glasses, shoving them on. Oh yeah, he thought as his fuzzy world came into sharp focus, revealing the gorgeously tousled woman astride him.

She was utterly beautiful.

And utterly perplexed.

An unexpected surge of affection hit him like a tidal wave, and he stroked her hair from her damp forehead and pressed his lips to her temple.

"What was that?" she demanded, voice hoarse.

"Great sex."

"Oh my God." She shifted with a wince. "There's a gearshift pressing against my ass."

He found a laugh. He was still buried deep inside her

and the movement caused her to shudder. Not from cold, he knew. The aftershocks of great sex.

"I'm not sure this is funny," she said.

He slid his hands up her warm torso.

"Wyatt—" She inhaled a sharply drawn breath when his thumbs gently grazed the underside of her breasts. Her bare skin was unbelievably soft under his touch, and he bit back a groan at the feel of it on his fingers.

"I think you're magic," she said.

He laughed again and she climbed off his lap, treating him to a fantastic view of her bare ass as she crawled back into her seat. There she snatched his shirt and tugged it over her head before she curled up and covered her face with her hands. "I really did totally instigate this."

"Yeah," he said with a grin. "I loved it."

"Oh my God. I took advantage of you."

"Uh-huh. It was hot."

"I had to *talk you into it*," she reminded him. "You were over there doing your Captain Platonic impression and I . . . I—" She covered her face and moaned miserably.

Leaning over her, he pulled her hands away from her face and waited until she lifted her gaze to his. "You're too sexy," she whispered. "You've really got to knock that off. I mean it, Wyatt."

He shook his head on a smile. "You're the most confusing woman I've ever met, and I've met lots of them. Hell, I live with the queen and queen-in-waiting of all confusing women."

"You think you're confused," she said, sagging back. "Imagine how confused it is inside my head." She reached for her panties, pulling them up one leg before apparently remembering he'd torn them. With a noise of frustration, she tossed them aside and went for her jeans, shoving her legs in, wriggling as she pulled them up.

Commando.

Sexiest thing he'd seen. Well, maybe the *second* sexiest

thing, the first being the way she'd moved over him, her eyes on his as she'd ridden him—

"Okay, *that* was absolutely our last time," she said. "I don't care how much your puppy and kitten tie pulls me in." She paused. "I'm going to resist you."

"Maybe you should put it in writing," he said.

"I realize you're mocking me, but that's actually a good idea." She pulled down the visor mirror and looked at herself. Her hair was wild, her eyes still a little dazed, and she was definitely wearing an I've-just-had-an-orgasm look as she groaned. She shoved on her shoes and opened the door.

He caught up with her on the sidewalk just as she stopped short. "What?" he asked.

"Hear that?"

He listened. The nights in Sunshine weren't quiet. Crickets chirped. Wind rustled through the trees. From a long way off they could hear the sounds of the river, and the very occasional car.

And the unmistakable howl of a coyote.

Emily hugged herself. "Never mind, I hear weird noises out here, I'm not used to the country." She moved to her door. "This isn't necessary," she said as he followed.

Not bothering to disagree, he took her keys from her fingers, unlocked her door for her, and held it open.

She stepped inside and turned back to him. "We've got to work on this."

"We?"

She sighed. "You're not taking me seriously."

His smile faded and he stroked a stray strand of hair along her temple, tucking it behind her ear, wondering what it would be like if they were even halfway suited for each other.

Pretty fucking great, he figured. "On the contrary," he finally said quietly. "I'm taking you very seriously."

* * *

The weekend was quiet. Emily woke up Saturday morning to Q-Tip sitting on her chest, staring into her face.

"Meow."

This translated to feed me, feed me now.

Knowing from experience that resistance was futile, Emily stumbled out of bed to feed the terminally hungry cat.

On her way to the kitchen, she glanced out the front window and saw her car in the driveway.

Wyatt, of course. She had a text from him telling her where he'd hidden her keys. When she went out to retrieve them, she found on her top step a to-go mug of hot coffee and several donuts from the bakery in town.

Which was almost more of a turn-on than his laugh.

She and Sara spent the weekend settling in, making the place theirs by painting their rooms. Sara went for a bold purple, Emily a muted, warm sea green.

On Sunday night, she called her dad to check in.

"How's Idaho?" he asked. Same question he'd asked last week.

Not wanting to worry him, she gave him the same answer. "Good," she said. "Two weeks down. How're you doing? You eating okay? Did you get the bills paid on time?"

"Two weeks down?" he repeated, ignoring her other questions. "Honey, don't tell me you're clock watching."

No, she was calendar watching.

"You need to enjoy this time in the wild, wild west," he said. "Go date a cowboy or ride a horse or something. Do what makes you happy."

This had been his life philosophy. He'd spent most of his career working as a vet at the homeless shelters. He had a drive to help, and she loved that about him, but at the same time, it had made it almost impossible for him to support his family. There were still medical bills from her mom to be paid, and he was making little to no headway there at all.

"I'm too busy at work for that, Dad. Did you look at the job apps I e-mailed you? There're a few openings that you're perfect for."

"I like my job at the SPCA."

"But it hardly pays," Emily said.

"Honey, some things are bigger than money. And anyway, I manage just fine."

She had to bite her tongue. There was no gain to pointing out that he managed just fine because she kicked in for rent and groceries and leftover medical bills whenever and wherever she could—after feeding and housing her and Sara, who like Dad, never could quite make ends meet. "You're eating?" she asked.

"Yes, I'm eating," he said. "*Now* will you go do something fun? Try it, you might like it."

She thought of what she'd done with Wyatt in his truck, how uninhibited and crazy it had been, and felt her pulse kick. She'd already had her fun.

Twice.

"Love you, Dad."

"Love you, too, honey. Tell Sara I tried."

She hung up and turned to Sara. "He tried what?"

"To loosen you up," Sara said.

Emily blew out her breath and looked at her phone when it rang.

Lilah ran the local doggy day care on the property next to Belle Haven, and as she was close to Dell and the guys, she spent lots of time in the office.

This worked for Emily, as she liked Lilah a lot. "I'm working on a big fund-raiser," Lilah said when Emily answered the call. "It's an online auction, with profits going to the local animal rescue shelter."

"I didn't know Sunshine had a rescue shelter," Emily said.

"Yeah, and it's me. Anyway, everyone from Belle Haven's donating stuff. Dell's offered ten free pet checkups.

Adam's offering a free puppy training course, and also S&R classes. Brady's giving out a one-hour chopper ride."

Brady was her husband, who was Dell's brother. He was a pilot for hire, and maintained a helicopter at the small airport across from the animal center, which he often used to fly Dell and Wyatt to the big animal ranch patients.

"And Wyatt?" Emily asked. "What did he donate?"

Lilah was silent for a beat, and Emily cursed her own mouth for revealing her interest.

"Wyatt's donating a shadow day," Lilah said. "The highest bidder gets to walk in his shadow all day long at the center. He's also giving away five home vet visits."

"Generous," Emily said, trying to sound not all that interested, also trying not to picture all the single women in the area bidding on him.

He's not yours . . .

"So," Lilah said. "You in? How about a night out with the highest bidder?"

"Uh . . ." Emily said.

"Just dinner," Lilah said.

Sounded harmless enough. "If you really think people will be interested," she said. "Because let's face it, the big draw's going to be the guys of Belle Haven."

Lilah laughed softly. "I take it you've seen the way women react to them."

"Yes, the Casserole Brigade has been very attentive."

This cracked Lilah up. "For the most part, the guys don't even notice," she said.

"Are you kidding?" Emily asked on a laugh. "Wyatt snags each and every casserole."

"That's more because he's always hungry. And by hungry, I mean his appetite for *food*," Lilah said. "He's actually a little bit shy in the women department."

Emily couldn't help it, she burst out laughing.

And in her ear, Lilah chuckled. "Okay, yeah, maybe shy is a bit of a stretch. Wyatt doesn't really have a shy bone in his body. But he's not exactly a man 'ho, either. He's just so damn busy all the time. Poor guy's got his hands full, what with the crazy growth of the practice these past six months, and trying to take care of his sisters and that big house, and planning the build on his own place. At least he's finally getting over Caitlin, though he's still protecting his heart pretty good—not that a man would ever admit to that, and certainly not a man like Wyatt."

"Who's Caitlin?"

"Uh . . ." Lilah's voice suddenly became professional-like. "Hey, I've got another call coming in."

"Okay, but—"

But Lilah was already gone.

By ten o'clock on Monday morning, Wyatt's ass was dragging. It had been a long weekend rewiring the downstairs bathroom, and an even longer morning. Having been called out to the front desk, his stomach growled like Pavlov's dog when he saw another casserole dish sitting on the counter.

Gertie hoisted herself to her feet and bounded to Wyatt for some love, leaving only a little slobber on his thigh.

"Rosa Martinez," Jade said, patting the casserole. "Homemade enchiladas. She left a note that I accidentally on purpose read. She wants to jump your bones."

"Jump your bones," Peanut said.

Wyatt pointed at the parrot, and the bird flopped dramatically to Jade's desk like he'd been shot.

Wyatt turned to Jade. "The note does *not* say that."

"It says, and I quote, 'call me, Dr. Stone, *anytime*.'" Jade waved it. "In women-speak that means she wants to jump your bones."

"Women are crazy."

"True," she said, not insulted in the least.

Emily came up to the counter holding a file. Wyatt gave

her credit, she met his gaze smoothly, as she had all morning. He wasn't sure if she blushed slightly, or if that was his imagination. One thing she hadn't done was speak directly to him.

Apparently, they weren't going to discuss Friday night. Fine by him, as every time he so much as thought about it, how she'd climbed into his lap and rode him like he was a bronco, he got hard.

"I need some copies made," she said to Jade, and then stopped to eye the casserole. "Another delivery from the Casserole Brigade?" she asked.

"Yep," Jade said.

"What's going on?" she asked Wyatt. "Are they auditioning for the role of your next girlfriend?"

Jade cackled.

Peanut cackled.

Wyatt slid both Jade and the parrot a look, but neither appeared at all repentant. "What?" Jade said. "It's not a bad idea. You deserve a new girlfriend since—"

"Jade."

"And speaking of girlfriends . . ." She handed him a stack of phone messages. "I almost didn't give you the first one, but last time I interfered, Dell told me to butt out of your business. So this is me, butting out."

He looked down at the first message and felt tension grip him. "Caitlin called?"

"Yeah," Jade said softly, no longer sounding amused. "From Haiti. I told her you were too busy screwing blond triplets in the back, that you'd call when you were done, but it might be awhile seeing as you were a God among men."

At his side, Emily sucked in a breath.

Wyatt shook his head. "Nice going on staying out of it, Jade."

She winced with guilt but kept her head high. "She deserved it. And since I've already stuck my nose in, let me finish off by saying if you call her back, I'll . . ." She paused.

"I'll call all the cougars in town and tell them your favorite foods, and that you need some lovin'."

"Do it," Wyatt said. "And I'll teach Parrot how to fake an orgasm, loud and proud, Meg Ryan style."

"You wouldn't dare," Jade said, eyes narrowed.

"Try me," he said.

She tried to stare him down, but he'd learned how to handle strong women from the masters: Zoe and Darcy.

Jade backed down.

"Caitlin's the ex-girlfriend," Emily said into the silence, clearly asking for confirmation.

"Ex-*fiancée*, who screwed him over," Jade corrected, then she caught Wyatt's gaze as she grimaced. "Sorry," she said. "That one slipped out. I'm going to control myself now."

Yeah, right. He felt the weight of Emily's surprise, but ignored it *and* Jade. Fucking Mondays. He headed back to his office with the messages. He dumped Caitlin's into the trash and then stared down at it. "Shit," he said, and pulled it back out.

"You gonna call her?" This from Dell in the doorway. "Don't tell Jade."

"Speaking of Jade, you need to control your woman."

Dell laughed. "I'm going to do you a favor and not tell her you said that."

Wyatt crumpled the message and tossed it back into the trash.

"Wise decision," Dell said.

Wyatt nodded.

Dell didn't leave.

Wyatt looked at him.

"Want me to take the trash out for you?" he asked, no smile, utterly serious.

"Christ." Wyatt scrubbed his hands over his face. "Yeah."

Dell grabbed the entire trash can and left.

Wyatt nodded to himself. That part of his life—while one of the best parts—was over. There would be no going back. He didn't need to hear whatever it was Caitlin could possibly have to say. He walked down the hallway and stopped in front of exam room one to take the file from Mike. "What do we got?"

Mike was unusually solemn. "Not good, man. It's Rebel, with Lizzy."

Rebel was a big biker dude who had a pet iguana. He and Lizzy had been together for fifteen years. Lizzy rode on Rebel's bike. They were a team, and Lizzy was the love of Rebel's life. Problem was, Lizzy was old for an iguana, and there was nothing any of them could do to stop time for Rebel.

Wyatt entered the room to find the biker sitting on the floor in all his leather and studs, knees up, Lizzy cradled to his chest. Wyatt set the file on the exam table, and crouched low next to the biker and iguana. "Hey."

Rebel nodded a greeting but didn't take his eyes off Lizzy. "She's sleeping."

Wyatt nodded.

Lizzy wasn't sleeping.

Wyatt slid his back down the wall to sit at Rebel's side.

"You gotta do something," the biker said, voice gruff. Dangerous.

Wyatt met his gaze. "You know I'd do whatever it took, man. But—"

"*Fuck*," Rebel said. And burst into big, noisy, gulping sobs, dropping his head to Wyatt's shoulder. "I know people don't understand," he gasped, "but Lizzy and I've been together for a long time."

"I know."

"I don't wanna go back to an empty house without her . . ."

Wyatt thought about all the lines he could utter. Time

will heal all wounds. You'll get another iguana. Don't try to stifle the grief, let it come.

But it was all bullshit. "It sucks," he said.

Rebel went still and then choked out a half laugh, half sob. "Yeah," he said, and head still down, held out his fist.

Wyatt bumped it with his own.

Rebel sniffed noisily, very carefully transferred Lizzy over to Wyatt, and rose to his full six feet six inches. "Take care of her," he said, and walked out of the room.

Emily looked at Wyatt still sitting on the floor of the exam room. She'd been caught up with Mike and another patient, but had come quickly when she'd heard the crying.

Her heart had broken at the sight of the big biker, still cradling his beloved iguana, and Wyatt comforting him.

Wyatt rose to his feet, pushed up his glasses, and very gently carried Lizzy's body to the back room, and the special cooler there that held the deceased. Lizzy would stay there until Wyatt determined what Rebel wanted done, and then they'd follow out his wishes.

One thing few people realized about being a vet was how much death they saw. It was a big part of their job and heart wrenching, and Emily's eyes stung thinking about Rebel's loss. "Does it ever get easier?" she asked softly.

Wyatt studied her for a moment. "No," he said quietly, voice gruff with his own emotion. "It doesn't."

Eleven

A few days later, Emily washed up for their first patient, then moved over and watched Wyatt do the same. The way he moved mesmerized her, all easy-paced economical grace, so innately male she could feel her pulse speed up just watching him.

So she tried not to watch.

Instead, she concentrated on the job. Their next patient made that easy. Monster was a Great Dane who'd been disturbing his people the night before with a new habit—dragging his butt on the carpet during a cocktail party the mayor had attended.

"Apparently it's only okay for pizza night," Wyatt said, making Emily laugh. She had to hand it to him, he could do that, make her laugh, even when she didn't want to.

Monster's owners had dropped him off so Emily and Wyatt were alone in the exam room. She'd managed to avoid this until now, which meant she had questions saved up.

He'd been engaged? To a woman named Caitlin who

still called him? Emily had tried to ask both Lilah and Jade about it, but they'd clammed up. Oddly enough, it had been Mike who gave her a glimmer of what had happened, because, as it turned out, there were no sacred secrets at Belle Haven.

"Caitlin dumped him and he's still working through that," Mike had said. "Dude's not ready."

Ready for what? To share his heart?

And why did it matter to her so much?

She watched as Wyatt tugged on the exam gloves and hoisted the huge Great Dane onto the table with ease, the movement stretching his lab coat taut over his broad shoulders.

She felt herself shiver.

What the hell was that? And why was everything he did so laden with sexuality? At least he wasn't wearing a tie today. Although his T-shirt said: *50% Vet, 50% Superhero.*

"This has to stop," she said, helping to hold Monster from the front while Wyatt stepped to the dog's hind end.

"What has to stop?"

She hadn't meant to speak out loud, but what the hell. "You being sexy."

He lifted his head and stared at her in genuine surprise. "I'm about to express this dog's anal glands. How in the world is that sexy?"

"I . . ." She blew out a breath and hung her head. "I can't explain."

He shook his head, a smile playing at his lips as he went back to Monster. "You've got a problem."

"I know!"

Dell popped his head in, brows raised quizzically. "Issues?"

"No!" they both said in unison over poor Monster.

Dell eyed them each and then vanished.

Emily watched Wyatt work, his big, tough hands gentle and yet firm and sure on the dog. His hands had been like that on her, too . . . "Gah," she said, dropping her forehead to Monster's. "Maybe there's a pill for this."

Wyatt laughed.

Monster licked her chin.

When Wyatt finished violating poor Monster, he tossed his gloves into the trash and grinned at Emily.

"What?"

"You want me again."

Again. Still . . .

"Should I put on a tie?"

She opened her mouth to respond but a question came out of her instead. "You've been engaged?"

He ignored this, and lifted Monster off the table, leading him back to his kennel. Then he moved to the sink and washed his hands.

"How come you never answer the good questions?" she asked.

"You didn't respond to mine, either."

She sighed and met his gaze, but he was the master at holding his silence when he wanted to.

"We're not discussing what happened last weekend," she finally said.

"You mean when you had your wild way with me in my truck?"

"I didn't—" But they both knew she totally had.

He grinned at the look on her face. "You know, maybe you should be thanking me instead of yelling at me."

"Thank you! For what?"

He arched a brow.

Okay, so she knew for what. She'd slept *great* that night. "Look," she said, "apparently you bring out my inner slut. I'm not going to thank you for that."

Wyatt smiled that sexy smile of his. "I could make you."

Her nipples went hard. Dammit. She pointed a finger at his nose. And then lowered it so it was pointed at another part of his anatomy entirely. "Don't even think about it."

"Oh, I won't," he said silkily. "But *you* will."

And she knew he was right.

Two hours later, Emily followed Wyatt into the staff room after a difficult case. He was quiet as he scrubbed his hands.

Emily met his gaze in the mirror over the sink. "You okay?"

"Yeah. Why?"

"Because that had to be hard, waiting for the owner to make the difficult decision."

Wyatt didn't say anything. He just turned off the water and reached for paper towels to dry off with.

"You were really great with him," she said to his back. "You let him make the decision without influence."

"It wasn't my decision to make," he said simply.

"But he could have easily made the wrong decision, and elected to keep the dog alive, letting it suffer through to the inevitable end."

He tossed the paper towels into the trash and turned to face her. She saw that he wasn't blowing off the conversation as one he didn't want to have, that he was indeed very seriously listening to her. In fact, she wasn't sure she'd ever seen him so serious—with the exception of the times he'd been buried deep inside her body.

This brought an odd little quiver to her belly that she did her best to ignore, fascinated as she was by his expression.

"I don't ever tell an owner what to do," he said.

"Not even when they're making the wrong decision?"

"I'll give my opinion when asked," he said. "Strongly, if it's needed, but I won't give an ultimatum. It's not for me to do."

"But . . ." This did not compute to a woman who'd spent her entire life making the hard decisions for everyone she loved, always. Her dad, her mom, her sister . . . "You're the one who's in a position to do the right thing for the animal," she said.

He looked beyond her for a moment, as if he was thinking about something extremely unhappy, then he brought his gaze back to hers. "I believe in giving a person all the information they need in order to make an informed decision, and then trusting them to make the right decision."

"And if they don't?" she pressed.

"They usually do." He looked at her for a beat. "You don't agree."

"I don't."

"Why?" he asked.

Since he wasn't being a smartass or making a joke, she decided to answer honestly and hope it didn't come to bite her on the ass. "All my life, I've had to make damn hard choices," she said. "And I've learned from each of them. If I can pass on some of that hard-earned knowledge and save someone the agony of a tough decision by making it for them, why not do it?"

"What hard choices?" he asked.

The question took her back. "They're . . . personal."

"More personal than you climbing me like a tree?"

She opened her mouth, saw the flash of good humor in his gaze, and sighed. "My dad was pretty occupied with his rescues most of my childhood," she said. "And my mom was often sick. My sister . . . she had her own problems. She coped the same way my dad did, by being busy, too busy. So any decisions, all decisions, from what was for dinner to how to handle my mom's medical care, were on me."

He was quiet a moment, soaking that in. "You know that our life experiences couldn't be more different."

"I'm getting that," she said.

"I never had a say in my own life. And now I don't believe in taking away someone's choices."

It was a stark reminder of why they'd made a great one-night stand—okay, a two-night stand—and yet it couldn't be more than that. At heart, they were two very different people. "I told you about me," she said softly. "Now maybe you can tell me about Caitlin?"

He looked at her.

She met his gaze, trying to look like the question was as simple as something like, *So, what did you have for lunch*?

He didn't buy it. Nor did he speak.

She let out a breath. "I'm just surprised," she said. "Seeing as we've discussed my love life."

"The almost, maybe, sort of boyfriend," he said, a ghost of a smile on his face.

Feeling defensive, she crossed her arms. "I'm just saying, you might've mentioned that you had a fiancée."

"Did you miss the ex part? *Ex*-fiancée," he said.

"You two still talk."

"No."

"She called you," she reminded him.

"Yeah."

Like pulling teeth. "She called you from Haiti," she said. "What does she do?"

"Caitlin's a doctor. Works for Doctors Without Borders."

Pulling teeth without Novocain . . . Emily couldn't have said why the idea of him having been engaged was so fascinating.

And compelling.

And . . . making her a little jealous. "Did she . . . break your heart?"

"We have patients," he said, and walked out of the room.

Twelve

"Bout time."

Wyatt ignored Darcy's snark and looked at AJ, who was standing in the doorway to his office, big arms crossed over his chest.

Clearly Wyatt had interrupted a standoff, a tense one.

"How is she?" Wyatt asked him.

"Crazy," AJ said, smiling grimly when Darcy sputtered, and then flipped him off.

"Right back atcha, sweetheart," AJ said. He looked at Wyatt. "She needs ibuprofen, a long, hot bath, and rest. I kicked her ass."

"And I'm going to kick yours," Darcy told him. "Just as soon as I can move. You should sleep with one eye open."

"Already do." And then he vanished into his office.

"Bastard," Darcy muttered. "Sadistic bastard."

Wyatt ignore this, as there was no real heat behind the words. He scooped her out of the waiting room chair.

"Seriously," Darcy said, wrapping an arm around his shoulders. "You're late. *Again.*"

"Had an emergency." Nodding to Brittney, the receptionist, he shouldered Darcy out of the office. He knew better than to make her walk after an hour with AJ. In fact, she was still trembling from the work out. "What was going on with you and AJ?" he asked.

"Absolutely nothing."

She was pale, eyes shut, unusually subdued, so he let it go as he set her on the passenger's side of his truck and buckled her into her seat belt.

"You're driving like Grandpa," she said a few minutes later.

Wyatt turned off the highway with more force than strictly necessary, and she banged her head into the side window.

"Hey," she complained, putting her hand to her head.

"Careful. You don't have the brain cells to spare."

"What the hell crawled up your ass today?"

"Nothing."

"*Something's* got you all pissy," she said.

He might have asked her the same question. Except Darcy, for all the things that drove him crazy; her wildness, her need to prove said wildness, her absolute drive to make sure no one ever loved her . . . could still do the one thing that few others could.

Read him.

And yeah, fine, she was right. He *was* pissy. That the reason for it lay at his own feet didn't help.

He was doing exactly what he said he wouldn't—he was falling for a woman who was just putting in her time. And he'd been there. Hell, he'd bought the fucking T-shirt. He had to be seriously messed up in the head to be even thinking of seconds—and thirds, and fourths, and whatever he could get—of Emily. He'd grown up with parents who'd chosen their careers over him. He'd then fallen for Caitlin, who done the exact same thing.

And now Emily was giving him that same vibe, and he was trying to play it cool, but inside he was wondering if maybe he was just the type of guy who women left.

"Earth to Wyatt," Darcy said. "Where did you go, Disneyland?"

"Maybe I was just tuning you out," he said.

She laughed. "You're incapable of tuning a woman out. It's why they all love you."

"Uh-huh."

"It's true. You're just too chickenshit to pick the right one."

He glanced over at her. "You are *not* giving me love advice."

"Well *someone* should. I know you let everyone think Caitlin dumped you, but I've figured out the truth."

He said nothing.

"You let her go, without a word."

"Shut up, Darce."

"Not because you didn't love her," Darcy went on. "But because you wanted her to pick you and Sunshine. You wanted her to stay without asking her. Because you'd never ask her to stay with you instead of taking that job she wanted."

He must have made some sort of "tell," given himself away, because she pounced. "You miss her," she said. "But she didn't deserve you."

"No. *No*," he said firmly when she just looked at him. "I don't." But he missed having someone.

"You need to stop dating the fancy girls," she said. "Date a homebody."

"Fancy girls?" he repeated with a laugh.

"Annie, Stace, Kennedy, and Christie," she said, ticking them off on her fingers. "A dentist, an attorney, a financial analyst, and some sort of executive."

And Emily, the vet, he silently added.

"Nothing wrong with any of them," Darcy said. "Well, except they all had sticks up their asses. But you need someone more . . . quiet. Someone happy here in Sunshine, like you are. Someone who won't bring more crazy into your world," she said.

"Because I have you for that?" he asked dryly.

"Exactly," she said. "I have gossip."

"I'm afraid to ask."

"Zoe heard from Kate, who heard from Holly, who heard from Jade that you like the new vet."

Kate was Griffin's girlfriend, Griffin was Adam's best friend, and Adam was married to Holly. "Jesus," he said, dizzy.

"She's the wrong one for you, Wyatt."

He sighed. "You don't even know her."

"I know she's exactly the wrong type."

"Yeah?" he asked, and reached over to tug her hair. "And why's that?"

"Because she's only here for a year. What's wrong with Brittney?"

"AJ's receptionist?"

"Do you know another Brittney?" Darcy asked.

"No, but—"

"She's quiet, sweet, smart, funny. She loves Sunshine, and—"

"You are not setting me up," Wyatt said on a rough laugh.

"Just for dinner."

"We've had dinner," Wyatt said. Several times, in fact. And Darcy was right. Brittney was quiet, sweet, smart, funny. She was also warm and caring, and, after ten years of travel, here in Sunshine for good. She'd sowed her wild oats and was ready to settle down.

And the two of them had zero chemistry. "Drop it."

"Fine. What was your emergency?"

"A patient came in just at closing," he said. "A dog got hit by a car."

She let out a soft gasp. "Did it—"

"Lived," he said. "Gonna be fine."

Eyes closed, she smiled. "You're a good boy, Wy-Ty."

The words made him smile. Their grandma used to say that to him. *You're a good boy, Wy-Ty. You're the man of the house.*

He'd been five years old the first time he'd spent a summer here in Sunshine with his sisters. Even back then the funky old Victorian house had been falling apart.

He'd loved it, every nook and cranny.

He'd been commissioned by his grandma to be in charge of the menagerie of animals she collected; a llama with three legs, a blind cow, a deaf Australian shepherd, an albino cat. The list went on and on. It didn't matter what type of living creature, if it needed saving, his grandma had taken it in—including her three wayward, emotionally neglected grandkids.

"Hey," Darcy said. "The gas is the long, skinny pedal on the right. Step on it, would you? I've got a nap scheduled."

"It's seven o'clock. Why don't you just wait an hour and then go to bed for the night? You can take a hot bath and relax a little bit."

She laughed. "No one goes to bed at eight."

"People who've survived an unsurvivable accident, gone through five surgeries and grueling physical therapy to learn to walk again do."

She turned away and looked out the window.

"Stay home tonight," he said. "Instead of napping until midnight and then going out."

"Nothing good happens before midnight."

"Darcy."

"*Mom*," she intoned, and then laughed.

Laughed.

The sound was music to his ears because for that one brief moment she almost sounded like her old self again.

When he pulled into their driveway and came around for her, she crossed her arms over her chest.

"I want my chair back," she said.

"AJ says you don't need it."

"AJ doesn't know shit. I want my chair."

AJ knew a hell of a lot, and he'd learned it the hard way and they both knew it. AJ had fought his own battles, and he'd come out on the other side.

Just as Wyatt hoped like hell that Darcy would.

Wyatt and Darcy's battle of wills was silent but short. Wyatt stared her down, but she'd never been afraid of him. Of being real, yeah. Of taking even a single care with her life, yeah.

But of him? No.

In the end, Wyatt once again hoisted her into his arms and carried her toward the house. Someone had weeded. The chore had been on his endless list of things to do. Zoe had texted him about it numerous times this week and he'd hit delete.

Clearly she'd gotten tired of the waist-high weeds lining the walk to the front door. Not that the grass—really more wild weeds at this point—seemed to notice. They'd had rains almost every night, and the entire yard looked more than a little neglected.

He needed more hours in his day.

"She's going to plant roses next, you watch," Darcy murmured with a tired sigh. "She thinks she can domesticate us."

"We could use a little domestication," he said.

"Hmmm."

It was a noncommittal sound, and Wyatt knew that of all of them, Darcy had no desire to settle down. She'd never admit it, but she was the most like their parents.

Free-spirited.

Bitten by wanderlust.

Happy to call the world home.

And in a single blink, it had almost all been taken away from her. But at least she was still breathing, and by the looks of things, finally on the mend.

With a sigh, Darcy set her head against his collarbone. It was more a testament to her hour of brutal therapy than any affection for Wyatt.

But he'd take what he could get.

"You're thinking so hard you're making me tired," she mumbled against him. "What are you obsessing about now?"

"I'm concentrating on not dropping you on your ass," he said.

A lie, and she knew it, but she laughed softly.

Zoe opened the door for them. "You'd all best be hungry," she said. "I brought home Thai— Criminy, Wyatt, kick off those filthy boots before you walk across my floor. And that had best *not* be my favorite tank top, Darcy."

Wyatt bent to dump Darcy onto the couch, and their gazes met. She rolled her eyes, and Wyatt felt himself grinning again.

Yeah, she was coming back to them.

He turned and bumped right into Zoe.

His older sister was, hands on hips, staring at them. "You guys are pretty late."

"Yeah," Darcy said from the couch, eyes already closed. "That's all on me."

"How can that be, you didn't have your car."

Darcy huffed out a laugh. "If you don't think I can fuck things up with or without wheels, you've not been paying attention."

Zoe turned to Wyatt. "What the hell happened?"

"Don't bitch at him," Darcy said.

Wyatt felt the knot that was always in his chest lately,

loosen very slightly. Darcy opened her eyes and flashed him a smile that was so brief he might have imagined it.

Then she closed her eyes again and turned over.

Zoe stared down at her and then nudged Wyatt hard with her shoulder.

Her version of a long, hard hug.

Thirteen

Emily got home late. She parked in the driveway and got out, hesitating when she heard that odd sort of howling she'd heard several times now. Not a coyote, she thought.

A dog. And it sounded like it was in pain.

Unable to take it, she was going to have to check it out. It wasn't quite dusk, but getting there, so she grabbed the flashlight she kept in her car and walked down the street about twenty yards toward the sound, moving faster when she heard it again.

Where was it? She walked a little farther, searching. The houses here were spread out, many of them small ranches with horses and other livestock in the back. She saw nothing odd.

Nor did she hear the cry again.

She kept walking. As the last of the sun sank over the horizon, she came to the last house on the block.

It was a ranch style like the others, with acreage behind

it. All the lights were on and there were a handful of trucks in the driveway. As she stood there, the front door opened and a man appeared in the doorway.

She couldn't make out his features, but lifted a hand and waved, anyway.

He was still for a beat and then returned the wave.

"Did you hear an injured animal?" she called out.

But the guy had already turned back inside the house, shutting the door.

Frustrated and tired, and no longer hearing anything, she turned back and walked home. It was Sara's boxing night—she'd signed up for lessons at the gym and wouldn't be back until late. So as she entered the house, she was immediately accosted by Q-Tip.

"Meow!"

"Let me guess," Emily said, dropping her purse and crouching to pet the cat. "You're hungry."

Q-Tip bit her ankle.

Emily hissed out a breath and stood up. "I'm changing your name to Satan." She headed toward the kitchen to feed them both.

"Meow," Q-Tip said, and ran between Emily's legs, nearly killing them both.

After feeding the cat, Emily studied the sad contents of the fridge in order to feed herself. Nothing called to her, so she grabbed her purse, and headed back outside.

A quick drive-through would have to do, which she wished she would've thought of before getting all the way home—

She stopped, startled by a sudden flash of light that came around the side of her house.

Flight or fight? *Flight*. Always flight.

Slightly closer to the house than her car, she ran back up the walk while fumbling with her keys at the same time. "Come on, come on," she whispered on the porch, and finally got the key into the lock, shoving open the front door. Shutting it hard behind her, she hit the lock.

And then the dead bolt.

"Meow."

"Shh." Emily rush to the living room window. Still in the dark, she peered out.

Nothing.

"Meow."

"I already fed you," she whispered, staring out the window.

Q-Tip rubbed her face against the ankle she'd bitten only a few moments before. Happily fed, she was feeling friendly now. Emily appreciated that but she couldn't concentrate on anything but the light. She could see it again, farther away, maybe twenty-five yards. But it was on the *other* side of her house now, like maybe whoever held the flashlight had seen her coming and retreated behind the house, and then come out on the other side.

Why?

Then she heard the distant rumble of a truck engine starting, and headlights appeared, crawling down the street toward her, and she sucked in a breath. When the truck pulled into her driveway, she held that breath and shoved her hand into her pocket, finding the familiar and comforting weight of her phone. Should she call the police? She didn't recognize the truck, and was so frazzled she couldn't have said if it was one she'd just seen in her neighbor's driveway.

It idled in her driveway for the longest ten seconds of her life before slowly pulling back out and driving off.

And then nothing.

At her feet, Q-Tip pulled out the last trick in her arsenal. She began to purr, gazing up at Emily innocently.

In the still of the night, with the only sounds now the rumbly purring and Emily's own escalated breathing, her cell phone rang, startling her into near cardiac arrest. She answered while still staring out the window into the dark night. "Hello" she whispered.

"Hey," Wyatt said. "About tomorrow's schedule—I'm on surgery detail, so we're going to start half an hour earlier—" He paused. "You okay? You're breathing like you've been running."

"Yeah, I'm okay. Gotta question for you, what do you know about the local police response time?"

"Where are you?" he immediately asked.

"At home. I—" She heard the ding-ding-ding of a vehicle door opening, and blinked. "What are you doing?"

"Heading your way," he said.

"No, don't. I'm fine." She moved into the kitchen, with Q-Tip following right on her heels. Emily passed by her bowl and Q-Tip stared at her balefully. "I'm just wondering," Emily said into the phone. "Being out here in the boondocks and all, how 911 works."

"The same as in L.A.," he said. "Fast and accurately. Emily, what's going on?"

It was his no-fucking-around voice, the one that both animals and people never failed to respond to. It would have taken a stronger woman than she to disobey his unsaid command to *Speak, now*. "When I went out to my car," she said, "I saw a glimpse of a beam of light, like from a flashlight, on the side of the house. Except there's nothing back there. I mean, our yard isn't fenced in, so really, I guess it could be anyone out for a walk, but—"

"But who walks after dark in someone else's yard," he finished. "You inside with the door locked?"

"Yes. I ran in here, and when I looked out the window, the light had switched to the other side of the house. Only I didn't pass anyone, so they had to have changed directions to come out the other way. I can't think of why a casual walker would do that. It's probably nothing . . ."

"Doesn't feel like nothing," he said.

"No. And then there was a truck. It pulled into our driveway, sat for a minute, and left."

"Doesn't sound like someone just out for an evening stroll."

"No. But they're gone." She pressed her forehead to the window. "I'm fine now."

"So you don't want company."

The house was dark and warm. Sara was gone for the night. If Wyatt came over, it wouldn't be to guard her body. It would be to *worship* her body, and no one did that better than him. Even the thought made her weak. "No," she said. "I don't need company."

Q-Tip, who'd given up on getting more food and was back to staring at Emily, seemed to smirk.

Emily rolled her eyes at the cat.

"Need and want are two different things," Wyatt said.

"In this case, there's neither," she said.

"Liar. Double check your locks, Emily."

"I will," she promised, and disconnected. And then she did just that, checked the locks and shut all the shades while she was at it.

And then she turned on every light in the place.

Next up was a very hot, very long shower, and when she got out she put on her Mickey Mouse pj's. She'd lost her appetite, so dinner was off the table.

"Meow."

She scooped Q-Tip up and gave her a nuzzle, which the cat allowed for exactly five seconds before demanding to be set back down.

The knock on the front door nearly had Emily's heart leaping right out of her ribcage. Q-Tip hissed and took off, disappearing down the hall just as a text came through.

It's me.

Wyatt. Oh God. Her heart knocked against her ribs again, for a very different reason now.

Let me in.

She stared down at herself, winced, and then thumbed her response: You sound like the Big Bad Wolf.

His response was immediate: Yes. Let me in and I'll show you what pretty eyes and teeth I have.

She laughed in spite of herself and opened the front door. Wyatt's arms were up, braced on the threshold above, eyes dark and serious. "Are we going to be stupid?" she whispered.

"Define stupid."

"Anything that involves either one of us exposing our favorite body parts." Or their hearts . . .

"I'm going to want to hear about your favorite body part," he said. "In great detail."

She felt herself flush. "I'm wearing my birth control pj's." Which was a relief. They'd keep her from doing anything stupid.

He took in her Mickey Mouse pj's, and exaggeratedly waggled a brow.

She laughed. "You can't possibly find this look attractive."

His expression said he found *everything* she wore attractive, and especially everything she *didn't* wear, and little tendrils of heat slid through her belly.

And lower.

Wyatt followed her inside, turning to shut, lock, and bolt the door. Then he moved to her living room window, nudging aside the shades to look out into the night. "Is this where you saw the truck pull into your driveway?"

"Yes."

"He see you watching him?"

"I don't know," she said. "I had the lights off."

Wyatt stayed like that for another moment then turned to her. "Nothing since?"

"Nothing."

"Where's your sister?"

"Boxing lessons," she said.

"With AJ?"

"Yes. How did you know that?"

"AJ's got the only gym in town," he said. "He's a good friend."

Emily frowned. "I hope she doesn't hurt him. She doesn't know her own strength."

Wyatt laughed. "AJ's ex-navy, tough as hell. No one gets the drop on AJ." He moved to the kitchen and looked out that window as well. "I walked the perimeter of your house and didn't see anything," he said. "Your closest neighbor isn't all that close, and that house is dark and locked up tighter than a drum."

"It wasn't a little while ago. There were trucks in the driveway."

"Nothing there now." He turned and looked at her. "You still scared?"

"Unnerved, maybe," she said. "Not scared." Not with Wyatt standing there, strong and watching her back.

He studied her a beat, then crooked his finger at her in the universal "come here" gesture. She didn't even hesitate and when she got close, he tugged her into him. She burrowed deep, sighing as his arms tightened on her. Cheek to his chest, absorbing the comforting steady beat of his heart, she said, "I'm being silly, it was probably just someone who was lost."

"It's not silly to feel threatened," he said, his voice rumbling against her ear. "You're holding your breath. Breathe, Em."

She let out a long, shuddery breath and a low, embarrassed laugh when her stomach grumbled. "Sorry."

"You eat?"

"Not yet."

He pulled back, grabbed her hand, and headed to the kitchen. "Dinner, then. I'm starving."

"There's not a lot of food in the house right now. I was

actually going out to get some when I got spooked. I've got take-out menus to the places in town that deliver."

"That's a whopping total of two." He shook his head. "Trust me," he said, heading to her fridge. "I can make a meal out of anything."

"Really?"

"Yeah," he said. "Lived all over the world, remember? I was a professional latchkey kid. My sisters and I learned early on to make do with whatever was out there. And trust me, there was a lot of *out there* stuff. You know what I missed most about the States?"

Fascinated by the way his shirt stretched taut across the broad width of his shoulders as he bent low to survey the contents of the fridge drawers, not to mention how the material delineated the flex and pull of his back muscles, she took a moment to answer. "What did you miss most?"

Still crouched low, he craned his neck and flashed her a grin. "Big Macs."

She laughed. "Yeah?"

"Yeah. I told my mom once that I was going to run away. I was going to catch a train, plane, boat, whatever it took to come back here, and get a Big Mac."

"What did she say?"

"She said that as I was a scrawny, white boy all of eight years old, I wouldn't like the jobs I'd qualify for in order to be able to buy a plane ticket."

"She did not tell that to an eight-year-old!"

"She did," he said. "She never believed in sugarcoating the bad in the world." He pulled cheese and apples from the fridge and set them on the counter. "And I already knew the world was a rough place. Being scrawny and white had some serious downsides in Uganda and parts of South America. I learned to be tough early on."

"You got in fights?"

He laughed a little. "More like I got beat up a lot."

"Oh, Wyatt," she murmured. "No."

He shrugged. "It wasn't a surprise. I was almost always the wrong color, and then there was Darcy and her big mouth—which got us in a lot of trouble."

"I hope you don't mind," she said. "But I don't like your parents very much."

"It wasn't all bad." He'd been helping himself to the pantry, opening cupboards, perusing the shelves. He added peanut butter to his growing pile, and then tortillas. "I learned how to fight dirty, and to run real fast. Oh, and if all else failed, I was a pretty damn smooth talker when I needed to be."

This was true. She had firsthand experience at what a smooth talker he was. In bed, she'd do just about anything he asked, and all because he had a way of asking . . . She shook that off and looked at him.

His grin went wicked. "I don't know what you were just thinking about," he said. "But keep thinking it."

She rolled her eyes.

He found a pan and put it on the stove top. In five minutes he'd made two grilled quesadillas, cut up the apples, and spread peanut butter on them. "Not fancy," he said. "But high in protein, anyway."

Q-Tip magically reappeared when the food was ready. "Meow."

Wyatt smiled and crouched low to meet her, scratching her beneath her chin.

"Careful," Emily said. "She usually bites after about five seconds—"

Q-Tip rubbed her face on Wyatt's thigh and began to purr.

"Cats like me," he said.

Yeah, and dogs. And women . . .

They sat at the table, Wyatt with his long legs spread out, nearly touching hers. "Eating peanut butter always reminds me of my mom," she said into the comfortable silence.

He licked peanut butter from his thumb. The sucking sound made her nipples go hard. “She like peanut butter?”

“She loved the stuff. We’d watch reruns of *Friends* and eat right out of the jar with wooden spoons.”

“Was she sick for a long time?” he asked.

“Unfortunately. She got an MS diagnosis when I was ten. She didn’t pass away until right before I left for vet school. She fought the good fight.”

“How does your dad do without her?”

“He pretends to be fine, but I think he’s struggling. It’ll be better when I’m back in L.A. and can do more than just send money.”

“You send him money?”

She shrugged. How had they gotten here? “Sometimes.”

“And your sister,” he said. “You helping support her, too?”

“She just got a job at a local construction company,” she said. “So she’ll be pulling her own weight now.”

Hopefully . . .

“So you’re the mom, the sister, the provider, everything,” he said, nodding. “Explains a lot.”

“What does that mean?” she asked.

He leaned in and gently tugged on a strand of her hair. “Don’t get all defensive.”

“Too late.”

He smiled, like she was amusing him. “It means,” he said patiently, “that I get now why you’re a little . . .”

She narrowed her eyes. *“What?”*

“Anal.”

“I am not . . . *anal*.”

He picked up her cell phone from the table. Swiped his thumb across the screen and hit calendar.

“Hey,” she said.

He turned the screen so she could see, not that she needed to. The Plan—really just the calendar date with two entries:

— 341 days left in Sunshine
— Check your bid on Wyatt

He arched a brow at her. “Bid on me?”

“Lilah’s doing that auction.”

“You bid on me?”

“Well, yes,” she said. “But only because I felt bad for you. Dell had way more bids.”

He laughed. At her, of course. Dammit. “I forgot about that thing.” He pulled out his own phone, and after a minute of wild thumbing, he set it on the table, looking smug.

“What?” she asked.

“I bid on you, too.”

Oh good Lord. “You shouldn’t have. I was outbid on you by Cassandra, and I don’t intend to put in another.” She snatched up her phone, and rising to her feet, she shoved it in a drawer. “And so I like to be organized, so what?” When she turned back, she nearly plowed into him.

He stroked a finger over her temple, down to her jaw, then back to her chin to hold her gaze in his. “Sometimes the best things are unplanned,” he said quietly.

Her gaze dropped to his mouth. It was a really great mouth, and the problem was that now she knew *exactly* what he could do with it.

He paused then closed his eyes a moment. Finally he took their dishes to the sink. When he’d rinsed them and slid them into the dishwasher, he turned to her. “It’s late.”

“I know.”

He came toward her, took her hand, and led her down the hallway. The first bedroom had posters of half-naked women on the walls.

“Sara’s room,” she said.

He tugged her to the last bedroom without comment, pulled back her covers and turned to her expectantly.

She climbed into bed, and then gaped when he started out of the room. "Wait— You're . . . going?"

"To the couch," he said.

"But . . . why?"

"I'm not leaving you alone if you're still scared."

This left her torn. She wasn't still scared. In fact, she was convinced she'd completely overreacted. But if she told him so, he'd leave. "What if I said I wasn't sure what I was?"

He came back to the bed and looked down at her from fathomless, dark eyes. "I'd help you decide."

Liking the sound of that, she opened the covers and scooted over.

Gaze still on hers, he bent and swooped up the cat at his feet and gently set her outside the bedroom and shut the door.

"Meow!" sounded from the hallway.

"One female at a time," Wyatt told her, and kicked off his battered sneakers.

Emily's pulse kicked.

He reached over his head and pulled off his sweatshirt.

And then his T-shirt, which said: *To Save Time, Let's Assume I Am Never Wrong.*

She laughed, and then held her breath, hoping his cargo pants were next because, though she loved how he filled them out, she loved, even more, how he looked without them.

But he slid onto the bed with his pants still on.

"You forgot something," she said.

He pulled her into him and tucked her face into the crook of his neck. "I'm giving you a chance to make sure."

"You can't do that with your pants off?"

"Not around you. You'll act first, think later."

She laughed and gave him a shove, but didn't budge him. After a beat, he rolled to his back so that she was sprawled over the top of him. His hands immediately slid to her ass.

"Tell me the truth," he said, his voice rumbling through his chest and through hers. "You really still scared, or did you just hope to lure me into sleeping with you?"

She bit her lower lip.

He looked into her eyes and laughed softly. *"Emily."*

"I can't help it! We have all this stupid, ridiculous chemistry! And have you seen yourself?" She lifted her weight off him with her arms and glanced down at his bare, beautiful, chiseled torso. "You're a little bit hard to ignore, Wyatt."

With a groan, he closed his eyes but—she couldn't help but notice—he kept his hands on her ass. "You shouldn't tell me this stuff, Emily."

"Why not?"

"I'll take advantage."

She paused for a long beat then nipped his chin as she pulled off his glasses. "I wouldn't mind," she said.

He swore low and rough, sounding deliciously strained. It was a thrill, as was the erection he had pressed between her legs. "Would it help if I told you I totally lied about being scared?" she whispered, and kissed one corner of his mouth.

His hands tightened on her. Squeezed. "From the get-go?"

"No," she said. "Just from the time you showed up at my door and made me forget my troubles."

He was still for a beat, and then he rolled again, pinning her beneath him, his hands stretching her arms above her head. His muscled thigh spread her legs, holding her open so that he could rest between them.

"Ding, ding, was that the right answer?" she whispered hopefully. Breathlessly.

He was laughing when he let go of her long enough to divest himself of his pants, produce a condom—thank God someone was thinking clearly!—and set it on the nightstand. "Just in case," he said.

"I love just in case," she said.

He laughed again, and kissed her.

She reached for the condom, and in the next moment he slid into her, and suddenly neither of them were laughing . . .

Fourteen

The next day Emily staggered home after twelve straight hours of being on her feet. A really rewarding twelve hours though, and she felt good about the animals she'd seen and treated, and in two cases, saved.

"Meow!"

She scooped up Q-Tip, gave her the allowed five second cuddle, and set her down before getting bit. She dropped her bag, kicked off her shoes at the front door, and followed her nose, which was twitching at the amazing scent coming from the kitchen.

Sara was there, still dressed in her construction gear, which today consisted of a man's large T-shirt with the sleeves cut off, a black sports bra beneath, and a pair of guy's cargo shorts. Oh, and steel-toed shit-kickers.

"I could kiss you," Emily told her.

"Because I cleaned the place?"

"Because you're cooking dinner."

"Would you feel less like kissing me if I said I used your

debit card to buy the groceries?" Sara asked. "Because my entire paycheck went to college debt."

Emily sighed. She was tired of always being broke, but it was a way of life. She sniffed and nearly moaned as she headed toward the stove, shedding her scarf and sweater on the table. "I'm torn between feeling really guilty, and incredibly grateful."

"Why the guilt? Because you're a total slob who had shit all over this house, including two weeks of laundry that I finally did for you? Laundry that included a pair of torn panties stuffed into your jeans back pocket?"

Emily went still. "That's old news."

"And the whisker burn on your throat? Or the sound of a man walking down the hallway this morning, swearing when he tripped over Q-Tip somewhere around the crack of dawn?"

Emily grabbed the scarf and put it back around her neck, ears burning. *Not such old news* . . . "Let's talk about you. Why are you becoming Miss Sara Homemaker all of a sudden, cooking and doing laundry?"

Sara pointed a wooden spatula at her. "Don't make me hurt you. Grab a plate."

"You didn't have to do this," Emily said, taking out two plates and silverware. "I take it you haven't heard from Rayna."

Sara sighed. "I wouldn't know."

"Huh?"

"I sort of blocked her phone number so she can't call or text me."

Emily stared at her. "Why?"

"Self-preservation," Sara said. "Do you have any idea what it's like to fall completely in love with someone, and then have them accidentally squash you like a grape? She seriously has no clue why I broke up with her."

"And why did you break up with her?"

Sara went mum.

Emily sighed. They'd been doing this for a month now.

"Look," Sara finally said, "it doesn't matter why. What matters is that she was okay with me breaking up with her. So okay with it that she wanted to remain *friends*."

"But that's nice, isn't it?" Emily asked. She took in Sara's glare. "Okay, so *not* nice?"

"The *f*-word? Are you kidding me? I gave her the best two years of my life." Sara picked up the pan, and with a jerk of her wrist, flipped a crepe and then slammed the pan back down on the stove. "Whatever. It's done. I'm over her."

"Clearly. Maybe if you told me why you broke up with her—"

"Bring it up again and no crepes for you." Sara expertly deposited the crepe onto a plate and poured more batter into the pan. "So back to the torn panties and the man in our house."

"I'm pleading the fifth," Emily said.

"So I suppose you don't want to discuss the whisker burn on your throat then, either."

Emily tightened her scarf. "Don't make me block *your* texts and calls."

Sara's sharp gaze landed on her. "That bad?"

More like that good . . . "Um . . ."

Sara studied her for a heartbeat, and then smiled. "You've extended the one-night stand. *Nice*."

Emily plopped to a chair, set her elbows on the table, and dropped her forehead into her hands. "No. Not nice."

"You still dig him."

"No. Maybe." She sighed. "I don't want to dig him *or* his sexy self. But I keep losing my clothes when I'm with him. I was even wearing my Mickey Mouse pj's and he *liked* them."

Sara laughed. "You know, maybe these slut moments of yours are your body's way of saying you need to loosen up."

"Well, I can't get much looser!"

Sara's smile faded. "That's not true. You're still wound pretty tight."

"Yes, because I'm trying to adapt to this latest side trip from my plan," Emily said.

"Oh, for God's sake. How many times do I have to tell you? Screw the plan, Emily. Life can't be lived off a damn plan, babe."

"Yes, it can," Emily protested. "You have to dream it to live it, *babe*, and I have the dream all figured out."

"Right," Sara deadpanned. "L.A. Taking care of Dad. Some version of the John . . . There are so many stupid things wrong with your plan, I don't know where to start."

"Name one thing wrong with it," Emily said.

"Going back to Los Angeles to try to reconnect with a guy who doesn't even care what you've been up to? I mean, it'd be one thing if he'd called, e-mailed . . . texted."

It was uncomfortably close to what Wyatt had voiced to her. "I can kill my own spiders."

"Huh?" Sara asked.

"Never mind!"

"Listen, Em. Working at some fancy vet clinic isn't the right dream for you."

"Oh, but hiding out in Idaho and pretending all is well while hammering nails is?" Emily asked.

Sara stared at her, then turned off the stove and walked out of the kitchen.

Emily turned and looked over at Q-Tip, sitting on one of the kitchen chairs like she owned it.

Q-Tip gave her a long, slow, you-are-an-idiot blink with her yellow eyes. Emily sighed. Thunked her head on the table a few times—which didn't help much—and got up, following Sara into their small living room. "I'm sorry. That was out of line."

"Not really, since it's the truth." Sara had plopped onto the couch, feet up on the coffee table, her boots still on.

Emily bit her tongue over that, moved to the end of the

couch, lifted Sara's feet and dropped them to the floor. Then she sat, too.

Sara sighed and set her head on Emily's shoulder. "I'm hiding out rather than face my stupid heart. Happy now? And you've been charging forward ever since—"

Emily shut her eyes. "Don't."

"—Mom died," Sara finished.

Emily felt the stab of pain behind her left breast. It was a familiar pain by now. At first, after the funeral, she'd actually thought she was having a heart attack. In a very scary round of tests at the ER, she'd learned that anxiety could present like that.

Humiliating. Especially since Emily had refused to believe it at first. She wasn't an anxious person. She was a person who missed her mom like she'd miss a damn limb. That was all. It was pure grief, and that it could manifest itself so powerfully, in such a physical way had left her feeling weak and even more unhappy.

So she'd read some books and learned that making definite plans was one good way to cope.

So that's what she'd done.

She'd made some damn plans. "There's nothing wrong with charging forward with your life," she said.

"But it's like you're on a mission to live your life perfectly, without regrets," Sara said. "But Emily, regrets are a damn way of life."

"I know that. I'm living with that."

"What regrets do you have?" Sara asked.

Laying her head back against the couch, she stared up at the ceiling. They had some cobwebs up there. Hopefully no spiders.

"Em?"

"I regret that Mom died so young."

"I know," Sara said. "We all regret that. But she gave us a lifetime of love. Remember what she always told us? Follow your heart, cuz a heart's never wrong."

Emily smiled, but it slowly faded. "I just meant that I hate she died without having anything to show for her life."

"Nothing to show for her life?" Sara asked incredulously. "She *loved* her life."

"We were poor, Sara. Dirt poor. Our apartment—"

"Was her home, and we were her life. She didn't care about anything else. And I'm sorry, but you disrespect her memory by suggesting otherwise."

Emily got that, she really did, but Sara hadn't been around. Only Emily had known how much Mom had suffered in the end. "She could have had more. Dad—"

"Taught us to love ourselves and every other living creature. Sure, he's a damn tree hugger, and he'd save a rattlesnake if it crossed his path, but hey, snakes are people, too."

Emily choked out a laugh. "Face it, he could have provided better if he wanted to, Sara. He chose to spend most of his time at the shelters."

"Yeah, well, he does have a real savior complex." Sara slid her a look. "Like someone else I know."

"Not me," Emily said just as Q-Tip leapt into her lap for a rare nuzzle.

Sara laughed. "The apple never falls far from the tree."

"Not true," Emily argued. "Dad would save a damn ant crossing his path on the sidewalk."

"Hello," Sara said. "Have you met you? You had an ant collection when you were young and named each and every one of them. And Sassy. Remember Sassy? She was the bird you found on our back porch, the one who'd fallen out of a tree. You fed it baby food and made her a new nest on the ground until she could fly again. And how about Stinky, the baby skunk you rescued? You laid down the law, threatened to sleep outside in the grass alongside of him if Dad didn't let you keep him."

Emily stared at her. "That was different."

"How?"

She squirmed a little. "Well, for one thing, I was a kid. I never did anything to the detriment of my family."

"If that's how you're remembering things," Sara said, "I don't think we grew up in the same house."

Emily blew out a breath.

"We always had a roof over our head. And food."

Barely... But she knew Sara couldn't ever really understand because she'd already been at college when the MS kicked in, leaving their mom unable to care for herself. Most people took for granted being able to do for themselves, but that had been cruelly wrestled away from the woman who'd always prided herself on her independence. The simple act of getting bathed, dressed, doing her hair, feeding her, *everything*, had fallen to others.

Emily's dad had been drowning in his own grief knowing he was going to lose his wife, and as he had all his life when things got tough, he'd worked. Twenty-four seven. Whatever it took to keep him from having to face the truth.

"You weren't there when it got bad, you were in Chicago getting your PhD in philosophy," Emily said.

"I know." Sara sighed. "I'd call and Mom just kept saying she was fine, that I didn't have to come home."

"She didn't want anyone to see her, or how bad it'd gotten."

Sara reached out for Emily's hand. "You were both good at convincing me all was well."

Emily blew out a breath. "We were fine." Until they weren't.

"It's funny, because I hate philosophy now," Sara said quietly. "I've got this piece of paper, a very lovely gold-lined, framed piece of paper that says people should call me Dr. Stevens." She snorted. "Really comes in handy on the job site."

Sara squeezed her fingers, her expression unusually solemn. "You did great with her, Em. I know it was a lot, but you did it, you took care of her when neither me nor Dad could.

But ever since then, you've had this plan, and you're so . . . clenched. And I get it, I'm betting that for you, knowing what's coming every day is a comfort." She smiled. "Maybe you should put 'hot sex with Dr. Sexy' on your plan."

Emily choked out a laugh. "Not going to happen. I know you don't get it but I don't want to end up like Dad. I don't want to have half my patients be pro bono. I want to pay off debts and actually earn a living. I want to keep my eyes on the prize. And L.A.'s the prize. Plus, Dad needs someone to take care of him."

"Since when?"

"Since always. And you're not exactly earning a ton of money with those fancy degrees," Emily said. "The starting salary of that L.A. job is double what the Belle Haven position pays. I'm going to be able to take care of us."

"We can take care of ourselves," Sara said.

"Yeah?" Emily asked. "How?"

Sara's eyes narrowed, but she didn't respond. Couldn't, Emily knew. Emily paid the rent on this place. "It's the way it is," she said. "And if saying so out loud makes me shallow and cruel, well, then, that's what I am."

"You're not shallow or cruel," Sara said. "If you were shallow, you'd get a haircut that cost more than twenty bucks and you'd wear more than just a swipe of mascara and the occasional lip gloss. You'd tell me I was an idiot for dumping Rayna."

"You're an idiot for dumping Rayna."

Sara let out a mirthless laugh. "You're wrong, you know. Your family, what you have left of it anyway, me and Dad, we're fine. We're all fine."

"Yeah," Emily said. "Until someone gets MS."

They both stared at the ceiling like it was their job.

"I don't want to fight about this," Emily finally said.

"Good. Let's go back to you and Dr. Sexy instead. You know he's not my type, but if he was a chick I'd totally be into him. You need to go for it."

"I can't go for it," Emily said.

"Why?"

"I just can't. Drop it."

"Not until you tell me why."

"Because . . ." Emily hugged herself. "Because I'm not sure I can keep it casual."

Sara's eyes sharpened. "You falling for him?"

"No." God. She winced. *Yes*. "Maybe."

Sara stared at her as if she'd just broken out into a song and tap dance.

"I can't help it!" Emily said. "He offered to squish spiders for me!"

"Huh?"

"Never mind! Never mind all of it, it's stupid. I've lost my mind."

"Honey." Sara shook her head. "I didn't know this. If I'd have known this, I wouldn't have teased you about him. You're supposed to just sleep with him, *not* fall for him."

"Did you hear the stupid part?" Emily asked. "I *know* I can't fall for him—" She broke off and stared at Sara. "Wait. I know why *I* can't fall for him, why do *you* think I can't fall for him?"

"First rule of one-night stands," Sara said. "No falling. It negates the whole *one*-night stand thing. And . . ." She winced. "Okay, listen, don't hate me. But I'm here to tell you that a five can't fall for a ten. It won't work out."

Emily just stared at her. "Was that English?"

"I'm a five and Rayna is a ten. It didn't work out."

"Because *you* bailed," Emily said. She blinked. "Wait a minute. You think I'm a five and Wyatt's a ten?"

"Honey—"

"Oh my God," Emily breathed, staring at the guilt flashing on Sara's face. "You do. You think I'm a five and Wyatt's a ten." She shook her head. *"Ouch."*

"I think five's are *real*," Sara said. "Five's are the *best* kind of people, and that's what we are. Trust me, Emily, you *don't* want to fall for anyone over a five. They've been pretty all their lives. They've never had to struggle. They've never had to fight for a single thing or person, nothing. They've never been disappointed, or hurt. I'm just looking out for you, sister to sister." Sara scooted in and hugged her. "Let's find you a new one-night stand, okay? *He* can be a five. That way if it turns into more, you're ready."

"You're a nut," Emily said. "A certifiable nut."

"Yes, and luckily, it runs in the family."

Fifteen

One week later, Wyatt walked by the staff kitchen and caught sight of Emily sitting at the common table in front of her opened laptop, on the phone.

"Uh-huh," she said into the receiver. "Yeah . . ." She was still leaning into her laptop, clearly avidly reading whatever was on the screen.

Wyatt stepped into the room as she spoke again. "I'm on a lunch break," she said. "And absolutely *not* obsessively checking the auction bidding."

Except she totally was. Wyatt could see it. He scanned the list over her shoulder and grinned wide when he realized she had her mouse hovered over . . .

Him.

"I've been outbid by no less than five other people," she said. "Yeah, and now he's up to . . . *five hundred dollars*—" She broke off to listen to whoever was speaking on the other end of the line—he was betting Sara.

"Damn that Cassandra. No, I'm not going to bid five hundred bucks," she said. "Are you kidding me? With that much money, I could fly us home to visit Dad for the weekend. I could get that new transmission for my car. I could take us to a spa day and get the works— Yes, I realize we've never been to a spa, Sara, the point is that we *could* go to one if we wanted— I'm not being ridiculous!" She sighed. "Look, I've gotta go."

Wyatt watched as she ended the call without taking her gaze off the screen. He was still watching when she blew out a breath and hovered her mouse over the bidding block.

And then clicked.

"Dammit," she muttered to herself, typing in a new bid. "You have *no* will power."

"Sounds promising," he said.

She jumped about five feet in the air at the sound of his voice and whipped around. "*What are you doing?*" she demanded.

"I think the question is what are *you* doing?"

"Nothing." Her gaze skittered away. "Just . . . making a shopping list. You know, cat food, cookies, Mace for people who read over my shoulder . . ." She hit a key on the keyboard, clearly intending to put the screen to sleep.

Instead, it brightened again, revealing the auction site.

Wyatt smiled and leaned over her shoulder. "I thought you said you let the bid go."

"I . . . meant to."

"Uh-huh. Let's see how much I'm worth to you . . ." He felt his brows raise. "Five hundred and one dollars?"

"That's a typo," she said, and hit another button. This time the screen went black. "And it's for charity."

"So I'm a . . . pity bid?" he asked.

"Yes." She sucked in a breath. "Exactly."

He burst out laughing, and she frowned. "It's true," she said. "Brady and Dell and Adam are all getting up there in the bidding. I didn't want you to feel bad."

He was still grinning. "Look at you, digging yourself deeper."

She flushed, but lifted her chin. Heaven forbid she cave on anything. "Hey," she said. "I'll have you know that your Casserole Brigade has divided into factions. Some of them are now pooling their funds to take the bid on you up to one thousand bucks so that Cassandra can't get you. I'm just helping them get there, is all."

He bent low so that his jaw pressed against the side of hers as together they looked at the screen. "Such a pretty liar," he chided, and turned his head, letting his lips graze the sweet spot just beneath her ear.

She sucked in a breath and shuddered, and when he touched the spot with his tongue, a soft moan escaped her.

"So it has nothing to do with missing me in your bed?" he asked in her ear.

"N-no, of course not. I don't miss you in my bed."

"How about my truck? You miss me in the driver's seat of my truck?" he asked, sucking her skin into his mouth. Christ, he wanted to eat her up.

She moaned again, and he set his hands on the arm of her chair to spin her around to face him. He was just able to haul her out of the chair and show her exactly what she was missing when they heard footsteps coming down the hall.

Emily shoved free of him and was doing her best to look casual as Dell strode in. He snatched a bottle of water from the refrigerator and smiled at her.

She smiled back.

"You got some sun out there today taking care of those geese that were brought in," he said. "You're all flushed. Wear sunscreen tomorrow."

Emily's gaze slid to Wyatt's. "Will do."

"Did I tell you?" Dell asked her. "The head vet from the Beverly Hills center called me. Their intern isn't enamored with L.A. Her family lives in Coeur d'Alene, and she misses them."

Emily blinked. "No," she said a little faintly. "You didn't mention that."

Her smile had slipped so briefly, Wyatt would have said he'd imagined it if he didn't know her.

"I told him we were damned lucky to have you," Dell said. "Since you're so happy here."

Yeah, her smile was definitely a little short of her usual wattage, but Dell was oblivious as he turned to go. As he did, he slid Wyatt a brief glance.

Not oblivious at all, Wyatt realized. Just respecting her privacy.

When they were alone, Emily also turned to leave.

Wyatt caught her hand and pulled her back around, giving her a long, searching look.

"What?" she said.

"You tell me."

She pulled free. "I don't know what you're talking about."

"So I just imagined that quick flash of horror as you realized you could have switched places with that other intern and gone back to L.A. early?"

Again she tried to go.

And again he held her to him. "How many days left?"

"Three hundred and thirty-six," she said without hesitation.

Shit. He took a deep breath. "You're still not happy here," he stated flatly.

She closed her eyes.

He didn't know what he expected. That she'd have miraculously given up on her *plan* just because they'd slept together a few times?

But that wasn't what pissed him off. It was that he'd been hoping for more.

And she'd been hoping to be sent home.

"You should have told him," Wyatt said.

"He'd just said how much he valued me as a vet," Emily said. "Do you know what he's given me? *Everything.* I'm not going to tell him I'd rather be in L.A."

Wyatt drew a careful breath, trying to leave his personal feelings out of the mix. He was good at that. Hell, he fucking rocked at that. "He would've understood."

She turned back to him, with heartbreaking sincerity. "You think so?"

Christ. "Yeah," he said. "I think so."

And then, because what he really wanted to do was push her up against the wall and kiss the living shit out of her, until she was panting his name and tearing at his clothes to get him inside her, he shoved his hands in his pockets to keep them off her.

He walked out.

Lilah came by after work and dragged Emily off for "some fun." Turned out Lilah's husband, Brady, was on a team with—among others—Dell, Adam, Adam's BFF Griffin, AJ, and a player who ran onto the field at the very last minute.

Wyatt.

The guys were all in athletic shorts, T-shirts, and cleats, and since it had rained until about five minutes ago, they were also drenched. And muddy.

Nobody wore drenched and muddy better than Wyatt, a fact Emily did her best to take in while pretending not to . . .

Sitting in the stands around her were other wives and girlfriends. She also figured out, when one pretty twenty-something struggled to the stands using a walker and stopped to yell at Wyatt through the fence, "You need to kick ass, Wyatt Stone, to make up for last week's suckage!" that sisters were welcome as well.

Lilah waved her over to sit with them.

"Aw," Darcy said, sizing Emily up. "The new vet."

"You're one of Wyatt's two sisters," Emily said.

"How did you know?" Darcy asked.

Emily smiled. "I recognize the hostility and intolerance and deeply seated resentment." She held out a hand to Darcy. "I'm Emily, the intern vet."

"The one bidding on my brother."

"He didn't have as many bids as Dell and Adam, and I felt sorry for him," Emily said in automatic self-defense.

Darcy's smile went real as she shook Emily's hand. "I like you already."

"I'm really quite likeable," Emily said, and for the next hour watched Dell, Adam, Grif, and Wyatt, not to mention a whole host of other hot guys, run through a muddy, grass field tackling each other.

The guys all had red tags hanging off their hips, which were supposed to be pulled by their opponents instead of anyone getting tackled. But, though the flags were yanked and thrust triumphantly into the air, there was still enough body contact—and bone crunching and taunting and heckling—that Emily found herself both holding her breath in terror, and shaking her head in bafflement.

When Wyatt was grabbed and taken down from behind by not one or two, but *three* men, she clasped a hand to her heart until he spit out some dirt and grass and pushed up to his feet.

"I thought it was flag football," she said, "not tackle the shit out of each other football."

Lilah shrugged. "It's a guy thing."

Emily didn't take her eyes off Wyatt. He looked okay, but she didn't breathe until Brady came over and high-fived him, and Wyatt flashed a triumphant grin.

And then, while she was sucking in a lungful of relief, he turned his head and laid his gaze right on her. The relief swimming through her veins turned to something else entirely, something she wasn't even close to ready to accept.

* * *

At the half, Wyatt took shit for being late to the game from all the guys

"We almost forfeited," Dell said.

"Hey," Wyatt said in his defense, "I had an emergency."

His entire team gave him the stink eye.

"What emergency?" AJ wanted to know. "Because if anyone has an excuse to be late, it's me, since my last patient was your sister, and I'm not sure who got more worked over, her or me."

"You slept with one of your patients?" Adam asked.

"Forget that," Brady said. "You slept with your best friend's sister?"

"What?" AJ looked at both of them in horror and then turned to Wyatt. "No! God. I wouldn't—"

"You don't think she's hot enough?" Grif asked.

"She *is* hot," AJ said, and then grimaced at Wyatt. "No, I mean— She's my patient, and—" He broke off when Dell, Adam, Brady, and Grif started laughing. Narrowing his eyes, he crossed his arms over his beefy chest. "You think that's funny?"

"Yeah," Dell said, straightening, still grinning. "You should see the look on your face, man."

"Jesus, I'm sweating," AJ said, and swiped his forearm over his brow. "You made me sweat." He looked at Wyatt. "I'm not."

"I know," Wyatt said as they moved together to the side of the spectator stands for the huge water jug placed there just for them. Wyatt knew Darcy wasn't sleeping with anyone right now, she was far too pissed off at the world to have been getting any. "But it got the attention off me being late, so thanks," he said, and downed a cup of water.

"No it didn't," Dell said. "All the patients were gone when I left. Who came in?"

"Skylar Houghton."

"With her hamster?" Dell asked. "I treated the abscess yesterday, all was well."

"Yeah." Wyatt ran a hand through his hair. "She brought by a lasagna dish."

"Score," Dell said. "Since it's my night to cook."

"She made it for me," Wyatt said.

Dell stared at him. "You suck."

"Hey, I earned that lasagna the hard way, trust me."

Dell grinned.

"Not like that!" Wyatt said. "Jesus. You guys all need a life."

"Sucks, doesn't it?" AJ muttered.

"I'm confused," Dell said. "Skylar's got a normal job at the post office, and she's not crazy. You could do worse."

Wyatt was saved having to answer by his nosy older sister who interfered from the front row. "Hey, so where's this lasagna?" Zoe wanted to know. He should have known the women could hear their converstation.

Beside her was Darcy. She looked at AJ, and his expression went blank.

Darcy's did the same.

Wyatt would have to wonder later what the hell had happened during physical therapy, because he locked eyes with Emily and like he was some stupid high school kid, he forgot everything else.

Next to Emily, Lilah waved at her husband, and blew him kisses. Brady grinned at her, the badass ex-special ops soldier looking soft as mush.

"Yeah, yeah," Zoe said, nudging Lilah. "Save it for later. I want to hear more about the lasagna. What kind? Her usual meat and cheese?"

"Next time tell her whatshername brought you lobster ravioli," Darcy said. "Tell her that's our fave."

"Or homemade mac and cheese," Zoe said. "I wouldn't mind some more of that. Who made it? Kathy Anderson, right? We need her cat to get sick again."

Wyatt looked at Emily. *I'm not cooking you homemade mac and cheese*, her gaze said.

He didn't want or need her to cook him a damn thing. Yeah, Skylar was sweet and gentle and kind, and she could really cook.

But he wasn't attracted.

Not like he was to the not-so-sweet, not-so-gentle, curvy brunette watching him right now . . .

Zoe stared at Wyatt, then followed his gaze to Emily. She blinked, then looked back at Wyatt. "Or maybe we could just get takeout," she said.

Sixteen

As always, Emily woke up to Q-Tip sitting on her chest demanding food. One look at the bedside clock had Emily groaning. "It's only five. I've got another half hour."

"*Meow*."

"Fine. I get it. You're starving to death slowly." She staggered out of bed and tripped over the cat.

Q-Tip yowled at her in reproach, and ran ahead to the kitchen, her belly doing its usual swing back and forth.

Emily filled her bowl and had to smile at the rumbling purr of thanks. She sat at the table and opened her laptop. As a matter of habit, she went to her calendar.

Another week had gone by. Three hundred thirty days . . .

Could've been less if you'd spoken up to Dell . . . She closed the calendar and checked Lilah's charity auction page. Shockingly, there were bids for dinner out with "Sunshine's newest, cutest, prettiest vet."

People wanted to have dinner with her. She tried to process her thoughts on that and decided she was flattered.

There were also bids for Dell, Brady, Adam . . .

But topping the list was Wyatt himself. Seemed that just about everyone in town wanted to "shadow" him for a day. His top bid was for two hundred bucks over what she'd last bid.

She opened a new screen and checked her account balance. She'd been socking away every spare penny she had, which wasn't all that many pennies.

But she had enough.

You're crazy, a little voice said. *Certifiable.*

Which is the only explanation for why she upped her bid on one Dr. Wyatt Stone and became his highest bidder.

Two minutes later her cell phone rang. It was Lilah.

"Funny thing happened," Lilah said. "I get an alarm when someone bids on the auction site. And someone just bid on Wyatt."

"Huh," Emily said casually. "I imagine that's happening quite a bit."

"Yes," Lilah said. "Actually, this person has bid four times for Wyatt so far."

"Five," Emily said, and clapped a hand over her mouth.

Too late. Lilah snorted with mirth. "Honey," she said, "you do realize you don't have to pay to shadow him, you do that every single day. They pay *you*."

"I just wanted to contribute to the cause," Emily said, and grimaced.

"That's your story?"

"Yep," she said with much more confidence than she felt.

Lilah laughed at her.

Emily sighed. "You're not going to make a big deal about this, are you?"

"Oh hell yes," Lilah said. She laughed again and disconnected.

Great. Shaking her head, Emily got showered and dressed, and stepped off their porch to head to work, cutting across the wild grass growing in her yard to her car. They'd had rain several nights in a row now, and the grass had grown halfway up to her knees. She made a mental note to ask the landlord if she was responsible for cutting it.

She hoped not.

At the odd rustling sound, Emily went still, and then slowly turned around.

There, just behind her, was something moving in the grass. Hopefully not a snake, the only animal she wasn't crazy about.

When the rustle came again, she almost acted like a complete girl by turning tail and running, but something had her taking a step forward instead.

Parting the long strands of grass, she smiled. A turtle was on the move. He—or she—was about nine inches long, olive and black, and had a nasty-looking gouge on one side of its face from jaw to left eye. It was so puffy he couldn't possibly see out of it. "Oh," Emily breathed, and crouched low. "Oh you poor baby." She scooped the thing up in her hands to get a better look, and it retreated into its shell.

"It's okay," she said, moving back to the garage to grab a box leftover from when she and Sara had moved in. Gently, she set the turtle in the box and then set the box on the front passenger's seat of her car. "I'll fix you right up at work."

The turtle remained in its shell, but she could feel its misgivings.

"Really," she promised. "I actually know what I'm doing. At least when it comes to animals. Life, not so much, but we're not going to go there."

Her patient was polite enough not to respond.

Wyatt walked into the center to find Dell had beat him in. Jade had flown back to Chicago for two weeks to help her mom recover from knee replacement surgery, and she'd gotten someone to fill in for her.

Either that person hadn't shown yet, or her substitute was Dell, which was highly doubtful. Dell and Jade had a solid relationship, but Jade had a rule—her husband wasn't allowed in her domain. She called it the how-to-stay-married rule.

No one was more respectful of that rule than Dell himself. He had a caller on speaker phone as he tried to retrieve a pencil from Peanut, who didn't want to give it up.

"How's it going?" the female caller asked.

Jade.

"Great," Dell said, still playing tug-of-war with Peanut.

"Boner," Peanut yelled.

"Great, huh?" Jade asked doubtfully.

"Fantastic," Dell said, giving up on his pencil.

Peanut cackled in triumph.

"I'll be available if you need anything," Jade said. "Don't let Peanut eat any more pencils."

Dell looked at Wyatt and grimaced.

"I almost forgot," Jade said. "I saw you'd ruined your favorite shoes."

"Yeah," Dell said. "Gertie ate the laces and threw up on them."

"I bought you new ones," Jade said. "They're in your office closet. Keep her out of there."

Dell's face softened. "Thanks, babe."

"Anytime." Jade's voice was soft now, too, and filled with affection. "Love you, babe. Don't mess up my front desk or we'll have problems. Oh, and Wyatt's kicking your ass in the auction. Don't worry, I've put in a bid for you that'll top it. You can thank me in person." And then she disconnected.

Dell stared at the phone for a long beat, that warm, affectionate look still on his face, and Wyatt felt an odd pang.

Envy.

He was happy for Dell, even as he envied the hell out of what he'd found with Jade.

Wyatt had had that once, however briefly, with Caitlin. She'd worked in town at the local medical clinic, and they'd had about six months of bliss.

Until an opportunity had come up for her to go work for Doctors Without Borders. She'd promised to be gone only a year, two tops.

How the hell did a guy resent that? Easy answer—he shouldn't. He couldn't. Just because *he* wanted to settle down and grow roots and a family, and she wanted to save the world . . .

No, he couldn't have asked her to stay. For years he never had a say in where the wind took him. He'd refused to do that to Caitlin, to anyone. He wanted to settle down in one place without having to ask someone to want the same.

So he hadn't asked, not that Caitlin had given him any sign that she'd wanted him to ask. It had sucked, making the break with her, but he wanted to believe that there was someone else out there for him. A woman who would belong to him the way Jade belonged to Dell. A woman he could belong to the way Dell belonged to Jade.

"If I screw anything up," Dell muttered, hands on hips, looking uncharacteristically flustered, "she's going to kill me."

The chances of this happening was high. Dell was famous for screwing up the scheduling, the billing, whatever he got his fingers on.

So Wyatt understood the concern.

Adam walked in the front door wearing S&R gear, two yellow Labs at his side. He took one look at his brother behind the counter and shook his head. "Jade's gonna kill you, man."

"Whatever," Dell said, scowling. "I've done this before. I did this before Jade."

"And you sucked," Adam reminded him.

"Then *you* do it."

"And risk the wrath of your gorgeous wife?" Adam asked with a rare laugh. "Hell no."

Dell's shoulders sagged a little. "Who am I kidding, I totally can't do this. I promised I wouldn't, but the woman she hired to cover us got sick. I've called in some favors from everyone I know. I'm waiting to hear back."

"You're fucked," Adam said under his breath.

Yeah, Wyatt was getting that. "What are our choices?" he asked Dell.

"I've got a great choice, and one . . . not so great," Dell admitted. "And the last one is oh-holy-fucking-shit we're in trouble, but she's better than nothing." He paused, rubbed a hand over his head. "Maybe."

Adam gave Wyatt a told-you-so look.

The front door opened and Emily walked in. Weeks ago now she'd wised up and ditched the business suits for more practical clothing. Today she was in khaki pants and a knit top that was one of those snug wraparound deals that tied beneath a breast with a bow. He watched her walk toward them while having some pretty damn explicit thoughts about that bow. Like untying it.

With his teeth.

She had a box under each arm. She set the smaller box down and read the note out loud:

Dear Dr. Dreamy Eyes,

Heard you love homemade mac and cheese, so for treating my dear Boo-Boo yesterday, I whipped some up. There's plenty more where this came from, any*time.*

Sue Mason

Dell and Adam started laughing.

"What's so funny?" Wyatt demanded. "When you first

opened up this place, every single woman in town suddenly had a dog or a cat that was sick."

"Just happy to have passed the torch," Dell said. "Dr. Dreamy Eyes."

"Shit." Wyatt snatched the note from Emily. It read exactly as she'd read, with one notable exception. "Hey. It does *not* say Dr. Dreamy Eyes."

Dell wiped away tears of mirth. "I should give you a raise for that alone," he told Emily.

"Feel free," she said demurely.

Wyatt shook his head. "Payback's a bitch, you know."

"No hazing the new employees, especially the cute ones," Dell said.

Emily grinned at him.

Dell grinned back at her.

Wyatt shook his head again and grabbed a stack of files to go to the back.

"Have a good day, Dr. Dreamy Eyes," Dell said.

"Shit," Wyatt said, turning back. "You are not going to call me that."

"All day long."

Wyatt realized he'd forgotten about the other box Emily had brought in. "What's in there?"

"Our first patient," she said.

Wyatt reached into the box and pulled out a painted turtle—indigenous to Idaho. "Ouch," he said, checking out the little guy's injured, puffy, bloody face.

The phone rang.

"Shit," Dell said.

Another phone started ringing, and Dell swore again.

Adam quickly made his escape. Smart man. Dell looked over and Wyatt cracked up at the look on his face.

"Not funny," Dell said.

"Yeah, it is."

"It won't be this afternoon. I've gotta be up north," Dell

said. "Brady's flying me. So guess who's going to be standing right here if no one shows up to help?"

Wyatt stopped laughing.

Five minutes later he was in the back with Emily and her turtle. "A new pet?" he asked.

"No, he was in my yard."

He smiled. "So the apple didn't fall far from the tree."

She stared at him. "Do you know my sister, Sara?"

"No." He smiled. "Rescuing's a good quality. Especially in a vet."

"Maybe. But not so much in a father."

He glanced at her, but she was bent over the turtle. "He didn't take care of you?" he asked.

She shrugged. "He did his best."

"But?"

She lifted her head. "But what?"

"There's definitely a but at the end of that sentence," he said.

She looked a little embarrassed to have been so transparent. "No. No but. Think this little guy is someone's pet?"

Okay, so they weren't going to chat about her dad. "I don't know, your neighbors aren't very close. This poor guy's had it rough. And he's been rudely rebuked by his mate."

"How do you know?"

"The males use their claws to stroke their woman's face, to woo her when he wants to mate."

Emily's gaze flew to his.

He smiled at her.

She dropped eye contact and looked at his hands, maybe remembering how he'd stroked the hair from her face when he'd been "wooing" her. "If she's not in the mood," he said, "she uses her claws to ward him off. I'm taking it she wasn't in the mood."

"Maybe she was just nervous."

He looked at her over the turtle.

She bit her lower lip. "Or maybe she wasn't ready, I don't know."

"Maybe she's just prickly, and she has to be the initiator," he said.

Her cheeks reddened, and he laughed softly. "Hold him for me," he said.

Emily cradled the turtle between her two hands while Wyatt cleaned him up and put some antibiotic cream on the nasty cut. "You poor little man," she whispered, stroking one of his legs. "Next time choose someone nicer."

Wyatt smiled. "You're not returning him to the wild."

"Of course I am."

He gestured to the way she'd picked the thing up and cradled it to her chest.

"Hey," she said. "He's hurt, that's all."

He nodded, but he had sisters. He knew exactly when a woman was in denial, and this was a woman deep in denial. "We have extra crates," he said. "Take one of the small ones. It'll make a nice little home for him."

"I'm not keeping him!"

"Okay," he said, watching her stroke the little guy across the head. "Whatever you say."

She made a noise, grabbed a crate, and walked out of the room holding her turtle.

He was smirking when she stuck her head back in, looking quite pleased with herself. "What?" he asked.

"Dell says you're backup to Mike at the front desk."

"What about you?" he asked.

"He said I'm shadowing him on an out of office call. To one of the ranches he takes care of," she said, smiling, her eyes flashing good humor, the little minx.

"I like that expression you're wearing," he said. "But there's one I like better."

"What?"

He strode over to her, wrapped his hand around the nape of her neck, slid his fingers into her hair to hold her where he wanted, and covered her mouth with his. When she gasped, he took full advantage, stroking his tongue to hers, kissing her until she'd plastered herself full front to him. Her arms had snaked around his waist and up under his shirt, where the touch of her fingers against his bare skin was sending currents of electricity out to every nerve ending he had, including the ones currently pressed against her pelvis.

She blinked up at him, dazed, her fingers still fisted in his shirt at his back.

"There." He smiled down at her. "That expression. *That's* my favorite."

Seventeen

At the end of the day, Emily took Sammy home with her. Yes, she'd named the turtle. She couldn't help it, he looked like a Sammy.

She and Sara sat on the bottom step outside their front door, staring at the box Emily had tipped on its side so that Sammy could walk away when he was ready.

He waited a good five minutes before walking cautiously out of the box and to the start of the grass.

"There he goes," Sara said.

But Sammy stopped. Went still as stone.

"It's all good," Emily told him. "I'll be here if you ever need me. Enjoy the rest of fall, eat a lot of good stuff. Have a great life, Sammy. But pick a nicer girl next time, okay?"

"Not a supermodel," Sara said.

Sammy took a few steps and vanished into the grass.

Sara went inside to cook dinner.

Emily stayed outside until dusk, watching for Sammy. But he was gone.

* * *

The next morning, Emily once again woke up to Q-Tip on her chest, nose to nose with her. "We've got to stop meeting like this."

"Meow."

"Yeah, yeah." Emily slid out of bed and fed the bossy thing. Then she did her usual online thing.

And maybe placed a new bid on Wyatt.

Dammit. At this rate, she was going to need to take out a loan . . .

Shutting her laptop, she walked through the house, heading toward a hot shower. She took a quick detour to the front door and peeked out, not sure whether she hoped to see, or not see, Sammy.

He was at the bottom step, and Emily would've sworn he was smiling up at her. She whirled into the house, put some lettuce and a strawberry on a paper plate, and ran back outside, setting it before the turtle.

He went to work on the lettuce while she crouched at his side and looked over his injury. It was definitely getting better. "I have to go to work," she told him as he gobbled up his breakfast. "But if you want to show up here again tonight, I'll be back with more food."

"Talking to yourself?" Sara asked from the doorway. She saw Sammy and shook her head. "Nope, you're talking to your animals, just like Dad."

"Sammy isn't mine," Emily said, rising. "He was just hungry and needed some TLC, is all."

"Uh-huh," Sara said wryly. "You're halfway to a menagerie, you know that right?"

"Q-Tip belongs to the house, not me. And Sammy's a wild animal." And with that weak defense, Emily lifted her chin in the air and, in her Mickey Mouse pj's, strode past her sister toward a shower.

When she got home that night, Sammy was there, waiting on her. So was Q-Tip, and Emily had to admit the truth.

She *was* halfway to a menagerie.

The next day promised to be as long and busy as all the others had been, but Emily was used to long days. At school she'd put in at least eight hours, and then study for several more before working part-time at whatever job she'd managed to hold onto that month. Waitressing, usually. So she was used to running ragged on little sleep in difficult, stressful conditions.

What she wasn't used to was brushing elbows all day with the hottest vet she'd ever met. Today Wyatt had come in wearing sexy army green cargoes and a T-shirt that read: *Will Work for Food*.

"And you can't figure out why women bring you food?" she asked.

He stopped at the front desk. They'd been rotating shifts there, all of them, and they all hated it equally. They grabbed their files and headed to the back, where they both slipped into white lab coats. They were unflattering on everyone but Wyatt. Somehow they always looked different on him. Cool different. His hair was finger combed at best and he hadn't shaved that morning.

He was edible. "What?" he asked when he caught her staring at him.

"Nothing." Thankfully, at least at the moment, his talents didn't appear to extend to mind reading.

They worked together for four straight hours, practically on top of each other. At lunch, she sneaked out the back door for a breath of air that didn't include the delicious scent of Wyatt.

The day was bright, the sun warm, and she texted Sara almost blindly: he's got two-day scruff and is wearing army cargoes, and I want to eat him up with a spoon. Tell me no.

She waited a minute for a response, and didn't get one. Instead, the back door opened behind her. When she turned her head, she nearly swallowed her tongue.

Wyatt stood there holding his phone, his eyes lit with a good amount of trouble and even more heat.

Oh God. She looked down at her phone, squinting past the bright sun.

Yep.

She'd texted him instead of Sara.

This wasn't good. This was the *opposite* of good. This was bad, very, very bad. She strained for dignity, but fresh out, she had to settle for humility. Retreat, she decided, and tried to stride past him and back inside. But two things happened simultaneously. First, her body brushed against his and a shiver raced through her, the good kind that made her want to rub all over him. And second, he caught her arm, whirled her around and pressed her against the wall, covering her body with his.

"So," he said, watching her intently. "My cell buzzed, and I got a very interesting message."

"Oh yeah?" she asked as casually as she could.

Laughing softly, he ran the tip of his nose along her jaw. Her legs wobbled.

"I realize that both Adam and I are wearing army cargos," he said. "I'm trying not to make any assumptions about who you'd like to *eat up with a spoon* . . ." This time he used his teeth. On her earlobe.

Emily had to bite back her moan.

"So I have to ask," he murmured, and sucked a patch of her skin into his warm mouth. "Me?"

"Yes! Okay? Yes, *you*, and you damn well know it."

When he grinned like a cocky, confident alpha male who'd probably never once had to wonder if he was having a bad hair day, or if his jeans made him look fat, she shoved him.

The sexy bastard.

She didn't budge him. Instead he dipped his head and nipped at her lower lip, then soothed the ache with a single and devastatingly arousing stroke of his tongue.

"We're at work!" she hissed, trying to lock her knees.

"Mmm," was his only response to her struggle against him. He liked it, damn him. "You started this."

"I did not." Okay, she totally had. "I didn't *mean* to. You weren't supposed to see that text."

"So it was a Freudian slip?"

"Yes!"

His busy, clever mouth had made its way back to her ear, and when he let out a slow, long exhale, she shivered and realized she was clutching him to her with her hands fisted in his shirt. She let go and then tried to smooth the wrinkles she'd left. "You're going to need to pretend you didn't see that text."

"Why?" he asked.

"Because you're a good guy."

"Not that good."

"Wyatt."

His hooded gaze met hers. "I'm not making any promises."

Oh boy.

He kissed the tip of her nose and backed up to let her out from between him and the wall.

"All bets are off if you sext me again," he said.

"I won't!"

"That's too bad," he murmured, sounding disappointed, and then, recovering with shocking ease, he took his sexy ass back inside.

Emily didn't recover nearly so quickly.

The next morning, Sammy was once again at the bottom step waiting for Emily. Finding him there, she felt a little stab in the region of her heart. She'd put out a pie tin the night before with lettuce and a few strawberries on it.

Sammy had a red stain around his mouth, assuring her he'd enjoyed the goods. And just in case she couldn't tell, he reached out with one claw and banged on the tin.

She laughed. "Okay, but if you start biting my ankles like Q-Tip does, I'll—"

"Feed him faster?" Sara asked wryly, coming up behind her. She was dressed for work in cargo shorts, her usual wife-beater, and steel-toed boots. "Your menagerie's food bill is going to be bigger than ours."

"I've told you," Emily said. "Q-Tip belongs to the house, and Sammy isn't mine."

Sammy banged on the tin again and Sara laughed. "Right," she said, heading down the walk toward her truck. "Whatever lets you sleep at night, Dr. Doolittle."

Emily's day was like most of the others. The variety of animals they saw here at Belle Haven on a daily basis never failed to amaze her. Today alone she'd seen a llama, and then an ostrich.

The challenge came from trying to help patients who couldn't talk, point to what hurt, and tell her what was wrong.

And then there was the stress. Some of this came from being a thousand miles away from her father when his number popped up on her cell phone. Standing in an exam room with Wyatt and Dell admiring a new litter of kittens that had been born overnight and brought in to be checked, she looked down at her buzzing phone and froze. He never called mid-week. She must've made some sort of giveaway expression because Wyatt and Dell both looked at her.

"My dad," she said.

"Take it," Wyatt told her. "We're done for the day, anyway."

Dell nodded. "Go ahead and take off."

She stepped into the hallway and answered. "Dad, you okay?"

"Have you seen my iPod?"

She was stunned into momentarily silence. "Dad, I've been gone six weeks."

"Well, I know that," he said, sounding irritated now. "What do you think, that I'm going crazy?"

She paced to the end of the hall and stared at the wall in front of her, not seeing the framed certificates of all the various degrees and awards that the men who worked here had obtained. All she could see was her father standing in the living room that she knew by now probably qualified for an episode of *Hoarders*. He'd be in his baggy khakis and wrinkled shirt, lab coat opened, pockets stuffed, scratching his head as he turned in a baffled circle looking at the mess around him.

"I don't think you're crazy," she said. "I think you're probably working yourself into the ground without looking up. Have you been eating?"

"Today?"

She resisted thunking her head to the wall. "Dad."

"Kiddin', pumpkin. I ate. I nuked one of those frozen breakfasts you have Mrs. Rodriguez stuff into my freezer every week. You know, I can do my own food shopping."

She let out a breath, relieved to hear good humor in his voice. "I know you can, the question is *will* you?"

"I'm fine, Emily. I can feed myself. Last week's oven fire was a total fluke."

She froze for a beat, mentally calculating the balance in her bank account versus what she had available on her credit card for a last minute fare to L.A.

"Emily, I'm kidding. I haven't even used the oven. You take such great care of me that I haven't had to." There was love and affection in his voice, and she sighed again, softening.

"I just worry," she said.

"Well, don't. That's my job."

"But—"

"Your job's to enjoy your year in God's country," he said. "Speaking of which, aren't you on the job right now?"

"Yes."

"Well if you don't know where my iPod is, get back to it. I've got to get to the shelter, it's free adoption night. We've got pizza coming and everything."

He was already gone, she could tell, distracted by the night ahead. "Okay, Dad. I'll talk to you soon. Love—" But she could tell he'd already disconnected. "—you."

It was dusk, with dark quickly closing in. Needing to clear her head before she hit the road for the night, Emily stepped out the back door. It was indeed "God's country" as her father had said.

With the sun already behind the Bitterroot mountains, the amazing, rugged peaks cast shadows hundreds of miles across the valley floor.

She pulled out her cell again. She hit Sara's number as she leaned against the fencing of the horse pen and took in the beauty sprawled out for thousands and thousands of majestic acres before her.

"Hey," Sara answered, sounding harried. "I'm on a third-story roof with a crew, this better be good."

"Oh my God. Why did you answer your phone if you're on a third-story roof? *Hang up*."

Sara laughed. "I'm fine. I'm roped in. Got a crew around me. A bunch of shirtless men, too. Too bad it's totally wasted on me."

"I talked to Dad."

"He still can't find his iPod?" Sara asked.

Emily sighed. "He called you first."

"I was less likely to freak out on him."

"I didn't freak out." Emily paused. "Much."

Sara laughed.

"I don't think he's eating, Sara. And—"

"Honey, he's fine. He's happy. Stop borrowing trouble."

"I think we should fly to visit him this weekend," Emily said.

"And I think you should have some chocolate. Or get laid. Listen, I get that you're lonely, and I swear I'll pretend to watch *So You Think You Can Dance* with you tonight but for now, I really am on a roof, so . . ."

Emily sighed and ended the call. She inhaled some really fresh air before she felt a nudge.

Reno, Adam's horse, looking for goodies.

Emily searched her pockets and came up with nothing. "Sorry, baby."

Reno snorted.

"I know, rude of me." Emily sat on a fallen log and leaned back. When she was little, she'd loved to try to star watch. In L.A., this was tricky because of all the city lights, not to mention smog. Doing it here, in the land of the big sky, was a whole new ball game. "I'm not lonely," she said to the horse, who snorted again and swished his tail.

"Good. Cuz you're not alone."

Two long legs came into her peripheral. Wyatt crouched at her side and looked into her face. "How's your dad?"

"Fine," she said.

He nodded. "And you?"

"I'm fine, too," she said.

Nodding again, he sat on the log at her side and leaned back, presumably to look at whatever she was looking at. "Pretty night."

His shoulder and a part of his chest brushed her arm and shoulder. Actually it was more like he was encircling her within his arm span, which was considerable. It was a guy move, an alpha guy move, and it made her feel . . . protected.

She was getting far too used to that, she thought with a sigh.

"I smell something burning," he said.

"Where is everyone?"

"Gone," he said, and there was an odd quality to his voice that had her taking a second look at him. He didn't take his gaze off the sky so she got him in profile, the tousled hair, the fine lines crinkling the corners of his eyes from long days out in the sun, the square, scruffy jaw, and broad shoulders built to take on the weight of the world.

He'd been working his ass off, here at Belle Haven, helping Dell take up the slack for the out-of-town Jade, and then going home and helping his sisters with the monstrous house they were fixing up. He did so much for everyone, and she found herself wanting to do something for him. Make him smile. Make him relax. Make him forget, even for a few minutes . . . She nudged him with her shoulder.

He nudged her back and turned to look at her then, his eyes dark and unfathomable behind his glasses.

Chickening out, she turned her head this time, and stared up at the sky as he had been only a few seconds before.

"Emily."

When she didn't tear her gaze off the stars, he leaned in and nipped her ear.

Sucking in a breath, she looked at him again. His gaze was still dark, but there were things swirling in those dark depths now. Need. Heat.

Affection.

He stole her breath.

"Let the record state," she said, reaching out to snatch off his glasses, "that I don't *always* make the first move."

He blinked in momentary confusion, and probably also because he could no longer see. He opened his mouth to say something, but she sank her fingers into his hair and kissed him, hard and long and deep.

"Emily," he said when they broke for air, his voice rough and husky.

She climbed into his lap and then pushed him backward

off the log so that he fell to his back in the wild grass with her straddling him.

Laughing, he slid his hands beneath her top and up her back, drawing out a delicious shiver from her. Then his hands slid slowly down her spine, and into the backs of her jeans. "Let the record also state," he said in a delicious growl, "who made the *rest* of the moves."

"Please say that it's you," she whispered hopefully.

He rolled, tucking her beneath him, making himself right at home between her thighs. "Got it in one," he said against her mouth.

When Emily got home much, *much* later, Sara gave her a brow's up from the couch.

"Worked late," Emily said.

"Uh-huh." Sara got up and picked a piece of wild grass from her hair.

"Work hazard," Emily said, thinking of what'd happened between her and Wyatt in the wild grass by burgeoning moonlight—and then again in the staff bathroom where he'd bent her over the counter.

Sara studied her face. "Right."

"Did you see Sammy when you got here?"

"No."

Worry niggled at her. She dropped her purse and went back outside, walking to the edge of the grass.

"What are you doing" Sara asked.

"Nothing."

"Liar. You're looking for your turtle."

"He's not my turtle. Sammy," she called, wading into the grass. "*Sammy?*"

When he appeared at her feet, she had to sit down on the step in relief. "Oh God," she said. "He's totally my turtle."

Sara sat next to her. "Yep."

"This is how it starts, isn't it?" Emily, having bad flashbacks to their house growing up, filled with the rescues her father could never bear to let go, shook her head. "We keep him, and then the next thing you know, I've also brought home a dog, a cat, a sheep, and an iguana."

Sara went brows up. "Iguana?"

"It could happen. I've lost control. Every surface of this place'll be covered with cages and crap. We'll be a zoo."

"I don't actually think we have approval for that from our landlord," Sara said, looking amused. Her smile faded. "You're not going to turn into him, you know. Dad. And so what if you did? He saved a lot of animals over the years. Hell, babe, have you looked in the mirror lately? You became a damn vet."

"I love animals," Emily said. "I just plan to have a life as well."

"I know," Sara said. "Everyone knows about your damn plan. How many days left?"

"Three hundred and twenty-seven." Emily looked at Sammy. He was watching her with his obsidian eyes, and if she wasn't mistaken, there was some judgment there. She picked him up. "You'll be in good hands," she promised him.

But would he? Would the new tenant of this house feed him, look out for him? *Not* mow the lawn so as to avoid accidentally killing him? And what about Q-Tip?

Or her own heart?

"Uh-oh," Sara said. "You've got that look."

"What look?"

"Like you're at the edge of a cliff peering down."

Emily blew out a breath. "I made a tactical error tonight with Wyatt." She paused. "Horizontally."

Sara laughed. "Again?"

Emily sighed and stroked Sammy's head. He gazed up at her adoringly, or so she wanted to think. Probably he was hoping for more strawberries. "Just like a man," she said to him. "Flashing me the eyes to get what you want."

Sara took Sammy from Emily and set him down. "Emily," she said solemnly. "I thought we had this talk."

"I know. Me becoming an animal collector isn't a sign that I'm going to go bat-shit crazy like Dad—"

"No. You're not bat-shit crazy at all. You're just a woman who's always given everything to the people in her life who she loves, who's always looked out for everyone but herself, and now maybe you're a little lost, that's all."

"The lost part might be true," Emily whispered.

"So, Dr. Sexy?"

Emily covered her face with her hands. "It's not my fault. He's just . . ." Everything.

Sara reached out and pulled Emily's hands from her face. "He's your supervisor. He shouldn't be coming on to you."

"You don't understand." Emily huffed out a mirthless laugh. "It's not *Wyatt* coming on to *me. I'm* the one who can't control myself!"

Sara hugged her. "It's okay," she said. "You can tell me the truth. I'll bury the body deep."

Emily laughed again. "I realize you're not attracted to hot and sexy men, so you're going to have to trust me on this one. It's all on me."

Sara was quiet for a long beat, considering. "Well, I still think you need to talk to him. Tell him that this isn't fun and games for you, that you're going to get hurt."

"I can't do that," Emily said. "I've told him time and time again that this isn't in my plan. I'm trying to ignore his damn sexy ways."

"Well, you could always switch teams," Sara suggested. "It's better on my side of the fence."

Emily set her head on her sister's shoulder and sighed. "If that was true, then you wouldn't be hiding out here in Sunshine nursing a broken heart."

It was Sara's turn to sigh. "True that."

Eighteen

At the end of the next day, Wyatt stood behind the front desk watching Emily attempt to print one of her files. When she'd said "*Crap!*" for the third time, he leaned over her and did it himself.

"Are you kidding me?" she asked, craning her neck to glare at him. "Why didn't you do that five minutes ago?"

He smiled and showed her how to print the day's receipts as well. Still leaning over her, the inside of his arm brushed the outside of hers, and she went still.

"What?" he asked.

"Nothing."

"It's something. You moaned."

"Did not."

He stared down at her bowed head. Her hair had fallen forward, revealing the nape of her neck, a spot he badly wanted to put his mouth to.

As if she could read his thoughts she shivered.

Christ. They were in trouble.

A truck pulled into the lot. "Damn," he said, not sure if

he was grateful or frustrated at the interruption. Both, he decided. "So close to escaping on time tonight, too."

Emily let out a breathless laugh. "There's actually an on time?"

"Only if you run fast." He gestured with his chin for her to make her escape. "I'll take this, you head out."

"No," she said, stubborn to the end. "I'm not leaving you here by yourself."

He looked into her fierce eyes and felt more than a physical arousal. Far more. "Emily."

"I mean, what if it's another woman in the Casserole Brigade?" she asked.

"Then maybe I'll get something good for dinner."

"And if she wants something in return?"

He smiled. "Depends on how good the casserole is," he teased to lighten the mood.

Her eyes narrowed. "That's not even funny."

The driver of the truck walked in wearing jeans and a police sweatshirt, hoodie up, badge and gun on his hip, carrying a brown bag in one hand, the leash to a young pit bull in the other.

Wyatt recognized him as one of the players on the police team that he occasionally played flag football against. The guy worked for the county on Highway Patrol.

"We're just closing up here," Emily told him. "Do you have an emergency?"

The guy gave a nod to Wyatt as he came up to the counter and leaned on it casually, smiling at Emily. "No emergency," he said. "Just been hearing about our new vet in town. You're as pretty as they say."

Wyatt mentally rolled his eyes and glanced at Emily, figuring she'd be doing the same as she had a very accurate bullshit meter.

She was smiling back at the guy. WTF?

"That's sweet," she said.

Sweet? How about stupidly cheesy?

The cop removed his dark sunglasses and pushed back his hoodie. "Evan Russell," he said, and held out his hand.

"Emily Stevens." She shook the guy's hand and looked at Wyatt. "And this is Dr. Stone."

Evan gave Wyatt a cursory nod. "Brought you something, Dr. Pretty," he said to Emily. "I've got a ranch full of animals at home, so I thought knowing the pretty vet might come in handy." He set the bag in front of her.

"A bribe?" she asked.

He smiled. "Open it."

She opened the bag, inhaled deeply, and closed her eyes on a blissful sigh. "Chocolate chip cookies. Heaven."

Evan smiled. "There's more where those came from."

"I bet," Wyatt muttered.

Emily looked at him. Evan didn't take his eyes off Emily. "So how's Sunshine been treating you so far?" he asked her.

"Well, the traffic's not as bad as it was in L.A."

Evan chuckled. They all knew traffic was nonexistent in Sunshine. Well, except on the days that the errant cow escaped a ranch and stood in the middle of the road. "I think we've got more to offer you than better traffic. You ride?"

"You mean motorcycles?" she asked.

He chuckled again, and Wyatt had to resist the odd urge to put a fist through the guy's mouth.

"Horses," Evan said.

"Oh." Emily smiled. "No. Not yet."

"I'll take you. You live nearby?"

Wyatt shifted. If she told the guy where she lived, he was going to have to kill him.

And then her.

"Not too far," she said, reminding Wyatt that she was no pushover. She was in fact, a city girl, smart. Wary. Tough.

But so was Evan, and he wasn't easily deterred. "Name the day," he said.

"I'll think about it," Emily said.

Evan nodded, and gestured to the bag of cookies. "Enjoy."

"Thanks," she said. "I will."

He spent an extra few beats holding her gaze, and then walked out.

Emily dug into the bag and took a bite of cookie, sighed in pleasure, and then offered Wyatt one.

"You shouldn't eat stuff from people you don't know," Wyatt said.

She laughed. She laughed so hard she choked on the damn cookie and he had to pound her on the back and bring her a glass of water.

When she could breathe, she grinned up at him.

"You ever worry about eating the things all those women bring you?"

"No," he admitted. "But it seems different when it's a guy."

She just kept grinning. "Guess you're not the only one getting in on the Casserole Brigade, Dr. Sexy."

"Dr. Sexy?"

"Oh, like you don't know it." She took another bite of cookie.

"You didn't give *him* the almost boyfriend line."

Emily cocked her head at him. "You're jealous."

"Bullshit."

"Good," she said. "Because I'm perfectly willing to share." She opened the bag and held it out to him, smiling guilelessly.

He stared at her, realizing they were on entirely different pages, and found *himself* laughing. "You don't have a clue," he said softly.

Her smiled faded. "A clue of what?"

He leaned in close, but not to take a fucking cookie. "That *you're* the Dr. Sexy."

* * *

The next morning Emily got up early to waste a little time online angsting over the fact that she'd upped her bid on Wyatt yet again.

She needed an intervention, she thought later as she walked into Belle Haven and, as she had since Jade had been gone, found Dell standing behind the counter, pulling out his hair. "Whatever happened to your three leads?" she asked.

He shoved his fingers through his hair. "First Choice told me there wasn't enough money in the world. Second Choice told me that she'd love to . . . except she didn't want to."

Emily laughed. "And your last choice?"

Dell blew out a breath. "She'll be here soon."

"What does Jade say about all this?"

"She doesn't know," Dell said. "If I told her, she'd be home already, and I don't want her to miss out on time with her family because of this."

Emily smiled. "You're sweet."

Dell's mouth turned up at the corners. "Hope you still think so after you have to take your shift back here."

But she never got to take her turn behind the counter at all. Adam strode in, spoke to Dell for a terse minute, and then both men looked at her. "Field trip time," Dell said.

"Where to?" she asked.

"Rob from Camarillo Ranch just called," Adam said. "They need help. Three of their horses got spooked and tangled themselves in a downed barb wire fence. They need medical care ASAP."

"It's a good one for you to observe," Dell told Emily. "It'll give you a real taste of what's out there for this type of practice."

Camarillo Ranch was sixty miles north, and Dell contracted with them as their mobile vet care. Emily looked at her watch. "If we take a truck and go now, we could be there in an hour and a half—"

"One of the horses doesn't have an hour and a half," Adam said. "Brady's readying the chopper right now. Wyatt's already over there."

The airport was literally across the street. "Grab my ready bag from the staff room and run," Dell said.

She stared at him. "You want me to go in the helicopter and assist Adam and Wyatt in a horse rescue?"

"I want you to observe, and learn," he said. "Unless you'd rather stay here and run this entire center by yourself while *I* go."

Hell no. "But—"

"I'm offering, because it's a great opportunity for you, and also with Adam, Wyatt, and Jade gone, I shouldn't leave the center. You've got three seconds before I change my mind."

Emily whirled and ran for the staff room and heard Dell's low laugh behind her.

Twenty minutes later she was in the air, in her first chopper ride. It was terrifying and glorious at the same time. Adam was across from her. Wyatt sat next to her—Mr. Lived In Twenty Countries And Traveled The World Over—looking cool and calm.

Emily tried to look calm and cool, too. She failed. "Holy cow," she whispered to herself as the chopper banked a hard right.

Across from her Adam grinned, and so did Wyatt, making her remember her headset.

The three guys could hear every word she uttered.

She could only see the back of Brady's head but somehow she knew he was grinning as broad as Adam. She couldn't find it in herself to care that they were laughing at her. She was a city girl, through and through. As a kid, once in a blue moon her parents would drive her and Sara to the mountains for the day.

But the mountains for the day in Los Angeles were a lot different than these mountains.

And they'd *driven* there.

Now she was . . . well, she had no idea how many feet in the air exactly, seeing the countryside up high, coupled with the whistle and whine of the chopper. She was enthralled by mazes of mountains and valleys below, sprawled out for what was surely hundreds of miles. She could see forever, it seemed, nothing but crests of the ridges of the Bitterroots and beyond, countless lakes and rivers, and isolated, rugged territory as tough as . . . well, the men in the chopper with her.

Or maybe the land had made them so tough. She wondered if it could do the same for her.

In any case, it was a thrill, a rush, at least until Brady banked hard, and dipped hard toward the ground.

Emily gasped, a hand to her heart to hold it into her chest.

"Damn," she heard Brady say with great disappointment in her ear. "That usually gets a scream out of the first timers."

"She's pretty good with the self-control at work," Wyatt said, his warm tone making her belly go a little squishy.

She met his gaze and he smiled his bad-boy smile, and she knew what he was thinking. He was thinking that outside of work, specifically in bed, she wasn't nearly so good with the control . . .

Which was true.

Maybe she hadn't exactly screamed for him, but she'd come pretty damn close a couple of times.

He nudged her knee with his.

She opened her mouth to tell him to stop making her think about their . . . escapades. But the truth was, she thought of him all on her own, without any help from him. At least she could be secure in the knowledge that he was doing the same. There was comfort in that, that their misery was shared.

Except he didn't look miserable. He looked hot and sexy, and then there was that light of trouble and mischief in his gaze, like maybe he wouldn't mind having another . . . escapade to be teasing her about.

But that couldn't happen. The first time with him had been the one-night stand she'd always wanted.

Twice had been . . . well, magic. So had their third time. And their fourth.

And their fifth . . .

After talking to Sara the night before, she'd decided to own those memories, collect them in her mind, and file them under the label *Hot Fantasies to Pull Out as Necessary.*

But to continue on like this would only prove Sara right. Someone—she—was going to get hurt. To continue on would surely take things to the next level, a level she didn't even know what to call, other than a huge mistake, because as Sara had so helpfully pointed out, it could and would derail her life plan.

The chopper banked again, steeper now. Biting her lip, Emily reached out in blind panic, and felt her hand gripped.

Wyatt.

No longer laughing at her. "Okay?" he asked.

"Worried I'm going to throw up on your shoes?" she managed to ask.

"This is a no throw up zone," Brady said from the pilot's seat.

"Take your thumb and middle finger and press firmly on both sides of your wrist," Adam told her. "It's an acupressure point, and should reduce nausea."

Wyatt didn't take his gaze off Emily as he reached out and did the acupressure for her. "You're all right," he said, holding on.

She was very glad he thought so.

But he was right. She was fine. They landed on a concrete pad to the side of a huge ranching operation. And even better, she didn't toss her cookies.

They were met by Tex, the ranch manager, and immediately taken by truck to one of the back pastures.

"The rains have wreaked havoc and hell on everything," Tex said. "The creek overflowed, took down the northwest fence line. The horses got out at some point in the night, and a few of them tangled in the barbed outer line fence. We got all but Aurora free."

Emily knew the recent night rains had saturated the ground, but she'd had no sense of how bad it could be until they alighted from the truck near a line of fence that vanished around a hill.

Even making their way closer was difficult, her feet kept sinking in the mud, and then a terrible scream stopped her heart.

Not human.

Horse.

There were three men surrounding the downed horse, who was struggling wildly, entangled in the barbed wire. Both Adam and Wyatt turned to Emily at the same time.

"Stay here," they said in unison.

She started to balk because she wanted to help, but the look on Wyatt's face was steel.

So she stayed, watching in horror, at the horse stuck in the mud and barbed wire, fighting itself and the men already in place trying to help. With every movement, Aurora only succeeded in embedding the wire deeper and deeper in her flesh.

Wyatt, Adam, and Brady waded right in, not a single one of them hesitating in any way or dodging the possibility of getting caught beneath those wild hooves or the weight of the horse. She watched Adam take charge of the rescue while Wyatt did something with a syringe. Then he was adding his hands and voice to the mix. Calm. Sure. Absolutely one hundred percent in charge as he worked to soothe Aurora.

The horse thrashed and fought, not going down easy.

"The wire's beneath her," Wyatt clipped out to Adam.

"Get her up," Adam said.

Heedless of the danger to himself, Wyatt dug his feet into the mud and added his bulk to the efforts of getting Aurora upright. Meanwhile Adam tried to work around the flailing horse to cut the wire free, all while Aurora did her best to trample the shit out of all of them.

Wyatt grabbed Aurora's face and spoke right into her ear with calm authority, and Aurora's ears flattened. She was listening. Not necessarily liking, but listening.

And Emily was transfixed. Watching Wyatt in action was like watching a rock star. A vet rock star.

Like Adam, like Brady, like Dell—all men she'd come to admire—Wyatt never rattled, was always willing and ready to be in charge of any given situation.

Just as they got the horse free of the wire, Aurora finally began to succumb to the sedative. The poor, exhausted thing dropped her head and huffed, pressing close to Wyatt, knocking him back a step.

Wyatt just spread his legs for better balance and wrapped his arms around her, stroking her face, murmuring something low that Emily couldn't hear, while the other men pulled the rest of the wire as far from them as they could get it.

Wyatt gestured Emily in. "She's good now," he said, eyes locked on to Aurora's. "Aren't you, sweetheart?" He stroked her, loving her up, and the horse tossed her head. "I know," he murmured softly. "You're still beautiful."

The horse, bleeding from a dozen deep cuts, snorted her agreement and gave Wyatt a not-so-gentle head butt to the chest that once again knocked him back a step.

He just grinned at her. "Still feisty. I can understand that. You've had a rough morning. Emily, you ready?"

She was ready, and side by side they began treating her wounds.

"Stay sharp," Wyatt told Emily quietly as they worked. "She's still looking for someone's ass to kick after her ordeal."

And indeed, when Emily shifted too suddenly, Aurora whipped her head around, teeth bared.

She might have taken a nice bite right out of Emily's shoulder if Wyatt hadn't given Emily a shove, a move that sent her flying back.

To her ass in the mud.

Aurora bit Wyatt instead, getting him on the forearm. Emily scrambled up to her feet and reached for him.

"I'm fine," he said.

Great. He was fine and her ass was covered in mud and smarting from the fall. But this was the job. She knew this. She accepted this. So she pushed her own discomfort aside and dove into the work.

Wyatt showed her some quick bandaging techniques for temperamental, still pissed-off and frightened horses so that she didn't get almost bit again.

It was the sort of experience she never would have gotten in the Beverly Hills vet office, and she knew it. By the time they all got back on the helicopter an hour later, she was exhilarated, but aching everywhere and starving.

Brady was there ahead of them, ready and waiting with—God bless him—food. Hot pastrami sandwiches loaded with cheese and spicy mustard. The exact perfect food. She stuffed in her first bite and moaned. "I could kiss you," she told Brady.

Brady smiled. "That's what all the women say."

Adam gestured to her leg. "What's wrong?"

He'd seen her limping. "Nothing," she said quickly. Too quickly because Wyatt's gaze narrowed in on her. "I'm fine," she told them both. Sure, her butt hurt from the fall, but she'd probably just hit a rock or something. "I slipped in the mud—"

"You didn't slip," Wyatt said. "I pushed you."

"Yes, well, I was trying to be polite."

"You pushed her into the mud?" Adam asked him, voice low but a whisper of disbelief in the tone.

"To keep me from getting bit," Emily said. "That, or for the whole mud effect."

"I did it for the save-Emily's-arm effect," Wyatt said. "But checking out your bruise later might make it worthwhile."

She choked on the bite she'd just taken. He was checking out her bruise *never.*

The light of intent in his gaze said otherwise, and her inner slut sighed in pleasure.

She shut it up with the rest of her sandwich.

Nineteen

They made it back to Sunshine in one piece. Emily exited the helicopter and walked across the street toward Belle Haven ahead of Wyatt and Adam, who'd stayed behind to talk to Brady for a moment.

She was glad. She'd joked about the mud incident, but sitting in the chopper had made her muscles tighten up. The back of her leg, between her butt cheek and upper thigh, hurt like hell.

Intending to go straight to the bathroom to take a peek, she started to walk into the front door of Belle Haven, but a hand clamped on her wrist.

Wyatt.

Without a word, he pulled her around the side of the building, through the back, and then nudged her into his office.

"Um," she said, when he shut and locked the door behind him.

Leaning against it, his crossed his arms. "Strip."

She choked out a laugh. "Excuse me?"

"I want to see your leg," he said.

"What leg?"

"The one you're rubbing."

Dammit. She dropped her hand from the back of her thigh, which she'd indeed been unconsciously rubbing. "I'm fine."

"No doubt of that," he said and reached for the button on her pants.

She squeaked and danced back, right into his desk. She winced at the contact.

"Okay, that's it." His big hands settled at her hips and her belly quivered.

The good kind of quiver.

Before she could give that any thought, he turned her away from him, sandwiching her, her back to his front, between his body and the desk. Again, he reached around her for the button on her pants.

She sputtered. "You can't just—"

He could, and did. Before she could finish her statement, he had her pants down to her thighs.

She tried to turn, but he put a hand between her shoulder blades and pushed her flat to his desk.

"Hold still," he said.

She opened her mouth to tell him she'd hold still when he was good and dead, which would be as soon as she managed to get her hands around his neck, but then he stroked his fingers very gently, very lightly high up on the back of her thigh.

"Wyatt—"

"Shh," he said, and then his fingers spread a little, and she was thinking she couldn't be as hurt as she thought because those fingers felt shockingly good.

His thumb slid beneath her panties and scooped the material aside, giving her a first-class wedgie. Once again she started to squirm but then he set his whole palm on her butt.

"I'm sorry," he said, his voice low and gruff.

"For bending me over your desk?" She tried to inject a pissed-off tone into the words, and a sense that his life was on borrowed time, but she sounded annoyingly breathless.

"You're bruised," he said. He pressed between her shoulder blades again. "Stay right there."

"Like hell—"

"Stay."

Wyatt grabbed an ice pack from the staff kitchen freezer, and then headed straight back to his office. In the thirty seconds he'd been gone, Emily had straightened up from his desk. Her pants were still at her thighs, and her hot pink panties covered all the essentials—barely.

The view was heart-stopping.

She stood there, craning around, trying to see her own ass. And if he hadn't caused the huge blooming bruise from her sweet ass cheek to the top of her thigh, he'd really be enjoying the sight.

He moved to her and placed the ice pack against her leg.

She squeaked and jerked.

"Shh," he said.

"I am not a dog or a cat or a damn horse," she said through gritted teeth. "You can't animal-whisper me into a blissful, do-whatever-you-want-to-me coma simply because of your sexy voice!"

He adjusted the ice pack, smiling when she sucked in a breath. "Do-whatever-you-want-to-me coma?" he repeated.

"Yes," she said. "That's what happens when you talk to your patients. They melt."

"And you?"

She turned away to face his desk, profile stony.

He smiled at the back of her head. "You want me again."

"You're a pain in my ass," she said. *"Literally."*

He stroked a finger over the pink silk. "I like these."

"If you were a gentleman, you wouldn't notice."

"Emily, I've seen it all before."

"Not bent over your desk, you haven't!" she said.

"True," he said. "You were bent over the bathroom counter last time."

She whipped around, still holding the ice pack to herself. "You're enjoying this!"

He scrubbed a hand over his jaw to hide his smile, but nothing could stop it from creeping into his voice. "Yeah," he admitted. "You're the prettiest patient I'll see today."

She stared at him, and then rolled her eyes. "You can't sweet talk me like you can an animal, Wyatt."

Yes, he could. He'd done it. But he wasn't stupid, so he didn't point it out or respond. "Keep the ice on it for a few minutes. I'm going to start seeing our patients."

"I'm supposed to shadow you."

"Keep the ice for a few," he repeated, and then in spite of wanting to strip her out of the rest of her clothes and bend her back over his desk, he left his office.

It was the usual afternoon insanity. For the last few hours, Wyatt had completely forgotten that, with Jade gone and her replacement a no-show, Dell had been left to face the chaos on his own.

He expected Mike to be behind the front desk. Or anyone other than who was sitting there.

Darcy.

The phones were ringing wildly, and she was using her walker to stand and face off with Colonel McVey.

Colonel was an old-timer. He'd been army way back, Special Forces, and he'd lost none of his fierce intensity or the ability to slay anyone in eye-contact range. He lived alone on his ranch with his cattle and his twenty-year-old cat, Betty.

Betty was blind but other than that, she was still spry and kicking. In fact, she was in better shape than Colonel.

"She hasn't had a BM in two days," Colonel was saying to Darcy.

"A BM?" Darcy asked.

"Bowel movement."

"Oh." Darcy laughed. "She's plugged. Hey, it happens to the best of us."

"Plugged," Peanut yelled from his perch on the printer. *"Plugged."*

Darcy grinned at the parrot. "What else do you know?"

"Boner," Peanut said proudly.

Colonel wasn't amused. "I want to see Dell," he said, not cracking a smile. "And I want to see him *now*, young lady."

Darcy's eyes narrowed and she lost her smile. "Dell's with a patient right now. How about you just sit down and take a load off, and I'll do my best to work you into the schedule—"

"I'm not going to 'sit down and take a load off'!" Colonel boomed. "There are *dogs* in the waiting room." The tough, badass *kissed* the top of Betty's bony head. "Betty doesn't like dogs."

"Well I don't like people who yell at me," Darcy said. "But we're all stuck with each other, so sit down, zip it, and I'll be right with you."

Colonel glared at her, and Wyatt moved in to save his annoying sister's ass, but Colonel spoke, his tone softer now.

"You got gumption, girl," he said. "I like that."

"Great," Darcy said. "What's gumption?"

Unbelievably, Colonel grinned. "You're ex-military, right? Where did you get injured?"

"I'm not military, ex or otherwise," Darcy said. "I'm not good with following orders. I got hurt by my own stupidity."

This shocked Wyatt, since as far as he knew, she'd never once spoken about her accident.

Colonel took a seat and Darcy met Wyatt's gaze as he came in close. "Betty here is a walk-in," she said. "I'm putting her on your schedule. And before you blow a gasket, Dell asked me to come and answer phones."

"Did he happen to mention that these people are his livelihood, and mine as well, and that you should be nice, even when they piss you off—which, trust me, they will?"

"I'm perfectly nice," she said.

When Wyatt just stared at her, she shrugged. "If they're nice to me."

"It's hard to be nice to someone who has a perpetual frown on her face," Wyatt corrected. "Maybe you could try smiling."

She flashed him a smile, only called such because she bared her teeth. "How's this?" she asked.

"I said smile, not scare people away."

"You know," she said, "I don't like your attitude. I'm going to double book you if you're not careful. Maybe with Cassandra. And I have the power, too, you're at my mercy, big bro."

Wyatt considered strangling her but there were witnesses. That's when Emily came out from the back. The mud on her pants had dried but she looked like she'd been wrangling wild horses. "Who's in what exam room and where do you want me?" she asked Darcy.

"See?" Darcy said to Wyatt. "A little bit of professionalism and kindness goes a long way. Oughta try it sometime." She looked at Emily again. "Dell's in exam one. We're full up, so if you want to hop into exam two, it'd be greatly appreciated."

Emily smiled at her. "Will do."

Darcy smiled back, and Wyatt wondered if the muscles around her mouth hurt from the fact that she hadn't used those muscles in a damn long time.

Emily turned to get to work but froze when the front

door opened and a twentysomething woman walked in. The first thing Wyatt noticed was that she didn't have an animal with her.

The second thing was that she waved at Emily, who was standing there looking surprised. "Sara," Emily said. "Everything okay?"

The sisters didn't look very much alike, but that might've been because Sara had platinum blond hair, cut in short spikes, and more piercings and tats than clothes.

"Yes, everything's okay," Sara told Emily. "I just thought I'd stop by on my way home from work and meet your people."

Emily's eyes narrowed slightly as she gave her sister one of those sibling looks that Wyatt recognized all too well. Sara was up to something and Emily appeared to know it. She came back to the center of the room to make the introductions. "This is Darcy," Emily told Sara. "Our lovely temp receptionist."

Darcy and Sara bumped fists.

"And this is Dr. Stone," Emily went on, gesturing to him next.

"Wyatt," he said, offering his hand.

Sara was slow to take it. "So you're him," she said.

"*Sara.*" This from Emily, and there was no mistaking the *knock it off* in her voice.

"What?" Sara said. "He is, right? Dr. Stone, aka Dr. Sexy?"

Emily's face turned a lovely shade of pink.

Darcy grinned.

Wyatt had no idea what the hell was going on, but no one knew better than him exactly how a family dynamic could work against you, not to mention how insane a sister could be. Or two.

"Dr. Sexy," Darcy repeated. "That's a new one. Personally, I think of him as Dr. Pain In My Ass, but hey, whatever works." She took a second look at Emily. "So you and my brother have been taking office politics to a whole new level, I'm guessing."

Emily made a strangled sound and shot Sara a look that Wyatt recognized well. It was an I-plan-to kill-you-later-and-slowly gaze that he could really appreciate right about now.

"I'm busy," she told Sara, possibly through her teeth. "Go home."

"Sure." Sara smiled and held out a brown bag. "But first I brought some brownies. I've got extra for everyone."

"Nice touch," Darcy said. "I should try that sometime."

Wyatt snorted. "You've never brought me food. And if you did, I'd probably need a taste tester."

Darcy rolled her eyes and looked at Sara. "Out of curiosity, what did Wyatt do to piss you off?"

"*Nothing*," Emily said, answering for her sister.

"He took a piece of her," Sara told Darcy.

"*Sara*," Emily said.

"I'm sorry," Sara said to Wyatt. "I realize it's unprofessional of me to come here during your workday, but Emily's never going to tell you this shit. She's not going to let you see that your . . . relationship with her is only further messing her up."

"Further?" Wyatt asked.

"Oh my God," Emily said. "Sara, *go home*."

"She's a giver," Sara said, ignoring Emily, speaking directly to Wyatt. "You know that by now. She'll do anything for anybody, and that includes animals, too."

"Out," Emily said to Sara, pointing to the door.

"My point," Sara said quickly to Wyatt, clearly knowing her time was limited. "Is that she's a giver, and sooner or later everyone takes advantage of her good nature."

"I'm right here!" Emily said.

"We've all taken a piece of her," Sara went on as if she hadn't spoken. "And that's on us. Me, my dad, even Mom, rest her soul. And her friends, too. Although she doesn't have many right now because she was in school so long and worked a bunch of hours, but mostly it's because she got hurt there, too. Her first boyfriend cheated on her with her best friend. Knocked out her entire posse in one, right there."

Emily reached for Sara and began to push her to the door.

Sara dug her heels in. "And then there was John Number Two," she told Wyatt over Emily's shoulder. "He took a piece from her without even knowing it. So you can't take your piece. You can't," she said, struggling with Emily, "because I don't know how many pieces she has left to give, and she's everything to me." Her voice cracked, her eyes shimmered. "So you need to stop playing with her, or you'll answer to me. You hear me?"

Emily had her halfway to the door by now, but Sara still hadn't taken her eyes off Wyatt. She was dead serious, and maybe not crazy, after all. At least not one hundred percent.

"I hear you," Wyatt said to her over Emily's head.

Relief burned fierce and bright in Sara's gaze, and she finally allowed Emily to boot her out the door.

"I'll deal with you later," Emily said, and shut the door on her sister's nose. She turned back to the room, which had gone silent.

"Holy cow," Darcy said. "That was better than *The Real Housewives* of *any* city."

"Sorry about that," Emily said. "She escaped the mental institution just this morning. She's got Tourette's and—"

"Why are you sorry?" Colonel asked. "My brother would've come in with his shotgun to make his point. You got a brother, Dr. Stevens?"

"No," Emily said.

"Want me to act as your brother?"

"No!" Emily said.

Darcy laughed and pointed at Colonel. "You know what? You're okay."

"I know," Colonel said.

"Work," Emily said, voice high, eyes a little wild, looking desperate to move on from this. "We must get to work!" And with that, she moved past them all, heading toward the back area of the center.

Darcy took one look at Emily's butt and choked out a laugh.

"What?" Emily demanded, whirling back.

"Nothing," Wyatt said, slicing a look at his sister that had her zipping her lip. "You just have some mud—"

"Oh my God." Emily craned her neck to look at herself and groaned. "I forgot about how you pushed me down."

Colonel stood up. "He *pushed* you? Hang on, I've got my gun in my truck."

"No!" Emily said. "It was my own fault, he was protecting me."

"You sure?" the man asked.

"Very!"

"All right, then."

"My God," Emily said, putting a hand to her chest, looking at the lot of them like she'd found herself in the middle of a reality show. "We're still in the U.S., right?"

"Yep," Darcy said, popping her gum, looking like a kid on Christmas morning. "I know, it seems like maybe Mars or something, right?"

"Or something," Emily said, and with one last unreadable look in Wyatt's direction, she vanished into the back.

Twenty

Emily managed to avoid getting stuck alone with Wyatt for their last hour of the day.

But Darcy was a whole different matter. She caught Emily in the bathroom and stood right outside Emily's stall. "That's messed up, what your best friend did to you," she said through the stall door.

Emily closed her eyes and resisted banging her head on the wall. "It was a long time ago." First year of undergrad. Old news.

Okay, so she still had a few trust issues, whatever. She was working on that. Sort of. "And I'm a little busy right now . . ."

"I mean, it's messed up what your boyfriend did, too, but guys are dicks. Your girlfriend, I hope she got vag-warts or something."

Emily stared at the closed door and felt her throat tighten with both the need to laugh and cry at the same time. "That's . . . gross. And sweet." She drew a deep breath. "About your brother, Darcy. I don't want you to think we're just . . ." She paused. Because she and Wyatt *were* just. She tried again. "We're not going to hurt each other. We've discussed it. We're on the same page. And I'm not a permanent fixture here, anyway. I'm eventually going back to L.A." She realized that Darcy hadn't answered, and as she exited the stall she nearly had heart failure.

Darcy was gone.

Wyatt stood there in her place, leaning against the sink, ankles crossed, hands in his pockets. Casual. At ease.

She bit back a sigh. "How much did you hear?"

"Enough," he said, his voice at odds with his laid-back posture, "and we're not on the same page. Not even close." He stepped toward her. "And you didn't tell Dell you wanted to trade places with the L.A. intern. If you'd wanted to go, you could have."

Was that true? That couldn't be true.

"And about Sara's little visit," he said, and her heart seized.

Oh, God. She wasn't ready to talk about that. She was never going to be ready to talk about that. "Wyatt—"

"You're not going to brush this off," he said right over her, expression firm. "We've done too much of that. What your sister said struck a chord with you, Emily, I could see it." He stared into her eyes. "The very last thing I want to do is hurt you."

"You can't," she said. "Because we're not a real thing."

"You sure about that?" he asked. "Because it feels pretty fucking real when I'm buried inside you." He took the last step between them, and his cell went off. He looked at the screen and swore.

"It's okay," she said. "You have to go."

His glittery gaze said he knew she wasn't being polite here, that he got she was as relieved as hell, and it pissed him off. "We're not done," he said. "We have to talk."

"Oh goodie," she said. She could hardly wait. But then again, as she was going home to kill Sara, maybe she'd land in jail, and with any luck, no visitation rights, and she'd never have to talk again.

It turned out a little better than that. Wyatt ended up having to leave with Brady on another emergency ranch call.

Dell and Emily took care of the last of their patients at Belle Haven, and finally, at the end of what had been a *very* long day, she grabbed her purse and sweater to leave.

And whirled right into Dell. His hands went to her arms to steady her. "You okay?"

Somehow she had the feeling he wasn't asking because she'd just plowed into him. "I'm great," she said. "Never better. I—" She broke off, deflating when he arched a brow. "You heard."

"That your sister jumped all over Wyatt's shit? Yeah. I just wish I'd seen it." His smile faded. "Emily—"

"He didn't act inappropriately," she rushed to say. "It happened months ago, before we even knew we'd be working together."

"Just the once then?" he asked.

She grimaced. "He didn't take advantage of me, Dell," she said quietly. "If anything, I've taken advantage of him." *Multiple times.* "So you're not going to sue me or anything, right?" she asked, trying to tease.

The ghost of a smile returned to Dell's gaze. "I think I can let it slide."

She patted his arm, pulled free and headed to the door.

"Emily?"

When she turned back, the smile had made its way to his mouth. "He's one of the good ones," Dell said. "You know that, right?"

Her heart squeezed, and she nodded.

When Emily finally pulled up to her house, she was still spoiling for a fight with Sara. But she paused in the driveway, hearing a not so distant howl. And then another.

Dog or coyote?

Coyote, she decided, and hurried to the front door.

Sammy was there on the walk, and Emily saw that he had fresh strawberries in his tin. It was going to be hard to kill Sara knowing she'd fed the little guy, but she'd power through it. It would be a loss because Emily really enjoyed Sara's cooking, but there was always takeout.

Even if there were only two take-out places in all of Sunshine.

Unfortunately, her plan was derailed by the sight of her sister sitting in the middle of the living room in a ball gown of all things, sobbing her heart out.

Q-Tip was sitting a few feet away, watching the human with detached interest.

"I found this," Sara said to Emily, gesturing to the dress, the four-inch heels, the tiara on top of her spiked head. Miss Butch America.

"I had it all in a bag with my stuff," Sara said soggily, and sniffed. "It's one of the outfits Rayna wore down the runway last year." The tears began again. "It smells like her."

Emily sighed as her anger drained away. She sat on the floor with Sara and pulled her in for a hug. "You could call her," she said quietly.

"Tell her what?"

"That you miss her."

"No. I don't want to interfere with her life."

"Right. You'd rather just interfere with mine."

Their gazes locked. Sara managed a short laugh. "Yeah. Lucky you." She stopped sniffling and blew her nose.

"Hungry?" Emily asked.

"Not if you're cooking," Sara said.

"We could go out. We *should* go out. I've never seen you in a dress before."

Sara choked out a laugh. "I thought you were mad at me."

Emily sighed and set her head on Sara's shoulder. "I was."

"But not anymore?"

"No."

"Why's that?" Emily asked.

"Cuz you're buying dinner."

Sara let out a low laugh. "Fair enough." She paused. "Can I borrow twenty?"

Emily sighed. "You know the two of us are really all sorts of screwed up, right?"

"In a very large way."

When Wyatt got back to Sunshine that night, he headed straight to Emily's.

You can't take your piece, Sara had said. *I don't know how many pieces she has left to give.*

His chest felt tight just remembering the look of misery on Emily's face. Take a piece of her? Hell, he wanted to do the opposite. He wanted to reclaim all the pieces she'd lost and give them back to her, kicking some serious ass while he was at it.

Her place was dark. He reached for his cell and called her, but she didn't answer, so he texted.

You can run but you can't hide.

No response to that, either.

Frustrated, he drove home. Zoe was waiting, needing his help with the leaking kitchen sink. He lay under the sink, staring up at the plumbing.

Drip. Drip. Drip.

Shit. He swiped at the water hitting him in the nose and scooted his head over an inch. Where was Emily tonight? "Wrench," he said.

Nothing.

He craned his neck and caught sight of Darcy's legs,

hanging from the counter, where she sat to keep him company. "You fall asleep sitting?" he asked. *"Wrench."*

Still nothing. He pulled himself from beneath the sink.

His sister was staring out the window, her eyes glossy, her mouth open. He stood up to see what she was looking at.

AJ was in the yard with Zoe, who'd managed to finagle him into helping her plant some shrubs along the front of the property. She'd done this by promising him all he could eat pizza, and that Darcy wouldn't be here.

But Darcy had decided not to go out for once, so Zoe had made her swear to stay out of sight.

"What are you doing?" Wyatt asked Darcy suspiciously.

"Nothing."

"Liar." She was *always* doing something, even when she wasn't moving. In fact, he'd learned that's when she was the most dangerous. "You're staring at AJ like he's dinner."

She slid him a look, and he grimaced. "Oh Christ." He scrubbed a hand over his eyes. "No, it's no good, I can't unsee that image."

"Oh shut up," she said. "*You're* getting lucky, as it turns out, so you don't get to judge."

"But it's AJ." Wyatt loved the guy, but AJ had made a career out of women. He loved women, all of them. The thought made Wyatt grimace again. "We're not going to talk about this."

"Do you know how many months it's been since I had a social orgasm?" Darcy asked.

"Shit, Darcy."

"You know what? *Forget it*." She kicked the wrench his way and snatched her walker.

He caught the back of her sweater. "I just don't want you to risk getting hurt."

Her face, when she turned to him, had softened, and she nudged him. "Well where's the fun in no risk?" she murmured.

* * *

The next day at work, Emily got an unintentional reprieve from having to face Wyatt when he was once again called up north with Brady and Adam, working some of Dell's ranching clients.

She wasn't sure if she was relieved or not. Maybe they did need to discuss, so that they both knew exactly where they stood.

And yeah, okay, there was some truth to what Sara had announced to the free world. Emily *had* let pieces of herself go. She was working on that, but the truth was, she wasn't all together. How else to explain why she was beginning to fall for this small town of Sunshine, which was literally the opposite of everything she thought she wanted?

And then there were the people in it, and the connections she'd made, like Dell, Adam, Lilah, Jade.

Wyatt . . .

She had no idea what she thought she was doing there, with him, no idea at all. And yet the thought of not having him in her life every day actually hurt.

What did that mean?

She had to give up thinking. She fed Q-Tip and Sammy, and grabbed the ice cream from the freezer, along with a microwaved bag of popcorn and her laptop. She sat on the couch to watch a *Say Yes to the Dress* marathon, finding it reassuring to know that other people's lives were more out of control than hers. Half an hour later, she'd checked on her auction bid on Wyatt to verify she was still on top.

She was.

Then she looked at the empty ice cream carton in her lap—Double Fudge—and the empty bowl of popcorn.

She didn't need a pity party—she needed an overeater's anonymous meeting.

When her phone rang, she frowned at the number she didn't recognize. "Hello?"

"Dr. Emily Stevens," said a velvety male voice when she answered. "It's Evan. Need another hit of chocolate chip cookies?"

Cute cop guy who made great cookies. She looked down at the empty ice cream carton. "Not right now, thank you. I'm on a dessert moratorium."

He chuckled low in his throat. "You're a hard woman to get a hold of."

He was referring to the three messages he'd left for her at Belle Haven. She winced and pushed Q-Tip off her lap. "I'm sorry. It's not a good policy to date a patient."

"So it's a good thing I'm not patient. I was hoping to take you riding on Saturday. You free?"

Her brain scrambled. He really was a very handsome man, and maybe under some other circumstances she'd be interested, but she had Wyatt. At least for right now she had Wyatt, and he was more than enough man for her.

Truth was, he was almost too much man for her.

And then there was the bigger truth, the one she wasn't ready to think about, much less admit—she had zero desire to be with anyone else but him. "I'm sorry, Evan. But I can't."

He was quiet a moment. "I understand. Good night, Emily."

She disconnected, remoted the TV off and looked over at Q-Tip.

The cat was watching her.

"I know," she said. "You're thinking I have no idea what I'm doing."

Q-Tip just stared. She turned to the aquarium on the coffee table, where Sammy now resided.

It was raining again, and she'd been worried about him. As much as she knew about animals, she had no idea if his type of turtle could swim.

He hadn't objected to his new home in the least. In fact, she kind of thought he liked it.

He was watching her, too, making her realize that she was Q-Tip's and Sammy's reality show.

Perfect.

"Okay," she admitted to the room. "So I don't have any idea what I'm doing." She thought of Wyatt, and how he'd reacted to Sara's tirade.

He'd given her a long, thoughtful gaze.

No obvious sympathy, which was good. But he hadn't given her anything. *Some* reaction might've been nice.

You could have returned his text, she told herself. She had a feeling she'd have learned his reaction by now if she had.

That's when she heard it. Through the sound of the steady rain hitting the roof and the wind beating at the windows, she heard the animal crying again.

The haunting sound went right through her. "Dammit." She grabbed a flashlight, shoved her feet into sneakers, and went outside. Standing on the porch, she cocked an ear and listened.

The cry came again, filled with pain and fear, raising every hair on her body.

Not willing to be the stupid chick in the horror flick, she got into her car, driving slowly with the windows down, getting drenched as she followed the haunting noise.

She came to her neighbor's ranch. The house was dark. There were no other places around here, so she remained still, chewing on her lower lip.

Get out of the car and walk around?

No. That was *definitely* the stupid chick in the horror flick.

Then she heard the sound again, clearer now. Definitely a dog. A dog in trouble.

And close.

Crap. She threw the car in park and got out into the rain, her sneakers making a squishy sound as she ran toward the sound until she found the dog huddled in a ball of misery just off the road, in a clearing between two trees.

She paused a few feet away and used her flashlight.

Definitely a dog, a young one, male, but hard to tell what breed in these conditions. "Oh you poor baby," she breathed, crouching at his side.

He lifted his head and . . . licked her hand.

Her heart stuttered in her chest. He was bleeding from multiple open wounds, attacked by a coyote? She let him sniff her hand a minute, during which she tried to see if he was in shock. Hard to tell in the dark without a stethoscope to check his heart rate, but the weakness wasn't a good sign. Cautiously she checked his limbs.

Nothing obviously broken. She ran back to her car, to the trunk, and yanked out her emergency kit. Returning, she wrapped the Mylar emergency blanket around the dog. Then scooping him into her arms, she brought him to her car, setting him carefully onto the passenger's seat.

By this time, she was shivering herself, and breathless. She slid behind the wheel. "You're okay," she whispered to her patient. "Well, you're not really, but you're *going* to be okay." Reaching out, she carefully crossed the seatbelt over him the best she could. "There," she said and hit the gas.

Wyatt sat hunched over his desk at Belle Haven, typing up the patient files he'd put off all damn week.

He hated typing.

He hated the glow of the computer in the dark of the night.

He hated the stack at his elbow that indicated he wasn't anywhere close to done.

He was just getting into his bad mood, looking around for something else to hate on, when he heard someone at the front door.

Earlier he'd locked it behind Dell. Being the last one in the place required a locked door. They were out in the boondocks, but that didn't stop the crazies looking for drugs, or stupid teenagers looking for kicks, or any asshole looking for trouble.

Not only was the door locked, but he had the alarm on as well. Half braced for it to go off, he strode down the hall through the darkened receptionist area as a key turned in the lock.

The door opened before he got there and he stared in surprise at Emily. Her arms were full, she was struggling to hold onto an animal and pound in the alarm code at the same time.

He got to her and reached for the . . . dog. A very bloody young dog who bared its teeth when he came close.

"Careful," Emily said, sounding distressed and possibly in tears.

His stomach clenched as he brushed her hand away from the keys and entered the code. Then he turned back to the dog. Definitely young, possibly not even a year old. Male. Lab, with some pit bull in him, approximately fifty pounds. "Aw, buddy," he said in a quiet, calm voice, "what happened to you, huh?"

The dog stopped showing his teeth.

"Someone hurt you," he murmured. "Let's fix you up, okay?"

The dog stopped growling.

"That's a good boy," Wyatt said, continuing to talk as he reached for him again.

This time the dog let him scoop him from Emily's arms. She straightened, visibly relieved at the loss of the weight. She ran ahead of him, turning on lights to the surgery room.

"What happened?" Wyatt asked, gently placing the dog on the table.

"I don't know," Emily said. "I found him like this. I think maybe he was attacked by coyotes, I keep hearing them near my house."

She came close with a stethoscope, and listened to the

heart rate while Wyatt stroked the dog's head, silent until she looked up at him.

"One eighty," she said.

Normal for a dog was sixty to one hundred and twenty. One eighty was too high, forcing the heart to pump too fast for it to fill adequately. Still, the dog wasn't behaving all that abnormally. He was clearly hurt, tired, and weak. He was panting, but that could be nerves from being on a table at a vet's office. He certainly wasn't disoriented or overly aggressive. Wyatt waited, watching Emily to see if she wanted him to take over for her. He could tell she was emotionally invested, and that was both a great thing and a curse.

He'd seen more than a few vets fresh out of medical school attempt this crazy life and then quit within a few months, unable to take the emotional strain. He hoped that wouldn't be her, she was far too good a doctor to walk away.

She moved around the table to check the dog's mouth. It was what he'd have done next as well, checking the color of the gums. Nodding to herself, she began to look over the injuries. "Pain meds, antibiotics, and a sedative," she said. "To keep him calm while we scrub out the wounds and stitch." She looked up, caught him watching her, and cocked her head. "What?"

He smiled. "You're going to be okay."

"I *am* okay," she said. "It's the dog who isn't."

"I mean you're going to do this. You're going to stick with being a vet."

"You think I accrued a mountain of college debt not to stick?"

He grinned. "Just checking."

"Well how about you just check his temperature and I'll clip, flush, and scrub?"

"Ah," he said. "You gave me the fun job."

She snorted, and at the sound, he felt better. He took the

dog's temp, found it normal, and was further relieved. He cranked up the heater in the room and used a Bair Hugger, a blanket that blew warm air around an injured animal in danger of going in shock.

She had the clippers and was already working on trimming fur away from the worst of the cuts.

"We going to talk about it?" he asked.

She didn't play dumb. "Yeah. Sure."

"It was serious stuff, the things Sara said."

Her mouth went a little grim as she administered the meds with a steady hand. "True, but it wasn't her stuff to say."

"Maybe not," Wyatt murmured. "But her heart seems to be in the right place." He hadn't liked knowing how hurt Emily had been in the past, but he'd needed to hear it. Something had begun to shift for him over the past few weeks when it came to his feelings for her.

They'd deepened. Far more than he'd ever expected them to.

She met his gaze, her own flashing a fierce independence and pride. "I'm fine," she said firmly. "I want you to know that much. I have all my stupid pieces." She rolled her eyes. "Okay, so maybe a few pieces are dented, but I'm not broken or anything. I really am fine."

He gave a little smile. "You are that."

"And we never talked about it before because we both know where we stand," she said. "We started this thing out as a one-time thing, and I get that its since turned into a *few* times, but it's still just . . ."

"Fun and games?" he asked wryly.

"You said it, too," she reminded him. "That night in your truck. You said that when we parted in Reno, you hadn't planned on seeing me again. I wasn't on your plan either, Wyatt. So yeah, this is fun and games. Well, minus the games, because I'm not playing games with you. I wouldn't even know how."

He took in her earnest expression and let out a long, slow breath. He knew that about her. He loved that about her. "Well, *I* know how," he admitted. "But I wouldn't. Not with you. Never with you."

"So . . ." She searched his face. "We're good?"

She wanted them to be okay. She needed them to be okay. And damn, but he did, too. He wanted a lot of things actually, most of which would have to wait. "Yeah. We're good."

They worked in silence on the sedated dog, flushing the wounds with disinfectant, suturing a few of the deepest wounds, treating and bandaging everything else.

"He's going to need antibiotics, pain meds, and bandage management daily for a good solid week," he said when they'd finished. "Are we releasing him into your care?"

She blew out a breath and picked up the still sleepy, sedated dog with a sweet gentleness that was more than doctor to patient.

Recognizing the signs well, Wyatt smiled. "Yeah, we're releasing him into your care."

"Just until I find his owner," she said. She looked exhausted, on edge, and deeply unnerved.

Shit.

"He's going to need watching over tonight," he said, "and I've got a lot more paperwork to do, anyway. Let me take him for you."

"I can't ask you to do that."

"You didn't ask." Together, they looked down at the dog in Emily's arms. His eyes opened and locked on Emily, big and forlorn.

She sucked in a breath.

Already, the dog knew how to charm a woman.

"I'm taking him with me," Emily said, and looked at Wyatt. She caught his grin. "Just until I find his owner," she repeated.

"Uh-huh."

"You can resist these warm, brown eyes?" she asked.

"Sweetness, I live with two sisters who are the *queens* of male manipulation. I can resist anyone and anything."

An empty, hollow untruth, because he'd never been able to resist the underdog, the injured, the weak. Ironically, he couldn't resist Emily either, though she was just about the least weak woman he'd ever met.

"So not true," she said, calling him on his bullshit. "You live with your sisters because you can't resist taking care of them. And you spend way more time with each animal you see than is necessary. And I've seen you treat them for free when their owners don't have money. You can't resist a damn thing."

No kidding, and especially not her.

Twenty-one

"You think you have me all figured out?" Wyatt asked softly.

Did she think that? No. Not in a million years. "Maybe not completely," Emily said.

He looked at her for a beat, then took the dog from her and gently set him inside a crate.

"But—" she started, stopping when he turned back and pulled her into him.

Her body instantly came alive. "Wyatt—"

"Shh," he said, lowering his head to press his jaw to hers. "I need a hug."

This wrung a laugh out of her because they both knew who needed a hug, and it wasn't him. But he was big and strong and warm, and damn.

Damn.

He felt so good that her limbs acted of their own accord and snuggled in, burrowing, inhaling deep the very male, very delicious scent of him.

"Did you just smell me?" he asked.

"No."

He laughed quietly, not bothering to call her on the lie. Stroking a hand up her back, he let out a low sound of regret. "Ah, Em. You're one big knot."

"It's my life," she said, closing her eyes, holding on tight, hoping he wasn't planning on letting go anytime soon.

Or ever.

She shifted to plant her face into his throat, loving the scent of him, the texture of his skin, the heat of him. God, she loved it when he held her like this, like for a moment he'd shoulder all of her problems.

"You need to make time to relax once in a while," he said, his big hand stroking up and down her back, making her want to stretch into him like a cat in heat.

"A drink might do it," she said. "So would ice cream."

"I've got something better."

She snorted.

He laughed softly and squeezed her tight. Her heart rate ramped up, which had nothing to do with the adrenaline rush of the rescue and everything to do with the man holding her. He was in his usual cargoes and T-shirt, sans the doctor coat tonight. She'd been too discombobulated earlier to see what the shirt said, but she couldn't deny that he was sexy as hell in everything he wore. Now he was all the more after watching him work on a dog that wasn't even his patient, and in no way his responsibility.

And yet he'd given one hundred percent to the dog.

And her.

When she'd first met him in Reno, she'd convinced herself he was a shallow, one-night stand guy. But over the past weeks, she'd come to realize how wrong she'd been.

He was strong, inside as well as out. He was smart and funny and protective, and incredibly sexy. But more than just about everything else, he was rock solid steady and unflappable. A guy you wanted at your back.

And he wasn't in her plan. Still wasn't, though she hadn't updated her plan in a while. She didn't even know how many days were left in Sunshine. If she opened her calendar right now, John would still be in it as one of her goals. "Dammit."

Wyatt went still, then pulled back just enough to meet her gaze. "Problem?"

"Sorry. You make me forget my plan."

"The one with an almost boyfriend on it, the almost boyfriend who you never talk to or about?"

"Hey, you're one to judge. You never say one word about Cissy."

He laughed. "You know her name isn't Cissy."

She crossed her arms over her chest. "Why don't you ever talk about her, about Caitlin?" Her gut squeezed. "Did she break your heart, Wyatt?"

His mouth curved. "You worried about me?"

"I do like to worry."

"Caitlin isn't a factor," he said. "Not with us."

Her heart fluttered, and she wasn't sure if that was because of the way he'd said Caitlin's name, with such aching familiarity, or that he'd said "us." She drew a deep breath. "There is no us," she said. "And how is Caitlin not a factor, when you can't even talk about her?"

"Do you talk about John?"

"You know damn well he's not really a factor."

"And yet you still put him between us."

There was that "us" again. "Look who's talking, the guy who's got a daily Casserole Brigade."

"At least those women are real."

She should have picked up the dog and headed out. It was late, she was tired. And her resistance was down—as evidenced by the urge to throw herself at him.

Wyatt looked at the dog who'd curled up in the crate and gone to sleep, the poor, exhausted baby—and then he grabbed Emily's hand and tugged her from the room and into his office. "I'm going to head out," she said. "I—" She broke off when Wyatt yanked her into him.

"I don't care about a stupid name on your calendar, a name of some dumbass who's too much of a dumbass to make you his," he said.

She stared up at him. His eyes were filled with heat, and a surprising temper, a really heady combination. Something wriggled deep inside her. It felt a little bit like a piece fitting into a puzzle. There were emotions, too. Affection, and hunger for this man who never seemed to care what a mess she was. "Crap," she whispered, still staring at him. Not again. Still . . .

"What?"

"This," she said, and tugged off his glasses. Then she tugged him down to her level, and kissed him.

He let her have her way for a minute, and then took control, hands in her hair, tongue in her mouth, hard body settling against hers. The heat of him seared into her as she tried to pull him in even closer. Hell she'd have climbed him like a tree if she could.

He pulled back a fraction, smiled a satisfied badass smile, and kissed her again until she forgot to breathe, forgot who she was, hell, she forgot *where* she was. All she could feel was Wyatt from the top of her head all the way to her toes, and *everywhere* in between.

When he pulled away again, she didn't have the brain cells left to protest. Instead she moaned as his lips trailed down her face, her neck, to the pulse racing at the base of her throat.

"Emily."

She had to clear her throat twice to answer. "Yes?"

"Now's the time to look me in the eyes and say this is still just a fun time, that this isn't going to hurt you."

She stared at him. His hair was more tousled than usual—from her fingers, she realized. His T-shirt was untucked. His gaze was heavy-lidded as he waited for her to process. "A *very* fun time," she said.

"And?"

So fierce. So careful with her. Her heart tightened. "And you'd never hurt me," she whispered, knowing it as the utter truth. The only way he could hurt her was if she cared more for him than he cared for her, but she could see that wasn't the case.

"Never," he agreed, voice low and utter steel. "But now is the time to say no if you're going to."

One of her hands was still fisted in his shirt, one of his thighs between hers, and when he rubbed it against her at the same time that his hand swept up from a hip to stroke a thumb over her nipple, she got a rush so strong it might have been an orgasm. The sound she made was horrifyingly needy and she tried to suck it back in.

"I'm taking that as a yes," he said, and swept a hand over his desk, knocking files and various piles of crap to the floor.

"So we're done talking?"

"For a few minutes." He ran his tongue along the outer edge of her ear, nibbling on the lobe as he brought her palm to his erection.

She shuddered and stroked him. "You think we'll be done in a few minutes?"

"Keep that up and it'll be a lot less."

She popped open his pants, tugged down his zipper, and slid her hand inside. He was hot velvet over steel, deliciously, heart-pounding hard, and every single inch of her trembled in desire and anticipation. "And if someone shows up?"

He backed up enough to hit the lock on his door.

"They might still hear."

"You'll have to be very quiet," he said, and stepped into her until she backed up into his desk. "Can you be very quiet, Emily?"

Oh, God, she thought, *that smooth whiskey voice*. "I don't know."

"Let's see." Hands to her waist, he plunked her onto his desk. "Take off your sweater."

She rushed to do just that but he lent his hands to the cause, stripping it off her himself.

She'd dressed for the day a very long eighteen hours ago, and couldn't remember what underwear she was wearing. She took a peek and groaned.

Wyatt ran a long, callused finger along the edge of her plain white cotton bra. "Problem?"

"I was hoping I was miraculously wearing black silk," she said. "Or something good to catch your interest."

He smiled and stroked her nipple through the cotton with a callused thumb. "Sweetness, you caught my interest a long time ago." And then her bra was gone, tossed as carelessly over Wyatt's shoulder as her sweater had been.

"Lift up," he said, fingers deftly unbuttoning and unzipping her pants.

"You want to see if my panties match?" she asked.

He smiled. "Among other things."

Yep, Wyatt discovered a minute later, her panties did indeed match the white cotton bra somewhere on the floor behind him. He wanted these there, too. Hooking his fingers in the soft material, he slowly pulled her panties down and took in the sight of Emily naked and sprawled out for his viewing pleasure. "I'm never going to look at my desk in the same way again."

"Wyatt . . ."

His name left her throat on a raspy whisper of longing. He liked that. He fucking *loved* that. Stepping between her spread legs, he slid a hand into her hair at the nape of her neck to bring her face to his.

"You're still dressed," she whispered.

He loved that, too, the way she could be so shy and yet climb all over him in his truck. Or in the yard by moonlight.

Or let him seduce her in his office . . .

He cupped her breasts and her nipples pebbled against his palms. "God," she said on a rough exhale, her arms wrapping around his neck as she leaned into him. He smiled, knowing she'd already forgotten to even try to be quiet.

He didn't care. He loved the sounds she made.

"Mmm," she murmured into his mouth, like he was the best thing she'd ever tasted. Her tongue fought with his for dominance, but he won the battle when he cupped her ass in one hand, the other sliding down her belly, between her opened thighs.

So wet.

At the feel of her, his entire body tightened, and his hips thrust into her reflexively. She moaned when he pulled away, and tried to reach for him, but he dropped to his knees. With a hand on each trembling thigh, he leaned in and put his mouth on her.

Above him, she made an unintelligible sound. Her head fell back, and when he used his tongue, rubbing in slow circles as he sank a finger into her, she closed her legs on him, like she was afraid he'd stop.

Not a chance.

He stroked her thighs with his hand to reassure her that he was here, right here and not going anywhere, staying close enough to feel every tremor, every quiver.

For him.

She was rocking into his mouth, speeding up, and, given the desperation behind her movements, needing to come bad. When he teased her by slowing down, she merely tightened her grip in displeasure.

Laughing softly against her, he once again increased

pressure, and she came for him, hard and fast. She was still shuddering when he rose to his feet, wrapped his arms around her and lifted. He took her the two steps to the couch against the wall, and turning, fell onto it backward, bringing her down on top of him.

She tugged up his shirt. He yanked it over his head and pulled a condom from his wallet. She tried to help him roll it down his length, but only succeeded in nearly making him come. Finally he grabbed her hands and tugged them behind her, squeezing gently.

Getting the message, she held still—well, except for her rocking hips, which was sexy as hell. She watched while he protected them both, eyes glossy, cheeks flushed to match her hardened nipples. He looked his fill, too, considering himself just about the luckiest bastard on earth when she lifted up on her knees. "In me. Please, Wyatt."

Yeah. He'd please.

She cried out his name again as he thrust up into her, and for a single beat the both of them went stock-still in utter bliss.

Then she bucked against the hands he had tight on her hips, an entreaty for more. When she didn't get it, she wriggled, the impatient gesture making him both groan and laugh. He loosened his grip, letting her take the reins she wanted so badly.

She flashed him a sexy-as-hell smile and began to move, looking hot as hell riding him. Reaching up, he wrapped a hand around her neck to pull her down to his mouth, his other hand sliding low, his thumb stroking her wet center.

She went off like a bottle rocket, and the beauty of her coming so hard for him was too much. Faces inches apart, eyes locked on each other, he let himself go, pulsing inside her as she panted his name.

When she collapsed over the top of him, he gathered her damp, quivering body in close and concentrated on gulping air into his lungs. Each time with her got more intense, more intimate.

How was that even possible?

He had no clue, none. Pressing his face into her hair, he slid a hand down to cup her ass, holding her to him.

After a long moment, she let out a shaky, contented sigh and went boneless on him.

He traced a random pattern across her skin with his fingers, until she shifted restlessly. Her movement went right through him, making his cock twitch.

"Again?" she asked with a whisper of hope.

He rolled, tucking her beneath him, letting his body answer for him.

"I forgot to be quiet," Emily said some time later as she sat up on the couch, eyes wide, hair wild, cheeks rosy, her lips still wet and a little swollen. "Was I loud?"

Wyatt leaned over her and kissed her worried mouth. "I don't know."

"How could you not know, you were right here."

He grinned. "Well, the first time, your legs were around my ears, so I couldn't hear."

"Oh my God." She covered her face, then peeked out between her fingers. "It's your fault, you know. It's how you touch me. You make me forget myself."

He laughed and kissed her again. "I loved it," he said against her mouth.

She slid her fingers into his hair and pulled him back enough to stare into his eyes. "And the second time?"

"Loved that, too."

She let go of him to smack his chest. "I mean why don't you know if I was loud the second time?"

He held her gaze. "It's how you touch me," he said, echoing her words. "You make me forget myself."

She stared back at him. "Dammit." And then she leapt at him.

"Again?" he asked, laughing.

This time she let *her* body answer for her, and he had no objections.

Twenty-two

The next morning, Wyatt drove into work with a silent and brooding Darcy. "Hey," he said, turning to her when he turned off the truck and met her pissy gaze. "I'm not the one who agreed to work the front desk for a week."

"I'm not mad at the fact I'm working," she said.

"Then what are you mad at?"

"You."

No surprise there. She'd been mad at him since birth. "Why?"

"You're breathing, aren't you?"

That wasn't it and they both knew it. AJ had told her to stop using the walker and downgrade to the cane, but Darcy hated the cane and had refused to give up her walker.

So AJ had asked Wyatt for help. And Wyatt had done what had to be done.

He'd returned the rental walker.

Darcy had flipped out on him. She'd thrown one of Zoe's precious potted plants at his head, narrowly missing him, too. Good thing having two sisters had taught him how to duck quickly.

Then Darcy had done another of her vanishing acts.

Wyatt had just been grateful for the silence.

This morning, she'd mysteriously been back in her own bed, and had gotten up without any prompting, not getting irritated until he told her she still wasn't getting the walker back.

Tough love, her doctor had told him.

Tough love, AJ had told him.

Bullshit, she'd told everyone. But after ten full minutes of silence, followed by ten full minutes of chewing him out, she'd made her way out the front door, slamming it so hard she'd rattled the molars in the back of his head. She'd used the hated cane to get to the truck, bitching the whole time.

Now she shoved the truck door open.

"Wait for me," he said, wanting to help her navigate the exit from the truck, but by the time he came around the front for her, she'd slid out of the vehicle.

For a moment she wobbled and her knees seemed to give out. He reached for her but she thrust her hand out in a don't-you-dare gesture.

So he watched, feeling helpless and useless, as she clung to the opened truck door, trying to get her balance. With visions of her sliding to the ground and hitting her head on the way down, he had to bite his tongue and shove his hands in his pockets to keep them from reaching out and yanking her upright.

Finally, after a painfully long thirty seconds when it could have gone either way, she grappled and won her balance.

"There," she said so triumphantly Wyatt felt his throat tighten. "Got it." She was sweaty and flushed and breathing heavily, and he'd never been so proud of her.

But if he dared say that, she'd probably kill him in his sleep. "Use the fucking cane, Darce," he said instead.

He expected her to flip him off. Or light into him. Or simply glare at him as she'd been doing since the day of her accident.

Instead, she beamed. "Don't need it, Wy-Ty, I did it!"

Five painfully long minutes later, she also walked into the front door of Belle Haven by herself. He felt her trembling wildly as he held the door open and knew she was one more step from falling on her face. Fuck tough love, he thought, and reached for her.

"Thank God," she whispered, flinging her arms around his neck. "I'm about ready to fall on my ass."

Emily was at the front desk, making flyers with a picture of the dog she'd rescued, who happened to be sitting at her feet covered in bandages, but looking pretty good considering.

Emily's gaze met his and held for a long beat.

Then the dog at her feet lifted his head and barked.

Peanut startled and nearly fell off the printer. "Bad dog," the parrot said, feathers ruffled.

Emily looked down at the dog, and Wyatt would have sworn the little guy smiled.

"Oh my goodness," Emily said with a laugh as she crouched down to love the pup up. "That's the first peep I've heard out of you."

The dog sat adoringly at her feet and wagged his tail at her. "What did you name him?" he asked.

"I can't name him," she said, rising. "He's not mine."

Wyatt could've told her that once she flashed her smile, anyone and anything could be hers. "What would you name him if you could?"

"Woodrow." She smiled. "Because he looks so serious."

Darcy had made herself at home behind the counter and lifted a bag to Emily. "This has your name on it."

Mike, standing at the counter flipping through files, lifted his head. "Some dude brought it in for you. Fresh chocolate chip cookies. Said you'd know who they were from."

Emily went still for a beat, and then opened the bag and handed one out to everyone. When she got to Wyatt, he waited until she met his gaze.

"No thanks," he said.

Oblivious of the odd tension, Mike removed his baseball cap and set it on Woodrow's head, scratching his ears for him.

Woodrow licked his hand and returned to gazing at Emily like the sun rose and set on her.

Mike added the sunglasses that had been tucked into the collar of his shirt, setting them very carefully on Woodrow's nose. "Now you look the part," he told the dog. "Own it, dude."

Gertie had been sleeping behind Jade's desk. She lifted her head to see if she was missing anything. Apparently she decided she wasn't because she went back to sleep.

They all went to work, and it was an insanely busy day. Wyatt took the time to get bitten on the shoulder by a temperamental sheep in the throes of an allergic reaction to a bee sting. During a rare late afternoon lull, Emily cornered him in his office, leaned back against the door she'd closed behind her, and crossed her arms over her chest.

"Strip," she said.

He felt himself start to get hard. He stood up and made to clear off his desk like he had the night before, but she choked out a laugh.

"Not for that," she said.

"So . . . you just want to look?"

"Yeah," she said. "I want to see your arm, you're babying it."

"I'm not babying shit."

She laughed again. "Such a man. Drop the shirt, Wyatt."

He tugged it over his head and lost his glasses in the process. He replaced them and focused in time to see Emily was staring at his chest and abs. "Want to kiss it and make it all better?" he asked.

"Yes." She visibly shook her herself. "No! You're insatiable."

"Pot, meet Kettle."

She blushed and rolled her eyes as she stepped up close, gasping softly at the bruise on his shoulder. "I could make that sheep a mouth retainer from this impression," she said, and ran her finger over his skin. "God, Wyatt, she really got you."

He craned his neck and showed her a red spot on his neck.

"There, too?" she asked in disbelief.

"No, this one's from the other female in my life," he said.

She stared at him, and then gasped. "I didn't—"

He just arched his brow.

"Oh my God," she said, horrified. "I'm so sorry—"

He set a finger against her lips. "I enjoyed every second of it."

She dropped her head to his chest and huffed out a soft laugh. "This is getting out of hand."

"Yeah."

She lifted her face and studied his. "You don't look broken up about it."

"A beautiful, smart woman gets off on me. What's there to be broken up about?"

"Well," she said slowly. "For starters, I'm the exact wrong girl for you, you need someone more quiet, someone rooted here in Sunshine like you are."

He stared at her, the words almost verbatim what Darcy had said not that long ago. "Where did that come from?" he asked, having his suspicions.

"The grapevine, so I can't cite its origin."

He bet he could.

"I heard it three different times earlier when I called everyone in town to find out if anyone knew who Woodrow belonged to," she said.

"Darcy." He wondered if she realized she'd started calling the dog by a name, but that would have to wait. "Definitely Darcy."

"She loves you," Emily said.

"Yeah," he said. "And so does my mother. And we both know how much that means."

She didn't smile. "Do you remember our plan?"

"You and the *P* word."

"It was to get to know each other," she said. "And we were going to *not* like each other."

"How's that working out for you?"

"Right now?" she asked. "Pretty good."

He flashed a grim smile. "Ditto."

"So we're on the same page. We have no problem," she said.

"Absolutely not a one," he agreed.

They stared at each other, and the air crackled. His body did that annoying-as-shit thing where he got hard from just looking at her. "Fuck," he muttered.

"Yes, please," she said, and threw herself at him.

He caught her. "You know what this means, right?" he asked, hauling her up his body.

She was already panting, taking little nips along his jaw, heading for his mouth. "What?"

"You're *all* crazy."

"Women? Yes, I know." She got to his mouth.

He met her halfway, tightening his arms around her, pulling her in hard just as his door opened.

Dell and Darcy stood in the doorway.

Both stared at Emily and Wyatt—still shirtless—and had the same brows-up reaction.

"Playing doctor?" Darcy asked.

"Would you believe yes?" Emily asked.

"No," Darcy said, and turned to Dell, palm out. "I'll take my fifty now."

"Christ." He fished through his wallet and paid up. Then he pointed at Wyatt. "You owe me fifty bucks."

When they were gone, Wyatt looked at Emily, who had her hands over her face.

"Not good," she said, and dropped her hands. "We've got to get a hold of ourselves."

"We?"

She closed her eyes. "Okay! It's me! I know!"

He laughed. "It's not just you. Not even close."

She opened her eyes and stared at him, achingly unsure and vulnerable. Shaking his head, a little thrown off by how much he wanted to see her smile again, he stepped into her. "Not even close," he repeated softly.

"This has to stop," she said, just as softly, her big eyes entreating and desperate. "We can do it," she said, and he wondered which of them she was trying to convince.

"Look, I'll show you," she said, and pulled out her phone. She accessed her calendar and shoved it under his nose. "Three hundred and twenty-three days left."

"That's wrong," he said. "You haven't updated. It's three hundred and twenty-two, see?"

She stared at the screen and blinked. "Huh. I guess I forgot."

He wondered if she realized that was a sign, and then decided by the annoyance on her face that it wasn't a sign at all.

Which made *him* the crazy one. Shit. He'd been here, right here in this place before, and he'd promised himself not to do this again.

Emily was looking into his face. "You look like you just had an epiphany."

Yes, and it wasn't all that pleasant. He shook his head.

She opened her mouth to say something but Mike called for her from down the hall.

With one last long look at Wyatt, she left his office.

When Darcy poked her head in five minutes later, Wyatt was still standing in the exact same spot.

She barely reached his shoulder, to which she gave a good shot with her fist, right where he'd been bitten.

"Jesus," he said, rubbing it. "What the hell's your problem?"

"You," she said, and did it again.

He caught her fist in his hand. "Knock your shit off, Darcy. I don't have time for your games."

"Even if I give you a hint?" she asked, and leaned in close. "You're an idiot."

He let out a breath and scrubbed a hand over his face. "Go away."

"Can't. It's my job to give you your messages. And this one's from me. You got screwed by Caitlin. She left you for a job, and you don't even get to be mad about it because it was noble and all that bullshit. But that didn't negate your feelings for her, did it? You'd have eventually married her, and then it would have been worse. You didn't deserve that, Wyatt, honest to God you didn't, and there's not a person in Sunshine that appreciates how she treated you in the end. But if you let yourself fall for Emily—another woman who isn't the right one for you, you *will* get exactly what you deserve. Disappointment—again."

"I'm sorry," came a quiet voice.

Wyatt and Darcy both turned to face a pale Emily standing in the doorway. She bit her lower lip. "I really didn't mean to hear that."

Darcy blew out a breath. "No, *I'm* the sorry one. Don't pay any attention to me, I'm crazy. Everyone knows that."

"No, it's true," Emily said.

"That I'm crazy?" Darcy asked.

"That if Wyatt falls for me, he'd be disappointed. It's a recurring theme in my life."

Shit. Wyatt started toward her, but she put up a hand. "No, we *really* don't need to discuss."

Mike had come into the front room behind her, a file in his hand. Behind him was Woodrow. Around the dog's neck was a badge on a braided lanyard, just like the ones all the staff wore. It had his pic, name, and addy—Belle Haven—just like a real one.

Emily took the file from Mike's fingers, bent to kiss Woodrow on the head, and vanished into an exam room.

Woodrow and Mike vanished.

"Nicely done," Wyatt said to his sister. "You really outdid yourself there."

"I'm sorry."

"Save it," he said. "It's my fault, anyway." He pushed past her and went after Emily.

She was with Mr. Myers and his thirteen-year-old golden retriever Buddy. "I've got this," she said without looking at him, nose buried in the file.

Wyatt smiled at Mr. Myers.

Mr. Myers smiled back. He was somewhere between eighty and two hundred years old. He hadn't worn his teeth today. Wyatt was counting on the fact that he wasn't wearing his hearing aid, either. The guy hated both with a well-known passion. "Emily—"

"Dr. Stevens," she corrected. "And I'm a little busy right now."

"I just want to be clear about why you're upset."

"Shh!" She slid a quick look at Mr. Myers.

"He can't hear you. He can't hear anything without his hearing aid."

She relaxed marginally but emotion still sparked from her. "I'm trying to be professional," she whispered.

"Professional?" he asked. "Is that what we've been doing?"

She flicked another glance Mr. Myers's way, found him sitting there humming to himself, and then glared at Wyatt. "We both know *exactly* what we've been doing. Fun and games."

"Which we both agreed to," he reminded her.

"Yeah." Her eyes shuttered. "Which apparently doesn't

include discussing your ex with me. Which doesn't matter anymore since we're done as of now. So if you'll go on your merry way, I have a patient."

Wyatt looked at Mr. Myers. "Excuse us a moment."

"Eh?" Mr. Myers cupped a hand over his ear. "Sorry, sonny boy, I forgot my hearing aid."

"Hall," Wyatt said to Emily. "Now."

"As lovely an offer as that is," she said. "No, thank you."

Wyatt held up a finger to Mr. Myers, signaling that they needed a moment. Wrapping his fingers around Emily's arm, turning her to face him, he pulled her into the far corner.

"Back off." She held up a syringe. "I'm about to express Buddy's anal glands."

Buddy let out a sigh and dropped his head to his paws.

"According to his file," Emily said, "he needs sedation first." The syringe got a little closer to Wyatt's face. "Get your hand off me or I'll treat you instead."

He paused and resisted the urge to smile. "Did you just threaten to sedate me and then express my anal glands?" He leaned in a little closer so that their noses were nearly touching. "Because I've gotta tell you, sweetness, I'm all for getting adventurous, but payback's a bitch."

She gasped and reared back, her gaze flying to Mr. Myers.

Mr. Myers smiled at her.

She gave him a shaky smile, blew out a breath, sent Wyatt a nasty look before heading back to the table. "We're done discussing this," she said. "All of it."

"All of what exactly? Spell it out for me."

"Everything, starting with that night in Reno. It's done, over, and finished. We're clearly not suited. In any way."

"Funny," he said. "That's not what you said last time you had your tongue in my mouth."

"Shh!" Her gaze whipped to Mr. Myers, who was studying the ceiling. "And that's exactly what I mean," she whispered furiously. "Listen, I realize this is my own fault, not yours. I've put out mixed signals. I'm not going to do that anymore. It's not good for either of us. We're done, Wyatt. We've got to be done."

"Maybe you'd better put that in writing," he said, feeling his own temper rise, hating how easily she said that. "And keep a copy on you, since you tend to forget every single time you jump me."

"Fine," she said through her teeth. "Now if you'll be so kind as to vacate my patient's room. I think I can handle this procedure by myself."

"Squeezing a guy's balls? Yeah, you got that one down."

Mike poked his head in the room. "Emily? Call on line two."

"Take it," Wyatt said. "I've got this."

She shook her head and left.

"Holy cow, you're bad at that, sonny boy," Mr. Myers said into the silence.

Wyatt turned to Mr. Myers. "Excuse me?"

"I was kinda hoping you were going to teach me something," Mr. Myers said. "But I've got more game than you. Hell, Buddy has more game than you."

Buddy licked Wyatt's face as Wyatt stared at Mr. Myers. "You're wearing your hearing aid."

"Nope, I got perfectly good hearing. I just pretend I don't cuz no one ever tells me anything."

Twenty-three

Sara had dinner going when Emily came in the door. She paused from stirring the pot on the stove as Emily removed Woodrow's leash.

"Thought you weren't keeping him," Sara said.

Emily hugged the dog into her and he licked her ear.

She hid her face in his fur. It had been a really bad day. She was pretty sure that whatever she and Wyatt had been playing at was over.

It hurt, so much more than she could have imagined.

"Right," Sara said. *"Dad."*

Emily lifted her head. "What the hell does that mean?"

"I don't know, let's see," Sara said. "You've got a turtle, a cat, and now a puppy. Our house is starting to resemble another vet's house—a vet we both know and love, one whose genes we share. I'm just hoping that the next thing you bring home is Dr. Sexy."

"We're done doing whatever it was that we were doing," Emily said, and rubbed a hand over the ache in her chest.

Sara shook her head. "You'll forgive me if I doubt that."

"It's true," Emily said. "And Woodrow's only staying until I find his family." Emily stared into twin pools of warm brown puppy eyes. "Right?"

He licked her chin again, and Emily felt a sharp stab of pain in her chest. "Great. And now I'm going to have a heart attack in Idaho."

Sara shook her head. "You're not having a heart attack. Your heart hurts cuz you're falling for a damn rescue. Like you're falling for Sunshine, *and* the people in it."

"Bite your tongue."

"Can't. My new tongue piercing is still sore. Stop being stubborn, Emily, and get your head out of your ass. Plans change. Change yours and move on."

She'd purposely not thought about her lifelong plan. So much that it'd taken Wyatt to point out to her that she'd forgotten to even look at it, much less update it. The fact was, she didn't know how to make changes to it and still do the right thing. What did one do when the right thing wasn't necessarily the right thing for her?

The next morning Emily got online to look at the bidding on the charity auction. Cassandra was now the high bidder. Crap. She had no business even caring who won Wyatt. None. She told herself to walk away. Instead, she bid again and drove to work. She sat in the car for a moment, engine off. Next to her in the passenger's seat, Woodrow lifted his sleepy head and blinked at her. He wasn't a morning dog. And since she wasn't a morning person, they were perfect soul mates.

However temporary.

With a sigh, she got out of the car and turned back for her patient. He was doing much better today, but was still moving slowly. She started to help him down, but he hopped out on his own.

"You okay?" she asked.

He sat at her feet and pawed the air at her. She was pretty sure he did this because he knew exactly how cute he was when he did. "Yeah," she said, heart squeezing. "You're okay." She kneeled in front of him. "I'm working hard at finding your owner, but I need you to be good for me. Can you do that?"

He licked her chin, and she hugged him. "Oh, Woodrow. What am I going to do with you?"

He panted happily in her ear.

"Okay," she said, pulling away to look into his eyes. "I like your attitude. But since I'm sure whoever lost you is dying to have you back, there's no use in us getting attached, okay? I get it's going to be hard, because I have the same problem. I'm temporary here, too. And inside this building there's this incredibly smart, incredibly funny, *incredibly* sexy guy. Only I can't fall for him, and neither can you. I know, he's got a great smile and amazing hands, and he always seems to know the right stuff to do to make me—I mean *you*—melt, but no melting, okay? We're going to be strong. We have to be, because I talked to him and we're not a thing. Not anymore."

Woodrow barked his agreement.

That, or he was telling her that she was a complete idiot. It was a toss-up.

"Don't make this harder than it is," she said. "It's best this way. You're not staying. I'm not staying. So remember, *no* falling for the hot guy." They shook on that, and then she rose to her feet. Turning, she plowed right into said hot guy. She thought of the things she'd said to him yesterday and had to lock her fingers together rather than reach for him.

Unlike her, Wyatt seemed to wake up in the mornings completely alert and ready to roll. His gaze was sharp on her, accessing but also somehow warm and affectionate. Either he hadn't let yesterday sink in, or he wasn't bothered in the slightest that they were no longer a thing. He was in low-slung cargoes, battered boots, and an untucked button-down, open over a T-shirt that read: *I like big mutts.*

Her stupid heart skipped a beat. “It’s rude to eavesdrop,” she said.

“I wasn’t eavesdropping.”

She searched his expression for the truth but couldn’t determine whether he was being honest or not. He was good at hiding his feelings when he wanted to. “Good,” she finally said, deciding to believe him, “because I wasn’t talking about you, anyway.”

Wyatt laughed. *Laughed.* And then he crouched on the balls of his feet and held out his hand to Woodrow. “Come here, little man.”

Wriggling in joy, Woodrow followed the demand.

Wyatt looked him over good, gave him a very careful body rub, working around his bandages. Woodrow’s eyes rolled in ecstasy into the back of his head. “He’s looking good,” Wyatt told Emily. “You did a great job with him the other night.” He rose up to his full height, looking disturbingly wonderful with Woodrow in his arms.

The dog licked him from chin to forehead, and Wyatt pressed a kiss of his own to the top of his head before setting the wriggling pup back on the ground.

Emily started to walk past Wyatt into the building, but he stopped her, a hand on hers. She looked up into his face. His hair was still damp, undoubtedly from his morning shower. It curled around his ears and at the nape of his neck. He’d shaved, and she . . . ached. She wanted to press her face into his throat and try to inhale him up. She had no idea what she’d been thinking, because she couldn’t imagine being just co-workers now that she knew how it felt to be in his arms. The problem was that she knew he wasn’t the guy for her. Not just because he wasn’t on her plan but because Darcy had said so and he hadn’t disagreed. He never lied, never misled, never misspoke. She could take him at his word.

Always.

A comfort.

And now, a nightmare.

He stepped close, until they were toe-to-toe, waiting until she tipped her head back to look at him. “If getting attached is the worst thing you do while you’re here,” he said quietly, the teasing light in his eyes gone, “that’s not such a bad thing.”

“You said you didn’t eavesdrop.”

“It’s not eavesdropping if a person’s talking to herself.”

“I was talking to Woodrow.”

He smiled at her and she was hit with another wave of longing for him that nearly took her out at the knees.

“I’ll be in surgery this morning,” he finally said. “You’re scheduled to shadow. Is that going to be a problem?”

“Of course not,” she said. “Is your shoulder—”

“Fine,” he said.

Not that he’d tell her if it wasn’t fine. He liked to chide her for keeping to a plan, but he’d kept himself a virtual island. He held the door open for her and Woodrow.

They were greeted by Gertie and Jade, who’d returned the night before. Woodrow sat patiently while Gertie sniffed him for the second morning in a row, taking a long time at his bandages. Woodrow’s tail was wagging with an air of hopefulness that made Emily’s throat tighten. When Gertie was done, Woodrow licked her.

Gertie licked him back, flopped to the floor, her hundred plus pounds shaking the place.

“Bed hog!” Peanut yelled.

Emily had put flyers up throughout town, and on several online bulletin boards as well. She’d gone by her neighbor’s house twice but no one had been home.

Jade handed her a stack of messages and watched Emily flip through them. Lots of people had called, wanting to adopt Woodrow. But no one had claimed to be his owner.

"You gonna adopt him out to one of the people who want him?" Jade asked.

"Can't. He's not mine."

They all looked down at her feet. Woodrow was sitting on them, eyes bright, tongue lolling.

Jade snorted. "Uh-huh."

Emily looked at Woodrow and felt her heart squeeze. Yeah. He was hers to the bone. She looked at Wyatt, who was back to giving nothing away. If the thought of losing Woodrow killed her, it was nothing compared to what she felt over imagining herself losing Wyatt.

But he was no more hers than Woodrow was. And she needed to remember that.

Three days later, Wyatt was spending his Friday night on the Victorian's roof, a tool belt around his hips, earbuds in his ears blasting loud enough to drown out the voices in his head.

The voices in his head belonged to his sisters, who'd had the blowup of all blowups earlier, over a trip to Target of all things.

Zoe had taken Darcy there on the way home from her PT appointment, and it had gone bad when Darcy got Zoe kicked out of the store. Exactly how this had happened was anyone's guess since neither of them would say. Wyatt had decided to escape the tension by knocking something off Darcy's never-ending to-do list.

The roof had been leaking over the attic's overhang and into the pantry for months. Maybe years. He'd just finished nailing down a new panel when a car drove up. From three stories up he watched Emily and Woodrow alight from her car.

Something clenched deep in his gut. For three days, they'd been perfectly professional at work, in sync.

He'd hated every moment of it.

He saw her look to his truck parked in the driveway, and then at the ladder leaning against the house. He saw her gaze follow the line of the ladder to the second-story roof, where he'd shimmied up the patio awning to get to the very top level.

Her mouth dropped open.

Far below him, he heard the front door open. He couldn't see who'd done so, but he was betting on Zoe.

Darcy never bothered to answer the door.

Emily and Woodrow disappeared inside the house.

"That can't be good," he said out loud.

"Sincerely doubt it."

He nearly startled right off the fucking roof at the sound of Darcy's voice. She was in the attic, her face level with his as she peeked out the window she'd opened. "*Jesus*," he said. "What are you doing up here?"

She shrugged.

"How did you even get up here?"

"I have my ways," she said.

She'd walked. Or crawled. Or hell, maybe she'd flown her broom. The woman had amazing staying powers when she set her mind to something.

"So why's Emily here?" she asked.

"Dunno," he said. "How did you get Zoe kicked out of Target?"

"Shockingly easy," Zoe said from behind Darcy as she came into the attic as well. "She grabbed a case of condoms and randomly dropped individual boxes into people's carts when they weren't looking."

Behind Zoe came Woodrow. Attached to the end of his leash was Emily, and she choked out what sounded like a horrified laugh.

Wyatt, on his knees on the roof, shook his head.

"That's not why," Darcy said.

"True," Zoe said. "It was because you also set every

alarm clock in Housewares to go off at five minute intervals."

Darcy smiled. "Still not why."

Emily stared at her. "How long were you in there?"

"Half an hour," Zoe said, tossing her hands up. "I was grocery shopping!"

"You weren't," Darcy said. "You were lingerie shopping. And I don't know why, he's not worth it."

Wyatt blinked. "He who?"

"Never you mind," Zoe said, and pointed to Darcy. "This is about *her*. When the manager put an announcement over the loud speaker to watch out for the crazy chick in the motorized wheelchair wreaking havoc on the store, Darcy put her hands over her ears and screamed '*The voices are back!*'"

"Hey," Darcy said. "This is what we do, we humiliate each other in public, it keeps us humble. And I humiliate Wyatt, too. Remember the last time he had a date over? We told her how he didn't potty train until third grade?"

"Which was a *lie*," Wyatt said.

"I don't remember that," Zoe said. "I remember telling someone that he slept with Petey the Bear until he was twelve."

Wyatt locked gazes with Emily, who was soaking this all up with avid shock. "Hi," he said. "Welcome to the house for the criminally insane."

"So what's the party for?" Darcy asked.

They all looked at Emily.

She clearly forced a smile. "I just came by to bring Wyatt his latest casserole dish from the Casserole Brigade."

"Who's it from?" Darcy asked. "Tell me it's from Rachel Masters. She makes a great enchilada casserole. I keep telling Wyatt to flirt with her, or better yet, take one for the team and sleep with her so that she'll make more enchiladas."

Emily gave another slow blink. "Um, no. It's not from Rachel."

"Damn, Wy," Darcy said. "You're falling down on the job."

Emily gestured behind her. "I'll just be going now."

"Oh, don't leave on our account," Darcy said. "Not when you made up such a good excuse to come out here and take advantage of my brother."

Emily's cheeks went red. "What? I didn't—"

"Sure you did," Darcy said. "But there's no need to be embarrassed. All the women in Sunshine go to great lengths to take advantage of him. So far he hasn't been real good at letting them, but there's always a shot, and we all know he has a thing for you. So go ahead, take advantage all you want—"

"Out," Wyatt said, pointing at his sisters. "Both of you."

"I—"

"*Now*," he said, ignoring Darcy entirely and giving the I-Swear-To-God eyes to Zoe.

She correctly interpreted the look and hauled Darcy to the door. "We're going out to dinner. We'll be late. Real late. So just carry on with . . . whatever."

Emily's gaze locked on Wyatt's. She nibbled her lower lip and went beet red, but she didn't turn tail and run. Neither of them moved, not until the front door shut far below them and Zoe's car started up and pulled out of the driveway.

"I didn't come to take advantage of you," Emily said into the silence.

He crawled through the window and into the attic. She was in black slacks and a soft sweater the exact color of her eyes. She was dusted in dog and cat hair, her own hair was falling out of its ponytail and framing her face, which was lined with exhaustion.

She'd never looked more beautiful to him. "Did you really come out here to bring me a casserole?"

"Yeah." She stared at his Adam's apple like she wanted to lick it. "It's in the car."

"Who's it from?"

She bit her lower lip.

"Emily." He was smiling. "There's no casserole, is there."

"No."

He put a hand on her hip. The other he slid into her hair, fisted gently, and tipped her face to his, letting his thumb rasp lightly over the pulse at the base of her throat.

She met his gaze, her own a little dazed. "You're dog-whispering me like you do to your patients at work, where you go all silent and alpha pack leader, and wait for them to surrender to you and tell you all their woes."

"I like the surrender part," he said.

She pushed him but she didn't mean it, and they both knew it.

"Okay," she murmured. "You were, right, okay? Does that make you happy?"

"Yes, *always*," he said. "But for the record, what am I right about, other than everything?"

A second push, and he laughed as he pulled her in against him. He hadn't laughed in days. Christ, he'd missed her. Even though he'd seen her for eight to ten hours a day, he'd missed this.

Them.

Which meant he was totally screwed, of course, but in that moment, he didn't care. Yeah, she had one foot out the door, so what. He'd survived it once, he'd survive it again. He pressed his lips to her jaw.

She shivered. "We said we're not doing this anymore."

"Actually, you said that. I didn't sign on to the not doing this anymore program." It was just about as revealing a statement as he could make without manipulating her into making a decision.

And he wasn't about to do that.

Ever.

She went still, then dropped her head to his chest and banged it a few times.

"You could take it back," he said.

She paused, like she really wanted to, but in the end she shook her head. "I can't because Darcy was right. I'm wrong for you, Wyatt. And even if I wasn't, I'm leaving." Her face was a mask of misery. "I'm sorry but I've got to go."

Twenty-four

At the morning's staff meeting, Darcy brought donuts. She was working the rest of the week, helping Jade catch up. Everyone dug in including Emily.

Wyatt knew this because he was watching her, unable to take his eyes off her. She was currently two fisting matching chocolate donuts, digging into them like they might solve her problems.

After she'd left him the night before, he'd gone to AJ's gym and worked himself into a near early grave. He'd needed to be beyond exhausted to sleep.

He hadn't examined his feelings too closely, and he could tell by the way Emily was avoiding eye contact that she wasn't any more eager to do so than him.

Which meant that they were just as messed up as ever.

The meeting covered the usual items on the itinerary, and at the end, when they'd all stood to head for the door, Dell looked at Emily.

"I took another call from the Beverly Hills animal center," he said. "The head vet there wanted to remind me that her intern's still unhappy. I reiterated how well you've worked out, and how lucky we are to have you."

Wyatt looked at Emily, waiting for her to say how she'd give up her right nut, if she'd had one, to switch.

But she said nothing.

And he didn't know what to make of that either, or the relief that swamped him.

That night, Emily made her weekly call to her dad. He'd apparently finally found his iPod, but then had gone on to lose his keys, having to call a locksmith to make a new set. He and the locksmith had traded services, and her father was going to give the guy's three cats a checkup.

He'd also lost his wallet, and had bribed the lady at the DMV to putting him to the front of the line if he immunized her dog as a trade.

"Maybe you could actually charge people for your services sometime," Emily said.

"But then I wouldn't have a new key or my license."

Emily didn't know how to fight that logic. "Dad, what if I said I could come home sooner. I could help you out more."

He laughed. "I think I'm beyond help."

"But if I could—"

"Honey, you can't. You know I'd love to have you here, and you will be. After you put in your time. Don't worry about me. As long as my head's still attached, I can't lose that at least. But do you happen to know where my Kindle might be?"

After they hung up, Emily went to her computer. She wasted a few minutes with the usual time-wasting techniques like Facebook, and then the charity auction. She was still top bidder for Wyatt.

Since this made her feel like she was on a boat at sea, she closed her browser and brought up her e-mail.

She started a new e-mail to Dell. It took her an hour to get it right and even then she stared at it for a long time before she hit Send.

She went to bed, but instead of sleeping, she found herself staring at the ceiling while her gut churned.

Finally she tossed the covers back and headed to the kitchen, going for the frozen cookie dough in the freezer.

Sara found her half an hour later, eating the dough with a spoon right out of the container. "PMS or SMS?" she asked.

"SMS?" Emily asked.

"Stupid Man Syndrome," Sara said.

"It's more like stupid woman syndrome." She paused. "The Los Angeles intern still wants to trade places."

"Yeah?" Sara took a big hunk of cookie dough. "She tired of treating the pink Pomeranians and hairless cats of the rich and famous?"

"I guess her family lives in Idaho somewhere, and she misses them, she wants to be closer to home."

Sara looked up, eyes sharp. "Wait— You're serious?"

"Yeah."

Sara set the cookie dough down. "You're going to do it? You're going to trade places and go back to L.A.?"

"Hello, have you been listening? She wants to come here for the same reason I wanted to stay in Los Angeles. We miss home. We miss Dad. We want to be closer to home."

Sara gave a slow shake of her head.

"No?" Emily asked. "What do you mean no?"

"I mean there's no we. I like Sunshine. You can see the stars at night. And I thought people would judge me, but as it turns out, there's a huge shortage of lesbians here and I'm in huge demand. Everyone wants the token lesbian friend. And I thought you were coming to like it, too. You're back with Dr. Sexy—" She broke off at whatever she saw on Emily's face. "You're not?"

"No."

"But on your first date, you came home with your panties in your pocket."

"It's not what you think," she said softly.

"Emily." Sara looked distressed, for her. "Are you *sure*?"

She thought of what Wyatt had said that first night they'd gone to dinner: *You're not the only one thrown off their axis here, Emily. We never intended to see each other again. Hell we didn't even know each other's last names. And that worked for me.*

It had been a month and a half, and never once in all that time had he alluded to changing his mind. There was no future for them. It wasn't because he was a commitment-phobe either—he'd been engaged. Which brought her to her last problem—the expression on his face every time Caitlin's name came up. He'd loved her. Maybe still did for all she knew. He hadn't let Emily in enough to discuss it with her. "Yes," she said. "I'm sure."

"You really shouldn't make any hasty decisions on this. Give it some time before you talk to your boss—"

"I e-mailed him." Emily gestured to the laptop sitting so innocuously on the kitchen table. "I told him I'd switch."

Sara just stared at her, disappointment and frustration clear. And worry.

"I know," Emily said. "It's risky."

"No," Sara said with a slow shake of her head. "The risk would've been to stay."

Dell was gone when Emily got into work, working one of the ranches he'd contracted with up north. She waited for Wyatt to say something about the internship, about the switch, but he didn't.

The reason for that didn't feel good. She wasn't sure if he was relieved, happy, or just plain indifferent about her decision. He'd been damn careful to keep things in the moment.

She needed to do the same.

When she got home that night, she fed Sammy, Q-Tip, and Woodrow, and then opened the fridge for herself. She was standing there staring at its contents when Woodrow went to the back door and whined.

"Now?" Emily asked. "I just let you out."

Woodrow pawed at the door.

"Okay, okay, hang on." She heard Sara come in the front door. "Hurry," she called out to her sister. "We're going for a walk!"

"We?" Sara asked, coming into the kitchen. "I hope that's the royal we. Or you and the mutt. Not me."

"You." Emily grabbed the leash. "It's almost dark, I need an escort."

"Oh sure, take the butch lesbian, she'll save you."

"Accusing me of profiling isn't going to get you out of this."

Sara sighed and out they went, heading down the street. Woodrow paused at every single bush and tree, but made no deposits.

"What, do you need an invitation?" Sara asked him.

When they got to the next property over, the ranch house where Emily had first thought maybe Woodrow had come from, the dog hunched in the middle of the grass.

"Crap," Emily said.

"Literally," Sara said, and fanned the air. "At least it's dark now."

"No, I mean crap, I didn't bring a baggie to scoop that up with—" She broke off when a long, unhappy howl of a dog sounded.

And then another.

At Emily's feet, Woodrow whined.

"Our neighbors have dogs?" Sara asked.

"I don't know. They're never home."

A few more barks sounded, and Emily looked at the house. Still dark. Quiet. Woodrow finished his business, but before they could move, a truck came down the street.

"Uh-oh," Sara said when it slowed.

Yeah, uh-oh. The truck was coming to the house. They turned off their flashlights and ducked behind a bush just as it pulled into the driveway.

Emily scooped Woodrow close and held her breath.

"We're going to get arrested for not picking up dog poo," Sara whispered. "We're going to end up as someone's bitch."

"Shh!" She went back to holding her breath. Beside her, Sara did the same.

And then, in the silence, her phone lit up like day with a call.

Shit. Emily reached into her pocket and reflexively swiped her thumb across the screen to answer instead of hitting ignore.

The truck door opened. Two long legs appeared out of the truck, heading around the back of the vehicle instead of the front.

Emily sucked in a breath. She could see boots. Denim-clad legs.

And a gun at a lean hip.

Oh, God. Her heart leapt into her throat.

"*Run*," Sara whispered.

The three of them ran like the hounds of hell were on their heels, Sara and Emily in terror, Woodrow barking like he was out for a joyride.

"Did you see—" Emily started.

"I saw," came Sara's grim reply.

"Cop?"

"Doubtful," Sara gasped as they flew. "This is Idaho. Everyone and their grandma is armed."

"Except for us," Emily managed.

"I've got a knife in my pocket."

Emily gave her a startled glance. "What?"

Halfway back, Emily got a stitch in her side and had to stop, hands on her knees, gasping for breath.

"That's . . . pathetic," Sara said, stopping besides her, but looking no better off.

Footsteps sounded, though it was hard to tell from which direction they came. It didn't matter. They both gasped and started to run again. Emily flew right into a brick wall.

Wyatt.

He absorbed the impact without moving and wrapped his arms around her. "What the hell?"

"Yeah," said a different male voice, from directly behind them this time. "What the hell?"

Big, Scary Neighbor Guy, Emily thought, shaking in her sneakers.

Wyatt flicked his flashlight upward and revealed the man who'd gotten out of the truck at the dark house.

Yep. It was indeed Big, Scary Neighbor Guy.

Woodrow got in front of Emily, backing his tush right up to her calves, standing on her feet as he barked sharply at the man.

Emily scooped him up and hugged him. "Good boy," she whispered. "Brave boy."

"Who are you?" Wyatt asked her neighbor.

"I'm the one who found Lucy and Ethel here in my bushes." His gaze went to Sara, and then Emily, and finally Woodrow. No flicker of recognition for the dog, which was a relief. No way could she have given him Woodrow.

"The question is," the guy said, "who the fuck are you?"

"We lost our kitten," Sara said. "We were looking for her and you scared us." She flashed a smile.

Emily didn't know why Sara lied, but she nodded her head in agreement.

Big, Scary Neighbor Guy didn't return the smile. Instead he pointed at her, and then at Emily. "Stay off my property," he said, voice low and menacing. "Watch yourselves."

Emily's heart went into her throat, and she opened her mouth to utter an immediate apology.

"No," Wyatt said, tall and strong at her back. "You watch yourself."

Neither man budged for a long beat. Finally Emily's neighbor made a low sound of disgust. "Handle your women, and I mean it, stay outta my business," he snapped, and stalked off into the night.

"I'm my own woman," Emily said to no one.

Wyatt didn't budge, watching the guy go. After a beat, he looked down at her and her sister.

"It was all *her* doing," Sara said, and pointed at Emily.

"I heard a dog in trouble," Emily said.

Wyatt didn't look happy to hear this. "Next time call me," he said. He'd dropped the tough-guy stance and was back to easygoing, laid-back Wyatt.

Except Emily was coming to realize he wasn't so easy-going or laid-back at all. He was just extremely good at compartmentalizing his life, and taking care of what was important, in the moment.

She could learn from that.

A whole hell of a lot.

But she wasn't feeling laid-back or easygoing. Her blood was still pumping. "Did you come by for anything important?" she managed to ask casually as they walked home.

Sara snorted.

Emily blushed. "I mean—"

"This is where I bow out," Sara said as they arrived back at the house. "I'm heading into town to play darts. Don't wait up."

And she and Wyatt were alone. She wondered if he'd come to discuss the internship, and her leaving.

But he didn't speak.

"So," she said. "How was it that you were our knight in shining armor tonight?"

"I came by and you didn't answer the door. When I called you, and you hit Answer but didn't say anything, I got worried. And then I heard someone say 'run' and just about lost ten years of my life as I came looking for you."

"Oh," she said, wincing, letting them into the house. "Sorry—"

She broke off when he kicked the door shut and then backed her to it. Somewhere along the way he'd removed his glasses. Setting a hand on either side of her head, he leaned in and kissed her until she couldn't remember her name, much less wonder what he'd come to see her about.

"I want you," he said, voice thrillingly rough. "Now."

"I know," she said, moaning at the feel of him, hard against her. "Me too. It's adrenaline."

"Bullshit." Sliding his hands down the backs of her thighs, he hoisted her up his body. Carrying her like that, he strode to her bedroom and kicked the door shut. "Don't make up reasons for what happens between us, Emily. For me, this has got nothing to with what happened tonight, and everything to do with you."

She stared at him, her heart doing jumping jacks against her ribs. If this wasn't adrenaline, and it wasn't a good-bye, what the hell was it?

He stared back, steady as a rock, a little pissed off, and hot as hell. "You're thinking so hard your hair's smoking." He rocked into her, letting her cradle the hardest part of him against the softest part of her. "Let me make this easy," he said. "Tonight. Yes or no."

She shivered with need and want, the two entwining so there was no telling which was which. Tonight? If that was all he wanted, she'd take it. "Yes."

Twenty-five

Emily staggered into the kitchen shortly before dawn. Wyatt had left a few moments before, leaning over her for a lengthy kiss good-bye that would've turned into something else entirely if they hadn't been out of condoms.

Sara was on the kitchen counter eating ice cream out of the container for breakfast, which was so unlike her, Emily stopped short. "What are you doing?"

"Rayna e-mailed me," she said. "She said she missed me, the bitch."

"Did you respond that you miss her, too?"

"No."

"Do it."

Sara sagged. "I can't. I'm the one that broke up with her."

"Which still makes no sense," Emily said.

"Because she's a ten, okay? And I told you, tens don't date fives."

Emily stared at her.

"She's a model," Sara said. "An L.A. runway model." She spread her arms wide. "And I'm a short, chunky construction worker."

"You're gorgeous," Emily said fiercely. "E-mail her back."

Sara dug for more ice cream. At her feet, on the floor, Woodrow was staring at Sara like the sun rose and set on her shoulders. Emily got why when Sara snagged another scoop and offered it to the puppy.

The wood spoon was quickly licked clean.

"Don't do that," Emily said.

"She's no fun is she," Sara said to Woodrow. "She doesn't get that having a broken heart requires a million calories to even *begin* to heal."

"You think you're the only one who's ever had a broken heart?"

"Of the two of us?" Sara asked. "Yeah."

"Hey," Emily said. "What about the Johns, remember them?"

"John Number One was a selfish prick and didn't deserve your heart. And John Number Two never had your heart. How could he? After John Number One and Becky, and then Mom, you never trusted anyone with your heart again."

Emily opened her mouth, and then shut it again. "Fine," she eventually said. "I've been stingy with my heart until now, sue me."

"Until now?" Sara pointed at her with the wooden spoon. "Does that mean what I think it means?"

"No. It means nothing." Not about to explain that Wyatt was interested in her body but not much more than that—especially when it had been all her idea in the beginning. Emily snatched the container of ice cream and the spoon and started to dig in. Then she looked down at the spoon that

Woodrow had licked. She loved him but she didn't want to eat after him. Tossing it into the sink, she reached for another from the drawer.

"Admit it," Sara said. "You're falling for Dr. Sexy."

Emily choked on her first bite. "Would you stop calling him that?"

"You do realize you're making roots," Sara said. "Making friends. Getting pets." She paused. "Bidding on hot bachelors."

"I only bid to make sure the charity gets a lot of money," Emily said. "Someone's gonna outbid me."

"How, when you keep checking it every day and upping your bid?"

Good point. She changed the subject. "And any day now, someone is going to claim Woodrow."

Sara hopped off the counter. "Good to know you're still the Denial Queen. I'm going to work. Maybe tonight we can have a discussion rooted in reality."

"Like what?"

"Like the fact that you're happy here." Sara gave her a long look, and then walked out of the kitchen.

"Yeah, well, I'll admit that when you admit you're a ten and a stubborn idiot!"

Sara slammed out the front door without admitting any such thing.

That night, Lilah, Kate, and Holly included Emily in the Girls' Night outing to the guys' flag football game. It was Bones vs. Firsts—the town's doctors, dentists, vets, and anyone in the medical field against Sunshine's first responders like cops, firefighters, and medics.

The Bones were down a member since Dell was on day two of being up north. Emily watched the rough game through worried eyes, sucking in a breath when Wyatt got taken down by a guy who had at least thirty pounds on him.

They rolled viciously around for a moment, and then Wyatt came up, still holding the ball triumphantly.

His opponent pushed to his feet, and Emily blinked in surprise.

It was Evan, the cop who made the amazing chocolate chip cookies.

The two men stared at each other for a long beat before going back to their own lines. Evan shot Emily a smile on his way.

"He's cute," Lilah said.

Wyatt strode by the stands, slowing to give Emily a long, steady look that had her blushing.

"He's cuter," Lilah said.

The next play involved both Evan and Wyatt rolling around on the ground again.

Kate looked at Emily. "There seems to be some tension there that has *'about a woman'* all over it."

Emily bit her lower lip.

"Spill," Holly said.

"I don't know what you're talking about."

"Right," Lilah said dryly. "That's why the both of them keep looking over at you, flexing their muscles."

"Honey, I'm all for a woman exploring her options," Holly said, "but you can't have two alphas sniffing around sharing air space like that."

"We have alphas sharing air space at the center all day long," Emily pointed out.

"But they don't want the same woman."

Emily sank down in her seat a little bit. "Evan brought me cookies. And wants to date me."

"What does Wyatt want?"

She knew what she *wanted* Wyatt to want, and that was for him to indicate that maybe he'd want her to stay, something she'd never have entertained in the beginning, but now . . . now she couldn't stop thinking about. But he'd not said a single word about a future with her, not once. She thought about the night before, when he'd taken her into her bedroom and given her so many orgasms she'd been boneless for hours afterward, making it perfectly clear what he did want from her.

Lilah took in her facial expression and burst into laughter, and Emily covered her face with her hands. "Oh my God. This is so out of my comfort zone."

"What, being sought after by extremely hot guys? Stop and smell the roses, babe, and take in the moment."

"Or," Kate said quietly, watching Emily's face, "you could pick one."

"Picking isn't the problem," Emily said, gaze on Wyatt. "Wyatt and I aren't a real thing."

He threw a hard, fast pass to Adam, who caught it in the end zone.

Game. Over.

The Bones team tackled Wyatt to the ground, pounding his back, victorious. After a few moments of this, the guys all headed off the field, eyes on their real prize.

The women in the stands.

Adam claimed Holly, who looked all too happy to be claimed. Same for Brady and Lilah. And Grif and Kate.

Wyatt strode past the kissing couples and came straight to Emily.

She nearly swallowed her tongue. "What are you—"

Yanking her in, he kissed her long and hard.

In front of everyone.

She pulled back and had to shake her head to put some sense back into it. "What was that?"

"A victory kiss," he said.

She wasn't one to bank her future happiness on a man, ever, but damn. She'd hoped for more.

But hoping was for dreamers, and she was a planner. To the bone. They'd outlined what their relationship was, she and Wyatt, way back in the beginning. Hell, she'd reiterated it to him many times, too many to count.

Which meant that this wasn't his fault at all.

Nope, this was all on her.

Twenty-six

Wyatt jackknifed up from a dead sleep to the sound of Zoe's scream. A spider, he thought, but it was worse than a spider.

He fumbled for his glasses and went running. He found her in the basement fighting a burst pipe. Wading into the mess, he turned off the water to the house, but that wasn't going to solve any problems. "This is bigger than me," he said. "I'll call a plumber from work."

"But in the meantime, we don't have water."

He looked down. They were in two inches of it. "We have plenty."

"Not funny, Wyatt. I have a flight in a few hours."

"And I've got surgeries. I'll call a plumber," he repeated.

"But—"

"Zoe," he said. "We both love this big ol' piece of shit, but we can't keep duct taping it together."

"Duct tape fixes everything," she said.

"Not this time. We need a major renovation, or we need to sell."

She gasped. "Mom put you up to this?"

"No," he said. "Look, I love the memories in this place as much as you. But—"

"But you're leaving us."

"You know I'm going to build a house," he said gently. "You know I want my own place, where there's no lingerie hanging in the bathroom—well, unless it belongs to the woman I'm sleeping with. I want to live where there's no need to tiptoe around for a whole week every month because we ran out of Midol."

"Hey."

"I want to live somewhere without roommates, aka sisters who are pains in my ass who remember and enjoy bringing up how when I was ten I used to save my gum on the bedpost for the next day."

She smiled. "I'd forgotten about that."

"You would've remembered the next time Emily came over."

She laughed. "Yeah. Maybe."

He squeezed her hand. "And when I go, I want to know that you're safe, and not drowning in the money pit."

"What if I promise to stop bossing you around?"

"You'll never stop bossing me around," he said. "And that's okay. I still love you. I just don't want to live with you. Are we going to be okay?"

"No." She sighed. "Yes. And the truth is, I don't want to live with you, either. Or Darcy— Oh, God," she said, clutching at his shirt. "Don't you fucking me leave me alone with Darcy!"

He laughed, and she kicked water on him, and he put his hand over her face and shoved.

Yeah, they were going to be okay.

"Who's going to tell Darcy?" Zoe asked, squeezing water out of her hair.

"Tell me what?" Darcy had appeared at the top of the stairs.

"Wyatt's leaving us," Zoe said.

"Good," Darcy said. "You finally told him we were tired of having him as a roommate then."

Wyatt slid Zoe a look.

She winced.

"*You're* tired of living with *me*?" he asked in disbelief. "What do I do?"

"Besides leaving the lid up, drinking out of the milk container, thinking that doing your dishes means getting them into the sink, and parking in the good spot every single night? You're a fun sucker," Darcy said.

"Darcy," Zoe said reproachfully.

"Gently," Darcy said, and smacked herself in the forehead. "You said to tell him *gently* that we don't want to live with him anymore. Sorry."

Wyatt looked at Zoe in disbelief.

"You're cramping our love lives," she said on a sigh.

"I'm cramping *your* love life?" he asked. "You don't *have* a love life."

"Because the last time I brought a date home, you told him he was an idiot."

"Because he used the wrong remote on the TV and unprogrammed everything," Wyatt said. "It took me three days to undo the mess. And that was a year ago."

"They were trying to watch porn and you came home on them," Darcy said. "The poor guy got nervous because you're about a foot taller than him and he was one of those skinny dudes who disappears when he turns sideways. Jeez, you're so oblivious."

Wyatt rubbed the heels of his hands over his eyes but he still couldn't undo the image of Zoe and that scrawny dude watching porn together. "You've done it," he finally said to Darcy. "You've driven me to drink. I need a beer. No, I need whiskey and it's five thirty in the morning."

"And I realize I don't have a love life right now," Darcy went on as if he hadn't spoken. "But someday I might. Because, unlike you, I'm ready to take a risk."

"You're a walking risk," Zoe told her.

"I risk," Wyatt said.

"Name one," Darcy said.

"Yesterday. In surgery. I—"

"Not at work," Darcy said. "With your heart."

He stared at her. At the both of them. Not liking where this was going.

Darcy softened. "You never have, Wyatt," she said. "You hide behind your let-it-happen attitude, because it's safe. If you don't ask someone to be yours and they don't pick you, well then nothing lost, right?"

"Wrong," he said. He'd risked with Caitlin, and she'd left. Excuse the fuck out of him for not jumping into it again with Emily.

Except . . . he had. Maybe he hadn't put it to words, but he'd let her in. Inside him.

A tactical error on his part, one he was hoping he didn't pay for.

His phone buzzed, and he looked down at the screen. Dell was back and needed him at work a few minutes early. Saved by the bell. "Gotta go."

"Wyatt," Zoe said softly when he started up the basement steps. "Darcy didn't mean to hurt your feelings—"

"Yes, I did," Darcy said. "Take a damn risk," she told him. "Try it, you might like it."

He risked plenty. Hell, he risked daily. And her name was Emily.

Risk personified.

Twenty minutes later, he strode into Belle Haven and headed to Dell's office.

"I'm finally catching up on the business side of things after all the running around," Dell said. "I don't see a reason not to make the intern switch if Emily's on board with it and wants it. You?"

Wyatt felt his gut drop. "What?"

"They're both on board. Emily e-mailed me about it days ago."

"When?"

"Right before I left."

Before her and Sara's Nancy Drew exploits. Before they'd made love all night long.

And she'd not said a word.

Dell's gaze remained even, steady. "I was surprised," he admitted. "I thought there for a while that you and she—"

"No." Apparently not. "No," Wyatt said again, trying to believe it, all while reeling.

Dell nodded. "I was going to go make the west ranching rounds. Three stops, Brady's flying. You want to switch and take it?"

Wyatt nodded, appreciating the out today, but he couldn't stop thinking *days ago.* Emily had e-mailed Dell days ago . . .

And not said one word to him.

Emily shadowed Dell for the day. He'd told her the switch had been approved and there were no hard feelings but it needed to happen ASAP for continuity sake.

He didn't say one word about Wyatt.

And neither did she.

Halfway through the day she received an e-mail from Lilah stating that Sara had won Wyatt in the charity auction. Sara was now the proud owner of a day of shadowing one sexy Dr. Wyatt Stone.

Emily couldn't believe her little cheat bid using someone else's name had worked. If she was a good person, she'd gift the shadow day with Wyatt to one of the other women who'd wanted him, but she totally wasn't that good of a person because she was keeping him.

At least on paper.

The day didn't end at the usual six o'clock because that night was Belle Haven's monthly immunization clinic. Emily had volunteered to work it, and then found herself surprised when the entire staff showed up to do the same, including significant others—minus Brady and Wyatt, who weren't back yet.

The atmosphere was more like a party than a work night. Lilah brought animals who needed adopting, and held an impromptu adoption clinic. Jade was giving out free pet visit coupons, and Adam was there teaching one of his dog training courses—which Darcy took—borrowing Woodrow to do so, who learned all sorts of things, including how to sit on command.

There was food, too, everyone had brought something, and the fun and laughter was plentiful. Anyone, even a perfect stranger, could've felt the love the place exuded. But it wasn't the place. It was the people. And their longtime connections to each other. Sunshine was like that, one of those places where history collided with the present, and it worked in a way Emily had never imagined it would.

Wyatt and Brady got back and when they walked through the door, Wyatt's gaze immediately zeroed in on her. Her chest got tight, like there wasn't enough room for her heart behind her ribcage. A montage of memories played in her head like a movie: running into Wyatt again at the hind quarters of a sheep in labor, climbing into his lap in his truck and fogging up the windows, saving that horse and getting a bruised butt in the process . . .

She would miss it here in Sunshine, she really would. She'd miss everyone so much, but Wyatt most of all, more than she'd ever missed anything or anyone.

You don't have to go, a voice whispered in her head. Except if she stayed for a man who'd never given her a single inkling that he wanted more than to be boinked, she'd never forgive herself.

Why hadn't he given her an inkling, dammit? It was time, past time, to ask. She actually started toward him to do just that, and a woman walked in the door.

She was a petite, auburn-haired beauty, with a sweet smile and deep green eyes that unerringly landed on Wyatt. She approached him with enough familiarity that Emily knew instantly who she was, even before she leapt into Wyatt's arms and kissed him full on the mouth.

Everything came to a skidding halt inside Emily, including her heart. No, wait. There it was, kicking hard against her ribs as she moved.

Fast.

She couldn't say what she was feeling exactly, but when she blinked again, she was out the back door, heading toward the horse pens. Reno and Kiki nickered a welcome. Blue was quiet but she did stick her head over the fence, looking for goodies.

Emily patted her. The view was nothing but inky blackness right now, the only light coming from a blanket of an infinity of stars.

It was a gorgeous night.

She climbed up on the fence and sat, and took her first breath since she'd seen Caitlin's mouth on Wyatt's. "Damn," she said, and scrubbed at her wet cheeks. Suddenly she *could* put a name to her emotions.

Red hot jealousy.

Envy.

Sadness.

Regret.

And perhaps the worst of all, loneliness.

Her phone buzzed an incoming text. Before she could reach for it, another text came in. And then another. And another.

First up was Lilah. Honey, come back.

Next was Jade. Girl, you left too early.

She didn't know what that meant, but read the next text, from Holly. You okay?

Kate texted, too. Get your cute ass back in here, you missed the good stuff.

Emily stared down at her phone as one last text came in from . . . Oh, God. Wyatt.

She squinted as she accessed it, because everyone knew that squinting while reading something potentially devastating made it easier.

Where are you?

She swiped her nose on her sleeve and typed: Gone.

It was silly and childish, but she figured she was past due.

Liar, came his next text. Your car's still here.

She hit Reply. I'm busy with a patient.

His own reply was so immediate she had no idea how he managed to thumb the words in so fast. Another lie. You're not going to be able to walk back inside with that nose, Pinocchio.

She choked out a soggy laugh and stared at the phone, having no idea what to reply. I just need to be alone for a few.

"No, you don't."

She jerked around, dropping her phone, staring at the tall, dark shadow coming around the barn. "Oh my God. You scared me."

He picked up her phone and held it out, and when she hopped down from the fence and tried to take it from him, his other hand shot out and grabbed hers, pulling her in. "Ditto," he said.

"Give me my phone back."

"Why did you run off?"

"I didn't. I told you, I had a patient."

"Yeah?" he asked, making a show of looking around. "Who?"

From behind her, Blue stuck her head over the fence and gave her a shove in the back that pushed her into Wyatt's chest.

Wyatt held on, but she stepped back and pointed to the damn nosy horse. "Blue. She's . . . not feeling good."

As she said this, Blue took advantage of how accessible she was and began to search her pockets for goodies, snorting her displeasure to find her goodie-less. She couldn't concentrate on that because there was an odd tension coming from Wyatt, which she didn't understand.

She was the injured party here.

Wasn't she?

He was hands on hips, staring at her. "So you expect me to believe that you came out here because Blue needed you, and not because Caitlin showed up."

Hearing the name of the woman he'd once loved, maybe still loved, fall so easily from his lips was like a sharp knife in the gut. "Caitlin showed up?" she asked with false casualness.

He narrowed his gaze on her and didn't answer.

Feeling defensive, and for good reason, as she was truly a crappy liar, she went hands on hips, too. "Why are you out here looking for me anyway? You were very busy a few minutes ago."

"So you *did* see her."

Fine. The jig was up. "Hard not to, since she was attached to your lips."

"Shit." Wyatt stared down at his boots for a long moment. Hard to tell if he was fighting the urge to strangle her or walk away. Then he met her gaze again. "I wasn't expecting her."

"As you don't expect much, this doesn't surprise me."

Wyatt shoved a hand through his hair, a very unusual "tell" from a man who was usually so comfortable in his own skin in every single situation that came along that she'd never really seen him so much as slightly rattled before. "I'm guessing she wants to start up again," she said.

He nodded, and it happened again, that stab right through her heart. "She missed you," she guessed.

"Yes."

"Not surprising," she managed, sounding oddly normal for a woman who could no longer feel her bones. "Seeing as when she broke up with you, it wasn't because she didn't love you anymore, but because she was going off to live a dream of hers and help people."

He said nothing to this.

"Why is she here?" Emily asked. "I thought she was in Africa or somewhere."

This got her a small lip twitch. "Haiti. And she accepted a fellowship at a hospital in Coeur d'Alene, working with a group of surgeons she admires."

Coeur d'Alene. Less than an hour away. "So . . . I guess congratulations."

He stalked past her to the fence. Leaning on it, he stroked Blue's face, shoving the horse back when she tried to frisk him. "Knock it off," he said, and she knew he was talking to her, not the horse. She stiffened and stared at his broad shoulders. "Excuse me?"

"You think she dumped me."

"Didn't she?"

"And in thinking that, do you really then *also* think I'd go back to the woman who walked away from me?"

She opened her mouth, and then shut it again as she stared at his back. She didn't know what she thought. He was so deceptively chill most of the time that she'd forgotten one important thing. He was strong, tough, and actually, pretty damn alpha.

He turned to face her, his eyes glittering with a dark emotion that she realized was temper, however rare. "*I* broke things off with *her*, Emily. I'm the one who sent her away, the one who said we were over. I knew she wanted to take the job, and I knew I didn't want a long distance relationship. I also knew that she wasn't ever going to be the right woman for me, regardless of my feelings for her at the time." A muscle jumped in his jaw as he stared at her. "And yeah, I had feelings for her. I loved her."

"Past tense," Emily whispered, feeling the teeniest flicker of hope deep inside.

"Past tense," he agreed. "I'll always care for her, about her, but she's not the one." He never took his eyes from hers, which made it all the harder to hear when he said, "I thought maybe I'd met the one for me, but I was wrong."

The tentative hope shriveled, replaced by dread. "What does that mean?"

"You got something you want to tell me?" he asked, voice even, face blank, like he was asking about the weather.

"Uh . . ." Her heart started to pound. "Yeah."

He leaned against the fence, all ears and bad 'tude.

"I won you in the auction by cheating."

He blinked. "You . . . what? How did you—" He shook his head. "Jesus, never mind. The internship, Emily. I'm talking about the internship. You're leaving. When the hell were you going to tell me?"

"Oh." Dread turned to fear. "That's not as easy to explain as the auction thing."

"Yes, it is," he said. "It's a sentence. Hell, Emily, it's two *words*: I'm. Leaving."

She shouldn't have been surprised at how angry he sounded, but she was. Still, she was more surprised at her *own* anger. "You know how much I wanted that internship," she reminded him. "It's in L.A., near home for me. It'll lead into a job that pays a lot more money than anywhere else. I've planned for that job, I—"

"Christ, are we back to your plan? Seriously?"

"Yes, and dammit, you know why. You know I don't

want to be like my dad, barely getting by. *Not* getting by. I want money in the bank, Wyatt, a house I can pay for. I want to be okay, for once I want that. I need that. It's not so different from your dream, you know. You gave up a relationship to stay here and build your home."

"And us?" he asked with his characteristic bluntness. "Did we not factor at all?"

"I wasn't sure there was an us."

His eyes merely darkened, his mouth going more grim.

"It was a difficult decision," she said softly.

"Doesn't sound like it was difficult at all."

"I told myself I couldn't pin my future on a crush," she said, and paused, waiting for a response. A bread crumb. Anything.

But got nothing.

"We both know this started out as just a fun thing," she said as calmly as she could. Not easy when she was so close to tears that she didn't dare blink. "Not a forever thing. How am I supposed to throw away everything I thought I wanted on a fun thing?"

"So you're what, going back to a job in a fancy zip code?" he asked. "And then what, Emily? You find your John? Is *that* the dream? Really?"

"I have to take care of my dad," she said. "Before he ends up in a cardboard box with eighteen dogs."

"Your dad's fine. Your dad's happy. Happier than you."

The barb hit hard. So hard she actually staggered back a step and put a hand to her chest, which didn't assuage the ache. "Why should I stay?" she asked. "Give me one reason."

He stared at her, a muscle ticking in his jaw as her heart shriveled a little bit inside.

"I hope this is what will make you happy, Emily," he finally said quietly. "You deserve to be happy."

And then he was gone, vanished into the dark night.

Twenty-seven

Emily sat straight up with a start and looked at the clock. She had no idea what had woken her. Beside her, Woodrow stirred and raised his head.

"Stay," she said, sliding out of bed. "I'm just going for some water."

He didn't stay. He hopped down off the bed and sat at her feet, looking up at her.

She sighed. "Okay, you can come. But you have to be very quiet."

She moved down the hall and peered into Sara's room.

Empty.

Figured. Even her sister, more of a city woman than Emily could ever hope to be, had found a nightlife here in Sunshine.

The night was warm, and they'd left a window open. As she pulled a glass from the cupboard, a long, thin howl of pain came through the screen, making all the hair on her body stand up.

Another dog, she was certain.

She was equally certain that she couldn't ignore it any more than she'd been able to with Woodrow. She ran to her room and threw on clothes.

"I know you're gonna hate this," she said to Woodrow, "but you're staying. There's another dog out there in trouble."

She ran to her car, following the cry that tugged at every heart string she owned. Three minutes later, she slammed on the brakes when her headlights caught the dark huddled form on the side of the road near where she'd found Woodrow. "No," she whispered, running out of the car, heart in her throat. "Oh, no."

It was another dog, this one much more injured than Woodrow. It hadn't been hit by a car, but in a vicious fight, and was bleeding from so many deep wounds she didn't know where to start. She flew back to her car, grabbed a blanket from the backseat, and carefully scooped up the dog, who whimpered in pain.

"I know," she whispered, heart in her throat. "Hold on, baby, just hold on."

She broke a few speed limits heading toward the clinic, and also the no cell phone law when she hit Wyatt's number.

He answered with a low-pitched, sleepy, "I hope this is a break-up sex booty call."

She let out a half laugh, half sob, and he came immediately alert. "Emily?"

She pictured him putting on his glasses to check the screen. "You okay?" he demanded.

She swiped her nose on her sleeve and swallowed hard. "I'm heading to the center."

"What's wrong? What do you need?"

"I forgot my keys and don't have time to turn around."

She heard some rustling and knew he was getting out of bed. Normally she'd wonder if he was naked, and maybe even indulge in picturing it, but right now she just wanted him to hold her, as much as that set feminism back fifty years. "Is there a set of keys hidden anywhere on the property?" she asked.

"No, but I'll be here waiting for you. What's the matter?"

"I don't want to get you out of bed—"

"Emily," he said, "I'm already halfway there. Talk to me."

She felt her eyes fill again and quickly blinked away the tears. What was it going to be like in L.A. without him in her life?

Your own doing . . .

"Emily?"

"I've got another injured dog."

"ETA?"

"Ten minutes."

"I'll have a room ready," he said calmly. "Drive safe, sweetness."

Because she didn't trust her voice, she nodded, for all the good that was going to do him. Then she ended the call and tossed her cell to the passenger's seat and drove.

Wyatt did indeed get to Belle Haven before Emily. He hadn't expected to hear from her, and for a moment, when her number had come up on his cell phone, his heart had squeezed, hard.

She'd changed her mind.

He'd been unprepared to hear her tear-ravaged voice, and fear had gripped him.

When her car pulled into the lot, he strode out into the night to meet her, opening the driver's side as she turned off the engine.

"The dog's in the backseat—" she started.

He pulled her from the car and gave her a quick once-over.

"I'm fine," she said, opening the back passenger's door. Wyatt gently pushed her aside and eyed the dog. Ah, shit.

"It's bad," she whispered.

Yeah. Real bad. He scooped the injured animal up while Emily ran ahead of him to get the front door.

"Where was he?" he asked her.

"About a quarter of a mile from my house, between my place and my neighbor. Right near where I found Woodrow. I heard him crying."

And she'd gone out alone. He hated that. He shouldered himself and the dog through the door, striding directly to the back. "You went out at this time of night by yourself."

"I had no choice," she said. "You'd have done the same thing."

The dog hadn't moved, but was breathing heavily, a distressed pant. He'd gone into shock and was badly damaged. Torn to shreds really, bleeding through the blanket from too many places to count. Wyatt gently set him down on the exam table and turned to Emily, who'd immediately shifted closer to stroke the dog's face and murmur softly to him.

She stood there, bent over the dog, tears shimmering in her eyes, balancing on her lower lashes. "It's going to be okay," she whispered.

Wyatt's heart tightened painfully. He knew that devastated look, he'd felt it all too many times himself.

It was one of the things that few people realized about being a vet, how much death and devastation they really faced every single day.

It took its toll on even the most distant and cool, levelheaded of people. And Emily was one tough cookie—he loved that about her—but she was never distant and only sometimes cool and levelheaded. Everyone had their breaking point and she looked to be at hers. "Emily."

"I . . ." Lifting her gaze from the table, she stared at him. She was covered in blood. The dog's, he told himself as she shook her head helplessly. "I—" Without another word, she whirled to grab some supplies and started assessing the dog as he would. "Shock," she choked out. "He's in shock."

"Yes," he agreed quietly. Waiting. It didn't take but another two seconds. "He can't take a surgery," she realized. "He can't—" She shook her head as it sank into her that the dog wasn't going to survive, that the humane thing to do was put it down. "I have to . . ."

"I'll do it," he said.

"No." She shook her head again. "This is on me. He's my responsibility—"

"Did you attack this dog?"

"Of course not!"

"Then it's not on you. Let me," he said.

"But—"

"I know, you want to handle it all on your own, and you do. You handle everything on your own better than anyone I know. But let someone help, just this once."

She was breathing a little heavily, telling him that the dog wasn't the only shocky one. He had no idea what it was about this dog that had gotten to her so deeply, but it happened. It was the job. And sometimes, the job sucked. "Can you get me a warming blanket?" he asked.

He wasn't going to need it. The dog wasn't going to need it. And if she'd been thinking clearly, she'd have known it.

But she went, leaving him alone to do what had to be done.

Emily was at the closet where they kept the warming blankets before her brain kicked in and she realized what Wyatt had done for her.

"Damn him," she whispered, and sat right where she was, on the floor by the closest. She pulled her legs into her chest, dropped her head to her knees, and tried to keep it together.

A few minutes later, footsteps came down the hall toward her and she busied herself with the blankets in the closest, like she was actually doing something.

"Come here, sweetness."

"I'm organizing the closet."

He sat next to her, right there on the floor, and then two warm, strong arms encircled her, pulling her into his lap.

"I'm sorry," she whispered, and lost it.

He tucked her face into the crook of his neck and pressed his jaw to the top of her head. And then he did what she couldn't remember anyone ever doing for her before.

He let her cry.

When she'd managed to curtail it down to noisy, hiccupping sniffles, he lifted her face to his. "Why did you become a vet?" he asked.

"To help," she managed. Her throat got tight again. "To help animals."

"And you helped him. You did," he said when she started to shake her head. "You rescued him from a night of pure hell and put him out of his misery, and that was your job. That's what we do."

She closed her eyes. "*You* did it."

"You went out into the night, heedless of your own safety, putting his life ahead of yours—which, by the way, we're going to circle back to later—and you saved him from being alone.

She gave a shuddery, exhausted sigh. "Wyatt?"

"Yeah?"

"I'm sorry I didn't tell you about the intern switch. I should have. I . . ." She squeezed her eyes shut. "I'm going to miss you," she whispered. "More than I know how to admit."

He blew out a breath. "Same. You came out of nowhere, knocked me on my ass."

She set her head on his shoulder and tried not to cry again. "Will I see you? After I'm gone?"

"You marrying anyone anytime soon?"

She let out a watery laugh. "No."

"Then yeah. I'll see you. It'll be okay, Em."

"I hate it when you do that."

"Do what?" he asked, stroking a big hand up and down her back.

"Act like a grown-up."

It was his turn to huff out a laugh. "Yeah, well, it happens sometimes. We've got to call this one in, sweetness."

"The police?"

"Yeah. That wasn't a hit-and-run. And that wasn't a coyote attack."

"What was it?"

"I think someone's fighting dogs." Still sitting on the floor holding her, he pulled out his cell, hit a number, and put the phone to his ear. "Kel? Yeah, sorry man, I know it's late. But we've got something you need to see." He shoved his phone back in his pocket.

"Who's Kel?"

"Local sheriff. He's on his way."

Kel arrived ten minutes later. He was a tall, lean, good-looking guy Emily recognized as one of the cops Wyatt played football against. Given his bed-head hair and unhappy expression, he'd clearly just dragged himself out of bed. "What's going on?" he asked.

"Remember what you were telling me the other night after the game?" Wyatt asked. "About the dogs? You said you suspected you had an illegal dog fighting ring in the county."

"Yeah."

"I've got something to show you. Wait here a sec," he said to Emily, and then he and Kel vanished down the hall.

A few minutes later they were back, Kel looking royally pissed off. "I don't know what kind of sick fuck could do that to a dog."

A half an hour later, Emily parked her car in her driveway, got out, and nearly screamed when a tall shadow materialized in front of her.

Wyatt.

"Need to be more aware of your surroundings," he said.

"Why are you following me?"

"Making sure you got home okay." He took her key from her and started to unlock the front door, but Sara pulled it open and gaped in horror at Emily's bloody sweatshirt. "What—"

"It's not her blood," Wyatt said, and shouldered his way in, hands on Emily, nudging her ahead of him. "She's just exhausted. I'm putting her to bed."

"Do you need a padlock to keep her there?" Sara asked his back as he strode down the hallway like he owned the place.

"I've got my ways," Wyatt called back.

"I bet," Sara murmured.

Wyatt took Emily into the bathroom and started her shower. "Need help?"

"No." It was an automatic response. She was good at not needing help. "I'm fine."

Wyatt let out a breath that was as close to a sigh as she'd ever heard from him. "Don't do that," he said.

"Don't what?"

"Don't try to be Super Woman, not with me."

She tried to laugh that off, but the sound was weak and she closed her mouth, afraid she'd go from laughing to crying again.

Leaning past her, Wyatt tested the hot water, and then he shocked her as he stripped quickly and efficiently, each movement economical and so masculine that she just stared at him.

When he was standing there naked and perfect, he began to remove her clothes, softening enough to smile when he caught her expression. "Don't look at me like that," he warned.

"Like what?"

"Like you want to eat me up."

But God help her, she did. He was all smooth, rippled sinew and male virility, and in any other circumstance, she would've taken at least a nibble. "I'm not."

He snorted, pushed her into the shower, and then followed, completely unselfconscious, even though he was quite obviously aroused. Eyes hooded, he washed her hair with firm, strong fingers, and she let herself enjoy the feeling of being taken care of. When his hands ran the soap down her body, her head fell back onto his chest. She closed her eyes so she couldn't see the dog's blood running off her, down the drain.

But it was embedded in her brain, and the shock of it, and her anger, hit her again, and she began to shake. She reached out for the wall but Wyatt turned her to face him and anchored her close. She rested her head on his shoulder and leaned into him as the tremors took her.

Wyatt set the soap aside and wrapped his other arm around her, too, and rested his head on top of hers, holding her until she calmed.

"I'm better," she said.

He didn't respond, nor did he let go of her. Instead, his hands glided up and down her back in a gesture she was sure he meant to be soothing and comforting, and it was. At first.

But then she started to tremble for another reason altogether, and that reason was directly related to being pressed up against his wet, hot, *hard* body. "If you want me to stop looking at you like that," she murmured. "You're gonna have to stop touching me."

"I can control myself if you can."

She stilled, then sighed. "Well that's just great."

He let out a low, male sound that went right through her to all her good spots, and lifted her chin so he could look into her face. "You can't control yourself?" he asked.

Of course she couldn't control herself, not with him, a fact she'd proven over and over again.

"Emily," he said, a bit strained now. "I shouldn't know that." He nudged her from him so she could rinse, during which time he soaped himself up as quickly and efficiently as he'd stripped them both, a fact that did nothing to lessen her sudden and desperate need for the oblivion he always brought her.

He turned off the water and wrapped her in a towel, and then grabbed one for around his hips, blocking her view. "Sleep," he said firmly. "You're going to sleep."

And then he practically shoved her into her bed.

She squeezed her eyes shut, not wanting to see him leave.

"Shit," she heard him say, and the sound of his towel hitting the floor spiked her pulse as he slid in next to her.

"Wyatt—"

"Shh." He flipped her away from him and hauled her back to his front. "Close your eyes and go to sleep."

"We're not going to . . ."

"What?" he asked.

He wanted her to say it? "Have sex," she whispered. "Like the last time you slept over."

"Besides the fact that we're not doing that anymore, we didn't have sex that night. Or any night here in this house."

"Then what were we doing?" she asked.

It took him a moment to answer. "I'm going to let you wrestle with that one," he finally said. "You let me know when you get it figured out." He had a sinew-lined forearm snug against her belly, one of her bare breasts cupped in the palm of his big hand. His mouth was resting at the nape of her neck to subdue her. When she tried to move, he gently sank his teeth into the crook of her neck. The move was incredibly intimate, a little protective, and a whole lot possessive.

And she wouldn't have admitted it out loud, but also arousing as hell.

Which wasn't helping her cause. "If we're not going

there tonight," she said, "you need to stop touching and biting my good parts."

"Can't help it that you're one all-over sweet-as-hell good part. Go to sleep, Emily."

"There's something poking me in my butt."

"It's just the blankets," he said. "Ignore it."

She squirmed a little, trying to get comfortable, and from behind her came a rough groan as his hands tightened on her. "Stop wriggling," he commanded.

She couldn't help it. The "thing" poking her had gotten bigger. "That's not the blanket, is it?"

"No, it's not the blanket." He ran his hand softly down her arm and took her hand in his. "Now stop talking."

Wrestling with the fact that she'd done this, she'd put the whole leaving Sunshine in motion, *she'd* ended whatever it was they'd had, she tried to remember why.

Los Angeles was her home.

Her dad was there, and he needed her.

The life she'd always wanted was there.

None of that helped. Wyatt was right here with her and she already missed him like hell. "Wyatt?" she whispered.

He let out a long breath. The alpha male version of *What the hell now?*

"I'm sorry," she said.

His arm tightened on her but he didn't speak.

She closed her eyes and tried to go to sleep. But it took a long time.

Twenty-eight

Emily woke up in the predawn to a grumpy Q-Tip on her chest and her phone buzzing. Since she'd fallen asleep what felt like only a few minutes ago, she was groggy as hell, but one thing was obvious.

Wyatt was gone . . .

Her heart clenched painfully as she reached for her phone. "'Lo," she answered without looking at the screen. "Who died?"

"Don't get mad," Sara said. "But I let Woodrow out the back door and he took off on me."

Emily tossed off her covers and sat up. "Took off? He never takes off."

"Exactly, but he did, and I didn't have my shoes on so I couldn't run after him. I thought he'd just go out and do his business and come back. Should have known better, men never do what they're supposed to. It's why I'm gay."

"Where's Woodrow now?"

"No friggin' clue. By the time I got my shoes on and made it outside, he was gone. I've got to get to work. Can you send Wyatt out to help me?"

"Wyatt's gone," Emily said, reaching out with a hand to touch the indentation on the pillow where his head had been.

"Why?" Sara asked.

"Because we're not a thing. He was here last night just to make sure I was okay."

"Bullshit. You messed this up by running chicken."

Emily sighed. "I simply moved up a situation that was going to happen anyway."

"If this is the part where you tell me how many days are left, I'm never going to cook for you again."

Emily stared up at the ceiling. "Go to work, Sara, I'll get Woodrow." She disconnected and pulled on the first item of clothing she came to, which was a pair of sweats she'd stolen from Wyatt. They dwarfed her, but they'd keep her warm in the morning chill. She shoved her feet into sneakers, grabbed a jacket, and took off out the back door. "Woodrow!" she yelled.

Nothing.

She followed the route they always walked in the mornings, calling his name as she went, getting more concerned when she got no response.

Woodrow wasn't a lone alpha type, he didn't like to be alone.

A minute later she heard a bark coming from the one direction she really didn't want to go—Big, Scary Neighbor Guy's house.

Once again the ranch-style house was dark. And thankfully, there was no truck in the driveway. Emily pulled out her phone and called Sara. "I think he's at Big, Scary Neighbor Guy's house."

"Don't go in!"

"No kidding! I don't think anyone's home—"

Another bark. Definitely Woodrow.

"I heard that!" Sara said. "Sounds like him."

"I'm calling Wyatt for backup." Emily ended Sam's call

and tried Wyatt's cell. When he answered, she told him what was going on.

"Go home," he immediately said. "I'll be right there."

"But—"

But nothing, he'd ended the call. She shoved the phone in her pocket and turned to go home—and then heard a fierce bark.

Woodrow.

Heart in her throat, she eyed the house. Still dark. Still no sign of life. She walked around the back, where she found three pens, no animals in any of them. There was also a barn and a shed, both open. From the barn came noises that were all too familiar—the yipping and barking and howling she'd sometimes heard late at night.

"Hello?" she called out. She wasn't anxious to run into anyone, nor did she want to be caught trespassing. With no one in sight, she poked her head in the barn and froze.

It wasn't filled with what she'd expected, which would have been horses and the equipment that went along with said horses. Pens lined both long walls. Dog pens filled with dogs of all shapes and sizes. In the center of the barn was an arena, like a fighting pen. "Oh, God," she said and quickly searched the locked pens for Woodrow.

He wasn't here.

She stepped back into the sunlight and heard his bark coming from behind her. His bark was immediately followed by a growl.

And then another.

She ran over to the shed and peeked in to find Woodrow huddled, cornered by two dogs, who were showing their teeth. "Hey," she yelled. "Back off!"

They turned to her, and when they did, Woodrow scurried around them, getting right in front of Emily. After that first night when he'd growled at Wyatt, she'd never seen him show an ounce of aggression, but he showed it now.

His fur stood up along the length of his neck and back, and he was in a fighting stance.

Her heart went to her throat. He was healing, but there was no way he'd win a fight with these two. "Okay," she said softly. "Let's everyone just take a nice, deep breath and—"

"What the fuck."

She craned her neck, and oh shit, felt a new wave of panic. Mr. Big, Scary Neighbor Guy was back, a big shadow standing in the doorway blocking her exit.

"I'm sorry," she said. "My dog trespassed, but your dogs cornered him—" She broke off when he didn't move, didn't do anything but just stare at her.

She bent and scooped up Woodrow. "We'll just go now."

Not even an eye flicker.

"I don't care what you're doing out here," she said. A big fat lie, of course. She cared to her bones, but she thought keeping that a secret until she got the police out here was a real good idea. "If you could just move aside," she said.

He did, slowly, and she slid out of the shed.

He followed, right on her heels, and suddenly it wasn't just Woodrow whose hackles rose. Every hair on her body stood up. She whirled around just as he was reaching for her. Heart in her throat, she danced back and yanked out her phone. "I'm going to call the police."

"No need. I'm right here."

Again she whirled and faced a man who'd stepped out from behind from the barn.

Evan.

"Dr. Pretty," he said.

She stared at him as he moved closer. Uh-oh. This wasn't good. "We were just leaving," she said, squeezing Woodrow close.

"You shouldn't have been here in the first place," Big, Scary Neighbor Guy growled, and took another step toward her.

"Bud," Evan said, his voice a low warning.

Bud stopped, and though his big, beefy arms hung loose at his sides, his fists clenched.

Evan looked at Emily. "You were asked to stay away," he said conversationally, still smiling a little bit, which she tried like hell to take as a good sign.

"I tried," she said. "Believe me. But I'm going now, and I'll stay away this time. Really. I promise."

"You promise," he repeated, sounding amused.

She nodded like a bobble head. "Yes."

"I don't believe you," Evan said. "You're curious as hell. And you're smart. You know what we're doing here."

"Killing dogs."

"No," he said. "Making big bucks."

"It's a felony to have dog fights," she said. "To gamble on dogs fights. To have spectators watching the dog fights."

"Actually, that part's only a misdemeanor," he said, still laid back and casual-like.

"Fascinating," she said. "Well . . . I really should be going now." She took a step, and Bud took another toward her. Woodrow growled, leapt out of her arms, and lunged at Bud.

"No!" Emily cried when he pulled his gun. "No, don't shoot him—"

A sharp whistle pierced the air. Emily glanced up and saw with shock and horror Wyatt coming around the back of the house.

Unarmed.

At his whistle, Woodrow sat on the spot, but he kept his sharp gaze on Bud.

So did Wyatt. "Emily," he said. "Come here."

She didn't hesitate, she ran to him. He grabbed her hand when she got close and pulled her in, gaze never wavering off the two men in front of them. He lifted his cell phone to his ear. "Got her," he said. "In the back."

Evan pulled his gun and pointed it at Bud. "Drop your weapon."

Bud stared at him. "What the fuck, dude?"

"Drop it, *now*."

Bud's mouth fell open. "You fucker. You think you're going to double-cross me?"

Kel and a handful of others suddenly swarmed the yard, and in less than twenty seconds, Bud had been forced to his belly in the dirt, hands behind his head.

Evan and Kel were in a standoff.

"Be smart," Kel said. "Down on the ground."

"I'm not the bad guy here," Evan said, not moving. "I was working undercover, trying to—"

"Bullshit!" Bud yelled, lifting his face out of the dirt. "This is your operation!"

"Shut up," Evan told him.

"Hell no, I'm not taking the fall for this—"

"Evan," Kel said. "One last warning. Drop your weapon."

He hesitated, and Woodrow—who'd run to Wyatt and Emily and was sitting on her foot—growled low in his throat.

Evan's gaze went to the dog, and in that split second Kel grabbed Evan's gun. The other cops moved in close and took him down to the ground.

Emily dropped to her knees and hugged Woodrow to her chest. "Good boy," she said, and he licked her chin.

Wyatt hauled her upright, gave her a quick once-over. "You okay?" he asked, voice low but utter steel.

Not trusting her voice, she nodded.

"No one touched you?"

"No. I'm fine—" That was the last word she got out before he crushed her to him. She pressed her face into his shirt, and breathed him in. He was warm and strong, and she burrowed in and held on, wanting nothing more than to never let go.

It was two long hours later before the questioning and sorting of the law was handled, and Emily was free to go. Five men had been arrested, fifteen dogs had been rescued, and Lilah and her team were handling the dog removal and treatment.

The adrenaline had let down and Emily was still shaking.

Wyatt was waiting for her, silent, tense. He drove her home without a word, and when they walked into the living room, they came to a shocked halt.

Sara sat on the couch, staring in stunned disbelief at Rayna, the gorgeous blonde kneeling at her feet holding out a ring.

A diamond ring.

"Oh my God," Emily whispered.

"I know," Sara said huskily, her eyes shimmering with tears and never leaving Rayna's face. "She just showed up," she said to Emily. "She's asked me to forgive her, to marry her."

"Neither of which you've answered," Rayna said softly.

Sara finally looked up at Emily, hope and love and joy all over her face. "I— You found Woodrow!"

Emily choked out a laugh. "Yes. Long story. Let's concentrate on you for a moment."

Sara sucked in a breath. "What do I do?" she whispered, as if Wyatt and Rayna weren't right there.

"A ten belongs with a ten," Emily told her. "And you're a ten."

Sara's eyes filled. "You sure?"

"Very. Follow your heart, Sara. Like Mom always said, a heart's never wrong."

Sara took the ring from Rayna and slipped it on her finger. "Yes," she said. "I'll marry you."

Rayna stood up, hauled Sara off the couch and spun them both in a circle.

"We need to celebrate," Sara said. "At the lake."

They were gone almost without a backward glance.

Emily closed her eyes. She needed Wyatt's arms around

her, needed him to hold her tight. *Needed him to love her.* Eyes still closed, she gave him the answer she should have given him the night before. "We've never had sex in this house because we've only made love here."

Before the words were out of her mouth, she was hauled in and crushed against his chest. His mouth took hers, hard. Hot. Deep.

"Wyatt—" she gasped.

"Not a good time to talk," he said, his hands all over her.

"But—"

He wrestled her down the hall and to her room, where he tore the sweats off her body. He took a nipple in his mouth, and the sudden, moist heat make her jerk. She arched up against him, seeking more.

"It's important," she said. A lie. She couldn't remember what she'd wanted to say at all. "I—"

"Should have mentioned it before you got naked."

"*You* got me naked—" She broke off with a moan when he took her down to her bed and his mouth latched on to her other breast, sucking hard before nipping it gently with his teeth and then soothing it with a kiss.

Her eyes rolled back in her head. "*Wyatt.*"

He flashed her a tight but wicked smile, and then his mouth traveled southbound. With no clothing to slow him down, all she could do was writhe against him as heat seared through her body.

He wrapped her inner thighs around his ears and sent her skittering with his tongue.

As she came back to awareness, he was kissing his way back up her body. She needed him with a shocking desperation that scared her. She was beginning to think that no matter how much he gave her, it wasn't going to be enough. It wouldn't be enough until she was his, body, heart, and soul.

Terrifying.

He put on a condom and pushed into her with one hard thrust that almost sent her over yet again. So did the slow, purposeful, knowing thrusts designed to take her to the very edge. She already knew he could hold her off for as long as suited him, drawing out her pleasure until she was mindless for release. "Don't stop," she begged. "Please, Wyatt, don't stop."

"Never."

Thank God, because this, with him. It was her air. It was her everything . . .

He broke from her lips, fisted his hands in her hair and locked his eyes on hers. She nearly came from the intensity of his expression, she was that close. He was, too, she realized, feeling him quiver against her with the effort it was taking to hold them both off. "Emily," he said, that was it, just her name, and she clenched hard around him, going off like a bottle rocket. She took him right along with her, the sound of his release refueling hers.

When she opened her eyes, he hadn't budged, his weight still holding her pinned to the bed, his heart thundering against hers. She loved that, feeling him breathing hard, knowing he was completely wrecked and that she'd done it. One of her legs was bent, her foot on the mattress, the inside of her thigh still tight to his hip. Her other leg was still wrapped around him, as were her arms, her hands gliding along his sleek, sweat-dampened skin. As the rest of her senses slowly returned, she wished for him to lift his head, meet her gaze, and say one word.

Stay.

His face was buried in her neck, his mouth brushing her skin softly. It felt sweet, and yet sexy. An affectionate just-had-an-earth-shattering-orgasm nuzzle.

"Was that good-bye?" she asked.

"I was thinking it was more of a 'damn I'm glad you're not full of bullet holes,'" he said.

Or that . . .

His arms tightened on her, and she felt a surge of hope, but before that emotion could settle, he looked at the three boxes along the wall, boxes she'd packed with her stuff. "I guess it is a good-bye of sorts," he said, and she stopped breathing.

Just stopped.

"You'll come visit," he said. "Your sister's here."

So are you, she thought.

"And I get to L.A. occasionally," he said. "And there's always vet conferences."

Ouch. Yeah, this was good-bye.

His back to her now, he pulled on his clothes. "I need to get to Lilah's and see if she needs help treating the dogs."

She let out the breath she'd been holding and sat up, pulling the sheet to her chin. Stupid to feel modest now, but she'd never felt more naked in her life.

Don't look back, she told herself. She wouldn't begrudge falling for him, or this place, *any* of it because she'd found herself here—not the person she'd thought she was supposed to be, but the woman she really was. And as it turned out, she was a lot more like her dad than she could have imagined.

And that was okay, too, because maybe, just maybe, she'd also learned to do what he'd always wanted for her—how to love without question, how to give her whole heart, no regrets.

But damn. Damn, it sucked.

Wyatt walked to her bedroom door, put his hand on the handle, and let out a long breath before facing her. "I really am happy for you," he said with his usual blunt honesty. "Everyone should get what they want out of life, but especially you, Emily. You deserve that."

He was gone before she found her voice. "You, too," she whispered.

Twenty-nine

Wyatt strode into Sunshine Wellness Center from the back. AJ's office was empty so he moved past the physical therapy rooms to the gym.

AJ was flat on his back on a bench, pressing weights. When Wyatt kicked his foot, he jerked. The weights clunked when he racked them, and there was lots of swearing as he sat up and eyed Wyatt. "Men have died for less," he said, and then frowned. "Damn, a dog die on you or something?"

"No."

"A horse?" AJ asked.

"No. Jesus," Wyatt said, and took the weight bench next to AJ.

"Something or someone died. It's all over your face."

"Nothing died. No one died." Wyatt shook his head and reached for the bar. "It's nothing."

"Bullshit." AJ stood and held Wyatt's bar down so that he couldn't lift. "You're not bench-pressing when you look like shit." He paused. "This about your sister?"

Wyatt's eyes narrowed up at his oldest friend. "What about her?"

AJ chewed on the inside of his cheek for a moment, as if carefully considering his next words. "I'm thirsty. You thirsty?"

"No."

"Good. Me too. Let's go." He hauled Wyatt up and shoved him out the door ahead of him. They walked down the street to the only bar in town.

"Two shots," AJ said to the bartender. "Whiskey." He slid onto a stool and glanced at Wyatt's face. "Actually, make that four shots. And keep 'em coming." He waited until the drinks arrived, lifted his, and knocked it against Wyatt's.

They tossed their drinks back.

"So," AJ said. "You didn't kill any puppies today."

"No."

"And it's not about your sister."

Wyatt gave him a long look. "Why do you keep asking about my sister?"

"No reason." AJ reached for his second shot and waited until Wyatt did the same.

The shot went down a little smoother than the first, and Wyatt gestured for another.

The bartender brought four more shots.

"She's leaving," Wyatt said, grabbing one.

"Darcy?"

"No." Wyatt clicked his glass to AJ's and drank. "Emily," he said, letting out a long breath. Finally. Finally he was feeling comfortably numb.

AJ blinked. "The pretty intern?"

Wyatt blew out a breath and picked up his fourth shot, gesturing to the bartender for still more. He wasn't sure how many it was going to take, but he figured he'd know when he got there.

"Man, I didn't realize," AJ said, matching him shot for shot. "Just ask her to stay, why don't you? Chicks dig that."

"No," Wyatt said, and shook his head. His befuddled head. "It's her life, and this is what she wants. I'm happy for her."

"Fuck that. Tell her to stay."

Wyatt laughed mirthlessly. "Is that what you do, you tell your women what to do?"

"Yes."

Wyatt pointed at him. "*That's* why you have no woman."

AJ frowned. "Hey. Well, okay . . ." He was speaking a little slowly, like his tongue wasn't working. "Maybe that's true right *now*," AJ said, "but this isn't about me. This is about you and your whole fucked-up family."

"We're not fucked up."

"*So* fucked up," AJ said, weaving.

Or maybe that was Wyatt.

"Growing up," AJ said, "you never had a choice or a say, like . . . *ever*, and now you won't tell a woman you love her and want her to stay because of it."

"Bullshit."

AJ raised a brow. "Which part?"

Wyatt wasn't exactly sure. He was fuzzy. Very fuzzy. "I won't take away her choices. She's gotta want to stay on her own. And she doesn't."

"Cuz you didn't give her *any* choices," AJ said. "That's as stupid as giving her too many."

Somehow, in some way, that actually made some sort of twisted sense. Wyatt stared at the empty shot glasses lined up in front of him. "I should fix that."

"Yeah." AJ pulled a pen from behind the bar and shoved it and a napkin at Wyatt. "Write it down. In a letter. It'll sound less bossy."

Way in the back of Wyatt's pickled brain he was well aware that he should actually *speak* to Emily and not write her a silly note, but he had to admit, it held some appeal. For one thing, it was hard to fuck up a note. He took the pen. Stared at the napkin. "Dear Emily," he wrote.

"Good start," AJ said, reading over his shoulder. "Keep going."

Wyatt bent to the task. It took about ten napkins, and some unsolicited help from AJ, and the guy on the other side of AJ, *and* the bartender. And then suddenly Wyatt found himself staring at Darcy. "Hey," he said. "What are you doing here?"

"Got a call that my shit-faced brother might need a ride home," she said.

The bartender shrugged unapologetically.

Darcy glared at AJ. "I blame you."

AJ, who'd been smiling and jovial all night, a happy drunk, was suddenly as somber as Wyatt had ever seen him as he stared at Darcy.

"This isn't my fault," he said.

"It's always your fault." Darcy slipped her arm in Wyatt's. "He's never like this."

"Maybe it's you," AJ said.

Darcy's mouth went grim. "No one can disappointment quite like you, AJ."

"It's a talent," he agreed.

Darcy turned to drag Wyatt out, and then paused. She met AJ's caustic gaze. "Come on, then. I'll drive your sorry ass home, too."

"Gee, as appealing as that offer is, I think I'll pass."

Darcy looked at the bartender, who nodded. He'd make sure AJ got a cab.

"Turn left here," Wyatt said halfway home.

"Why?"

"Just do it."

Darcy turned left. Wyatt gave her a few more directions to the route he had memorized. In three more minutes they were outside of Emily's place.

"Thought you'd already said good-bye," Darcy said, engine still running as they both looked out the windshield at Emily's car, clearly loaded and ready to go first thing in the morning.

Wyatt didn't answer. He got out of the car and went to the driver's side of Emily's car. Not locked.

She'd become used to Sunshine, he thought with a smile. Whether she knew it or not . . . He set his note against the gearshift.

And then he walked away. No regrets, he told himself.

But for the first time in his life, it wasn't true.

Emily gave Sammy one last tin full of strawberries, feeling her throat tighten when he dove right in. Then she tried to hug Q-Tip good-bye, and got bit for her efforts.

Woodrow was in the car. She wasn't leaving him behind, she couldn't. She kissed Sara and Rayna good-bye. "I still can't believe you're going to stay," Emily said.

Sara shrugged. "Sunshine grew on me." She paused. "This is really stupid. You know that, right?"

"Says the woman who invented stubborn," Rayna murmured beneath her breath.

Emily let out a short laugh. She and Sara had argued about this until they were blue in the face.

It was done. She'd agreed to go.

Sara rolled her eyes but wrapped an arm around Rayna's neck. "Straight people. They don't know how to communicate."

"Yeah," Rayna said softly, kissing Sara's jaw. "Because us lesbians do it so much better."

Sara sighed and turned to her sister. "Be happy, Emily," she said fiercely.

"I will." But she didn't feel happy. She felt anxious, like she was leaving something behind.

You are.

Your heart.

"I mean it," Sara said. "Promise me you'll be happy. You'll put it on your fucking calendar and do it."

She would try to do the happy thing, but that hadn't worked out so well for her last time, had it?

One week later, Emily left work at the Beverly Hills clinic. She walked out with Woodrow and the other intern, the one who'd spent three whole days in Sunshine before coming back.

Turned out she had a vicious allergy to horses.

Emily had talked in great length with Dell about it. He'd told her to stay in Los Angeles, that they'd brought Olivia back from her maternity leave for now, that they'd work it out.

He'd told her all of this before she could say a word.

Not that she knew exactly which word she would say. She had a bunch of them. Such as . . . How was Wyatt? Did he miss her?

She missed him like she'd miss a damn limb.

I'm so sorry, she'd nearly said. *Please take me back . . .*

But Dell had been happy for her that she was getting what she'd wanted, and . . . he was in a hurry. When he'd disconnected, she'd stared at her phone forever.

Now she swallowed the lump in her throat, the one that felt a whole lot like homesickness. She got into her car and drove. Not to her place—which was a guesthouse in the hills, a lovely little private cottage. Instead she drove herself and Woodrow into the valley, to her dad's house.

When she let them both in, Woodrow went directly to the kitchen, to the bowl of cat food he'd already discovered was always there just begging to be poached.

Emily plopped down on the couch next to her dad. He was reading *Animal Wellness* and eating from a bag of baby carrots. He had a blind parakeet on one shoulder, a three-legged cat on his lap, and two geriatric dogs at his feet, all of them clueless to the real world.

"How was work?" he asked.

"Fine. You look like Dr. Doolittle."

He looked up and narrowed his eyes on her. "Not fine."

And not so clueless . . .

"How long is it going to take you to realize that L.A. isn't going to work out for you?" he asked, going back to his magazine.

"Tired of me already?"

"Never."

Woodrow came into the living room still licking his chops and hopped up onto her dad's legs, upsetting the balance.

The parakeet squawked. The cat hissed.

And Emily would've sworn Woodrow smiled at the chaos. She knew he had to take his jollies where he could get them, as he wasn't allowed free reins at work the way he'd been at Belle Haven.

And no one had made him a badge or given him a hat.

Her dad tossed his magazine aside and hugged Woodrow. "Does he like carrots?"

"He likes everything but green veggies."

"Smart dog." He fed Woodrow a carrot, then looked at Emily. "Talk to me."

She sighed and leaned her head back, staring up at the ceiling.

"Truth?"

"Yeah, let's start with that."

"It's not that L.A. isn't going to work out," she said. "It's more that I don't want this life anymore." She let that sink in. "So what's wrong with me?"

"You want a list?" he asked.

She blew out a breath. "I've been here a week. I get a great stipend *and* a cute guesthouse to live in. It's a great practice. I've been given the keys to the kingdom, Dad. It's 'the life' on my plan. I go to work and if there's no smog, I can see all of the city of Los Angeles, and yet all I can think about are the mountains."

"I'm more of a desert man myself," he said conversationally.

"Dad. I'm serious."

"Me too."

She turned her head and looked at him. "Two months ago this was all I ever wanted. It's everything . . ." She shook her head. "But it's not."

He arched a brow. "Quite an admission, coming from you."

"What does that mean?"

"Life isn't in the planning, baby. Life's in the living."

She stared at him. "I can't believe you can say that to me with a straight face. With even a little bit of planning, you could've had everything you ever wanted. You have a degree from Tufts, for God's sake! You could've worked with the best of the best but you're here because . . . well, I don't know why exactly."

"Don't you?"

"No! And then when you didn't put any money away and Mom got sick, you were wiped out with her medical bills and *couldn't* go anywhere."

He looked around. "I like this place."

"But Mom could've been the one living in the Malibu Hills—"

"And she still would've died," he pointed out gently.

"Yes, but it could've been easier," Emily said, throat thick, remembering those lean, awful years.

"Honey." Her dad put his hand on hers. "You take great care of me. That's what you do, you take care of things. People. Animals. Whatever you can. I get that. You make a plan and you go for it, blinders on."

"You're missing my point, Dad."

"No, you're missing *my* point. I *am* living my dream. I've got two wonderful daughters, and I'm doing the work I love, and I married the love of my life. We had a great run."

She stared at him.

He squeezed her hand. "Do you want to know why I loved Sunshine for you? Because it wasn't on your plan. It wasn't even on your radar. And every time I talked to you, you sounded *alive*."

She sighed. "L.A. will work out, too. Even if I did treat a purple poodle today."

"Honey," he said in an amused tone, but there was something else there, something behind the laughter.

She was afraid it was a little bit of horror about the purple poodle, and also the knowledge that they both knew her life wasn't exactly going as planned, L.A. or not.

"Emily, I'm happy with my choices. Can you say the same?"

She opened her mouth, and then closed it.

"If your mom taught you one thing," he said. "It's to follow your heart. Always. No regrets. Yes?"

Yes. But she also knew that following her heart caused pain. So much pain. She'd watched him suffer so much when her mom had been dying, had watched him grieve . . . "I didn't follow my heart," she admitted. "I followed my brain."

And her calendar.

Yeah. So many regrets.

"You can change that," he said. "It's not too late. It's never too late."

"I can't."

"Why?"

Because Wyatt didn't care that she was gone. Her heart squeezed hard at that, and she rose to her feet. "I'm going to get us dinner. Thai or Mexican?"

He met her gaze but didn't answer.

"Dad, if you say follow your heart on this, I'm going to—"

"Italian."

"Okay, then." She and Woodrow headed back to the car. The dog jumped in, knocking her purse to the floorboard. She had to crouch down and reach beneath the driver's seat to gather everything—

She stared down at the napkin lying there next to her purse. It was a small square napkin with the words *Sunshine Bar* on it, but that wasn't what had her heart stopping.

No, that honor went to the scrawled penmanship—horrible penmanship—that she immediately recognized as Wyatt's. The first line read:

Dear Emily,

Don't fucking go.

That line was crossed out.

Twice.

She stared at the words, let out a choking half laugh, half sob, and covered her mouth with a hand as she read the rest, which wasn't crossed out.

I want you to have everything you want, even if it's not what I want. But I can't let what I want come before what you want.

Ever.

But . . . I want you to stay. Please stay.

Love, Wyatt

She stared at it until the words blurred.

"Honey." Her father stood in the doorway. "Your cell

phone rang and I picked up. Work wants to know if you'll go in early tomorrow."

She tore her gaze off the note. "No," she said. "I can't."

"It's your job," he said.

She clutched the napkin to her chest. "My job's in Sunshine."

Thirty

Still sulking?" Darcy asked Wyatt.

They were in the front yard of the house, Wyatt and his two sisters. It had been a mandatory Saturday clean-the-yard day. He was on a mission to get as much done for them as he could, because he'd hired an architect and gotten a building permit on his land. It was going to happen.

Zoe understood.

Darcy, not so much. She was still pissed off at him. "I don't sulk," he told her. "And *you're* the one barely talking to *me*. Even after you lied and said you wanted me to move out."

"I get why you want your own place," she said, ignoring this. "We cramp your style."

"*You* cramp his style," Zoe broke in. "I'm not the one who told Emily he wet the bed until he was twelve."

"Five," Wyatt said through his teeth. "Only until I was five."

Darcy was lying flat on her back in the grass that was

turning brown for winter, staring up at the sky. He nudged her foot with his.

She nudged back.

That she even could was a miracle, and he crouched at her side. "I'll be only three minutes down the road," he said.

"Maybe that's not far enough."

There hadn't been much to smile at this week, but he smiled now. "You're going to miss me. That's why you're being such a shithead."

"I'm going to miss the lobster ravioli."

"That's not what *I'm* going to miss," Zoe said.

They both looked at her.

"I miss you being happy," she said to Wyatt.

His smile faded. When he'd first come back to Sunshine, he'd let the familiarity, the sense of community, fill him. He belonged here, and it felt right. That rightness had only grown as he'd worked at Belle Haven. Settled into friends and a routine. Hell, even living with his sisters had given him a sense of belonging.

And then Emily had come, and she'd been like icing on the cake. The very best part.

They'd fit. With her, everything else in his life had gotten better.

"Sucks," Darcy said. "Falling in love."

Yeah. Sucked hard. He hadn't wanted Emily to leave. He'd been unnerved by the magnitude of what he'd grown to feel for her, but it was nowhere near the magnitude of how he felt about her leaving.

And yet he'd let her go. He'd let her go with nothing but a damn note.

"You should've told her you didn't want her to go," Darcy said.

"AJ has a big mouth."

"And you're a complete dumbass if you really let her go without a word."

"Don't." He shook his head. They'd been over this. In great detail, at high decibel volumes, several nights this week already. "We've had this fight. We were dragged around all our lives," he said. "I'm not going to tell her—"

"Oh my God!" Darcy burst out, and tossed up her hands. "Get over it already!"

"Just call her," Zoe said.

"Or take the pussy route," Darcy said. "And write her a *stupid note on a stupid napkin.*"

Wyatt scrubbed his hands over his face. "Not my finest moment," he admitted.

Which didn't matter, since Emily hadn't responded to the note in any way. Not even when their L.A. intern had left after three days because of horse allergies.

Or, as the staff had rumored, due to Sunshine's lack of Thai takeout.

"At least call her," Zoe said.

It was nothing he hadn't told himself every single moment of every single day all week. "I'm already packed," he said. "I leave in the morning."

Zoe blinked, and then grinned.

Darcy whooped and gave him a kick that would have knocked the feet out from beneath him, knocking him to his ass, if the sweetest sight he'd ever witnessed hadn't suddenly appeared.

Emily's piece of shit pulling into the driveway.

He was sitting up and straightening his glasses as Emily parked. The car was bug-ridden and covered in dust. She tumbled out, not looking much better. She had a left-side-only sunburn. Her hair looked like she'd stuck her finger in an electrical outlet, and he wasn't sure what the mysterious stains were on her clothes. Not to mention she smelled like the inside of a 7-Eleven, but she'd never been more beautiful to him. Five cans of Red Bull fell to the sidewalk before she shut the door.

Zoe gasped at the sight of her. "Were you mugged?"

Emily stopped short and looked down at herself. "Despite what it looks like, no."

Darcy grinned. "It's called two days of driving."

"Yeah. And I didn't have the route mapped so I nearly ended up in Canada by accident when I was practicing what I was going to say instead of concentrating on the drive."

"A speech!" Darcy said, and kicked Wyatt again. "She has a speech! Let's hear it!"

Wyatt gave her a long look and gestured with his chin to the house.

"Oh no," she said. "You've been brooding for days, you're not going to make us leave now."

"You've been brooding?" Emily asked him softly.

"Zoe," Wyatt said.

"Yeah, on it." Zoe grabbed Darcy and pulled her up. "We're going to give them privacy. I realize you don't know the meaning of the word, but—"

"Fine! Just hang on one second." Darcy pointed at Emily. "I know he screwed up, but he *is* screwed up. Don't you screw him up even worse, got me?"

Jesus. Wyatt opened the front door and shoved both his sisters inside before slamming the door. He turned back to Emily, heart pounding uncomfortably hard. "Hey."

She came close. "Hey," she whispered back.

He had to touch—*had* to—and yanked her into him. "God, you're a sight for sore eyes."

"You should probably know that I'm punch-drunk tired," she said muffled into his chest, her hands fisted at the back of his shirt. "Which isn't the same as being plain out drunk, of course." She shoved free and gave him a long look. "Because if it was, I'd be writing what I want to say to you on a friggin' *bar napkin*!"

"Is that why you're yelling at me?" he asked.

"No, I'm yelling because I've had five Red Bulls!" She stopped, drew in a deep breath and let it out slowly. "I'm yelling because you were careful to keep your feelings to yourself. I had to *guess*, Wyatt. Hell, I'm *still* guessing."

He opened his mouth, but she poked him hard in the chest with a finger. "You showed me with your body, and okay, you showed me with your actions all damn day long, every day, but you were stingy with the words. And I needed the words!"

"I know," he said. "I—"

"Who leaves a note under the driver's seat? Tell me that. *Who does that*?"

"It didn't start out beneath your seat," he said. "I set it against the gearshift. It must have slipped to the floor."

"I repeat," she said. "Who leaves a note"—she pulled it from her pocket and waved it under his nose—"telling a woman he wants her to stay?"

"Yeah, okay, it was a really stupid idea," he admitted. "But it made perfect sense to a drunk man."

"Oh good," she said, nodding. "You *were* drunk. I was afraid you'd paid a third grader to write it for you." She went hands on hips. "Let me make sure I have this straight. When I was here, falling for you, *hard*, you didn't say a word. When I was here, thinking that I'd finally found the first something really good in my life—" Her voice broke, which sliced at his heart as she poked him again, in case he hadn't figured out that it was *him* that was the something good in her life.

He caught her hand and pulled her in again, holding tight. "Emily," he said softly.

"Did you know?" she asked. "Did you know how I felt?"

"I knew you cared for me. I knew you wanted to be with me."

When she tried to pull away, he held her still and met her stormy gaze. "I didn't want to crowd you. I didn't want to make a decision for you, or worse, dictate your plans. My hope had been that if you wanted more, you'd say so."

"I wanted you to ask," she said softly. "Or better yet, tell me. I wanted to hear you say it."

"I know," he said with real regret. "I want to make that up to you. What I *don't* want is to lose you." He tightened his grip on her, and when she did the same, he felt the knot in his chest loosen. He sank a hand into her very tangled hair and tipped her head up to his. "I missed you," he said against her mouth. "So fucking much."

"Yeah? So much that you were just sitting on the grass having a little chat with your sisters?" she asked.

"It was more of an intervention, and if you looked inside my truck right now, you'd see my duffle bag. I was coming to you in the morning."

She went still. "You were?"

"Yeah." *Don't fuck this up . . .* "I had things I should've said before you left."

"Like?"

"Like he was scarred by being dragged all over the world without getting a say or having any choice in the matter," Darcy yelled from the living room window. "Only he's a stupid guy and can't seem to say it out loud."

Wyatt turned and gave Darcy a look that had her squeaking and slamming the window shut.

Sorry, Zoe mouthed through the glass.

Hell if she was. He turned back to Emily. "Have I ever told you that I like your sister better than either of mine?"

She laughed softly. "I love your family, Wyatt."

"Because they're entertainment?"

"Because they love you. And I should've figured out for myself what you were doing. Or rather, what you weren't doing. I should've understood that it wasn't because you didn't have feelings for me, but that you had so many. I know, because I had just as many for you."

He let out a breath and tightened his grip on her, burying his face in her hair. He paused, lifted his face and pulled a leaf from her silky strands. Her matted silky strands.

"It got really windy over the pass," she said defensively and lifted her hand to her hair.

He caught it, then her other hand as well, his own encircling her wrists. His fingers laced with hers and he brought them up to his lips, kissing each palm before looking down into her face. "I was coming to you to say I wanted you back in Sunshine. That I think we have something, something different than I've ever had before." His lips brushed hers. "I want you back because I love you, Emily. So goddamn much."

"Oh," she breathed softly, her eyes luminous. "That would've been worth the trip."

He smiled. "I know you have a plan, but if you think it can tolerate some deviance, then I'd be happy if you deviated in my direction."

She bit her lower lip. "What kind of deviation are we talking about?"

He laughed, and she closed her eyes. "Oh God, how I missed that, Wyatt. Hearing you laugh. I gave up my calendar. Thought I'd try winging it for a while."

He tightened his grip on her.

"And that," she breathed, snuggling in. "I missed that, too, feeling your arms around me. And your voice. And the way you make me feel." She opened her eyes. "I love you, too, Wyatt." And she graced him with a smile that made her seem as if she was lit from within, and took his very breath away.

"Stay," he said again. Not asking. Hell, no. He wanted to be perfectly clear on things this time. "Stay, Emily. Tonight. Tomorrow. *Forever.* Just stay with me."

Her smile widened and her eyes shone brilliantly with unshed tears. "I wasn't sure where my home would end up being," she admitted.

"You found it, sweetness. Me. I'll be your home. Seems only fitting, since you're mine."

Animal magnetism

Sunshine, Idaho, is a small, sunny town – the perfect home for man and beast. Well, maybe not for man, as pilot-for-hire Brady Miller discovers when his truck is rear-ended by what appears to be Noah's Ark.

As the co-owner of the town's only kennel, Lilah Young has good reason to be distracted behind the wheel – there are puppies, a piglet and a duck in her Jeep. Still, she doesn't find it hard to focus on the sexy, gorgeous stranger she's collided with.

Brady is just passing through, but there's something about Lilah and her menagerie that makes the temptation of staying in Sunshine one that's difficult to resist . . .

Praise for Jill Shalvis:

'From beginning to end, *Animal Magnetism* is a captivating story that will have you laughing out loud, rooting for a happy ending for Lilah and Brady, and hoping that this won't be your last visit to Sunshine'
Romance Reviews Today

Animal attraction

Sunshine, Idaho, is the perfect place to give injured animals a refuge . . . or to find one. Veterinarian Dell Connelly suspects there's a reason his clinic's uber-efficient receptionist has taken shelter here.

Jade Bennett couldn't be happier to escape the big-city jungle to work with injured animals . . . and enjoy the gorgeous views of her ruggedly sexy boss.

Jade is used to planning everything in her life, but Dell's seductive, alluring ways have sparked an uncontrollable desire. And though Dell has never had time for love, Jade's strength and sass is the kind of call no red-blooded male can resist . . .

Praise for Jill Shalvis:

'Funny and hot as hell . . . Moving, empowering, and engaging'
All About Romance

Rescue my heart

After a tragic stint in the National Guards,
Adam Connelly returns to his animal shelter
in Sunshine, Idaho, just wanting to be alone.
Then he opens the door to the woman whose
heart he once broke. Still gorgeous, still tough-
as-nails, but this time, unusually vulnerable.

Adam is the last man Holly wants to see.
But with her father missing, he is the only
one she knows will be able to find him.

For Holly and Adam, each with their ghosts, a
search this desperate, this unpredictable and this
intimate, will have its share of risks – including
opening their hearts one more time.

Praise for Jill Shalvis:

'I'm a big animal lover, and this series is
centred around animals. Animals and hot
heroes. How can you not love a romance
like that?'
Jaci Burton, *New York Times* bestselling author

headline
ETERNAL